THE
BUFFALO
FENCE

JESSICA McCLELLAND

I0616834

RED SKY INC.

This is a work of fiction. Names, characters, places and incidents are of the author's imagination and are used fictitiously and not based on actual events, or persons, living or dead. Any resemblance to actual locals, organizations or events is coincidental.

Red Sky Inc.
Grand Junction, Colorado.

First printing: 2013
Second printing: 2018

PRAISE FOR THE KILLDEER SERIES

You'll be compelled to race through North of the Crazies by Jessica McClelland's easy and addictive prose, but that means you'll lose the detail and the accuracy that make her a truly fine writer. Her knowledge of the contemporary West and her abilities as a storyteller makes her a welcomed addition to the new class of crime fiction authors.
-Craig Johnson, author of the Walt Longmire Mysteries, the basis of A&E's hit series Longmire

Jessica McClelland's Snow at Midnight bursts out of the chute with a fresh new voice an authentic Montana sense of place, and a flawed but endearing protagonist readers will cheer for. Welcome aboard, Marley Dearcorn.
–C.J. Box, New York Times bestselling author of Force of Nature.

Snow at Midnight highlights not just a murder, but the nuances of Western culture: the conflict between old ranchers and new money, the independent self-sufficiency that comes from living an hour down a dirt road from the nearest hospital, the power struggles, the endless sky arching from the jagged horizon.
-The Daily Sentinel

THE BUFFALO FENCE

CHAPTER 1

"How long has it been like this?" I asked.

Tatiana Phelps, owner of the Deep Creek Ranch, kicked the dry soil with her lace-up ropers and squinted in the sharp sunlight. "About a week, I guess. I hadn't really paid much attention, until yesterday. Thought it was odd I couldn't see any of the little barkers. I called you first."

The prairie dog town was silent. I couldn't hear a sound above the low August wind. It was early morning, but already growing hot, and the pasture in front of us should have been alive with activity. The sun had been up for a couple hours now, and the ground should have been crawling with barking, grazing prairie dogs. But the only thing moving was one curious raven circling us from a safe distance. As I scanned the deserted town all I could see was dry sagebrush and thirsty tumblegrass, and in spite of the rising heat I felt a shiver creep over my skin.

I knelt down and examined the hole at my feet. There wasn't a single track.

"What do you see?" she asked.

Tatiana Phelps was about as far away from looking like a Tatiana as was possible to get. She was in her mid-fifties now, but I honestly thought she hadn't changed much in all the years that I had known her. Her bowed knees and bent hips gave away the fact that she had spent half her life on the back of a horse. I wondered if a tube of lipstick had ever even gotten close to her face.

I scanned the dogtown until I spotted what I was looking for. A single prairie dog corpse.

I stood up and wiped my hands on my jeans. My palms were already damp.

"Stay put, Tatiana," I said, walking towards the dead prairie dog.

She gave a rueful laugh. "Girl, you got that right."

I pulled my strawberry blonde hair away from my face and tied it in a quick ponytail with my bandanna. I should have been at work. But, circumstances being what they were, I was on the other side of the mountain from my little library job. Risking my neck for a friend.

I was careful where I put my feet, watching to make sure I didn't kick up any more dirt than was absolutely necessary. When I reached the spot where the dead prairie dog was lying, my mouth went dry and I tried to swallow. Every instinct was telling me to get the hell out of there, but Tatiana had called me to come to her ranch and make an evaluation, and that's what I was going to do.

I had only been a librarian for about a year. In my previous life I had worked at the Montana Fish and Wildlife branch office up in Helena. And I had been the branch office manager, not a biologist, so why I felt qualified to make a judgment call concerning a mass die-off was beyond me. The branch office where I had worked was tiny, unlike the huge regional office that was staffed like a small city, and it wasn't as if I came across questions about diseases every day at work, but I'd held the job for almost a decade, and you picked things up.

I stood over the dead prairie dog, the dampness in my palms spreading to the rest of me. The little animal was on its back, twisted to the side. It had been dead for only a few days, but already the relentless heat was working on the remains. It was dried out and looked like a tiny mummy. I knelt down, checking for any sign of trauma. No bite marks. No broken bones that I could see. This dog had not died from the usual means. And if it had been killed by an eagle or a coyote, the predator would have carted the body off for lunch. I stood up quickly and tried to determine the best way for getting out of there.

I could see that my initial guess had been right. I knew what had wiped out the dogtown.

"Tatiana, you should start backing up now." I eased my way backwards.

"Was it the plague that got them?" she called.

I winced as I stumbled, caught my footing, and a fine cloud of dust wafted over my hiking boots. "Yep. We should go. Like, right now."

"Oh, hell. Marley, get on out of there and I'll go round up the horses," Tatiana called over the wind.

She turned and trudged down a shallow drainage towards the dry creek bed to collect our mounts. We had left both animals tied to a sturdy shrub in case our worst fears were realized. No sense in having a couple of horses sniffing around a pasture filled with the Black Death.

The dogtown had obviously been completely decimated. I sidestepped another dead prairie dog as I tried to ease my way out of the colony. This second corpse was also unmarred, and partially concealed under a clump of sagebrush. I

3

almost stepped on it as I hurried from the colony, but I managed to shift my foot in time and avoided landing right in the middle of it. Since the plague was spread from animal to animal by fleas, I knew that coming into contact with an infected prairie dog was a very bad idea.

I stopped for a moment and shuddered. What was I doing out here? I wasn't really qualified to evaluate what had caused these animals to die. But Tatiana had called my father at 6 that morning and asked him to get in touch with me. My father, in turn, had called me at 6:05 at Leif's house. Leif had rolled over and answered the phone, roused from a sound sleep, climbed out of bed and searched the entire household for me, finally locating me in the kitchen next to the coffee machine, and told me about Tatiana's request. Since everyone had gone to so much trouble just to track me down, I felt it would have been selfish to say no. I'd called up my boss at the branch library in the tiny town of Fable and asked her to trade days with me. She had agreed to it after I threw in an offer to work that Saturday for her. Three hours later, Tatiana had saddled two horses and we'd left her stables, riding at an easy pace and squinting against the bright morning sunlight.

I took a breath to steady my nerves. Thanks to my former job, I had developed a phobia of the plague. One summer, back when I had been a green hire for the Fish and Wildlife office, the Helena biologist had convinced me to work for a week on the black-footed ferret reclamation project in the badlands. It had been challenging to begin with, because of the late nights spent driving the trapping truck from cage to cage in pitch blackness, guided only by a GPS unit and the angry snarls from the trapped ferrets. I'd loaded each ferret into the back of the truck carefully, enduring their threats, and driven them back to the field tent for testing and evaluation. The days were spent sleeping. If it could be called that. The biologist snored like a diesel engine. By the end of the week I was half-crazed from lack of sleep and the stress of getting hopelessly lost each night.

During the six-hour drive back to Helena, the biologist had taken great delight in describing to me in minute detail what happens to a person who catches plague from handling infected ferrets. He'd gone on and on about fevers, swelling, delirium, and seizures and finally described very graphically the bleeding from eyes, mouth and other places I didn't even want to think about. I took four showers in a row when I finally made it home. The experience had left me with a phobia when it came to the plague that I couldn't shake.

Now here I was, deliberately wading around an infected area. I searched the ground for the easiest path away from the colony and started walking. The quicker I could escape the better. My entire body crawled with shivers.

I saw Tatiana riding her big roan and leading the little paint she had saddled for me towards the draw that emptied out below the ridge. She was being careful too, avoiding the dogtown, and she skirted the slope that marked the leading edge of the colony.

I had to adjust my direction so I could meet her down in the shallow draw, and as I came down the slope at a trot I ran into a thick tangle of tall junipers.

My path was completely blocked.

"Great." I started picking my way around the sprawling shrubs.

Prickly branches jutted in all directions. I would need to circle around to the other side to get back on track.

I saw Tatiana ride down the slope and into the draw just as a stiff gust of wind caught her straw cowboy hat and lifted it off her head.

The hat flopped wildly and sailed past the paint horse she was leading beside her big roan. The paint immediately spooked and bolted, stripping the reins from the ranchwoman's hand and tearing off down the draw like he was being pursued by a mountain lion.

"Dang it, Peanut!" She shook her head and cast a frustrated look in my direction. "I'll be right back."

She reined her big roan around and chased after the little paint at full gallop. I knew it wouldn't take her very long to catch him. Tatiana's roan could outrun just about anything within a hundred-mile radius. She liked to prove it once a year by participating in the South Pass, Wyoming, reenactment of the Pony Express Run. She joked with everyone that if the Pony Express had used the horses she raised on her ranch, they wouldn't have ever had to bother with inventing the telegraph.

I worked my way around the juniper, and thinking about the Pony Express event reminded me the Killdeer rodeo would be coming up soon. In fact, I realized that the rodeo was this coming weekend. I also remembered at exactly the same moment that I had volunteered to work Saturday. No wonder my boss had been so agreeable to switch days with me.

"Of all the bad luck," I said, irritated with myself. I had been looking forward to taking Leif to the street dance. Well, it wasn't the end of the world. We would still be able to go. But we would miss the pancake breakfast and the bed races down Main Street. Killdeer was a silly place during the rodeo. Silly, but a hoot.

I was concentrating on the fact that I had just negotiated myself into working on the biggest party weekend of the year, and not paying attention to where I was putting my feet, when my boots came into contact with something that definitely should not have been there.

For a moment I thought it was Tatiana's straw hat, blown there by the wind. But as I leaned forward and pushed a stray juniper branch out of the way I could see it was a sleek, gray Stetson.

"What are you doing here?" I said to the hat. Like most people, when nobody else was around, I tended to talk to inanimate objects as if they could answer.

I crouched down and slid my fingers under the brim. The dry soil was warm to the touch and grainy with tiny pebbles. The hat looked pristine, in spite of the blowing dust. Pristine and expensive. It sported a sterling silver hatband and I could tell just from looking at the quality it had to be worth more than five hundred bucks.

Somebody would be wanting that back. The hat had to belong to one of Tatiana's ranch hands. Maybe there was a name stenciled inside the brim? I flipped it over and when I saw what lay on the ground beneath it, I stood bolt-upright and backed up until my knees collided with a juniper branch. My legs buckled and I fell square on my ass, my heart thudding with shock. I couldn't move, in spite of the sting of pain as a branch dug into my back.

I sat there in the dirt, gulping air and trying to get myself under control, when Tatiana rode up the draw. She stopped when she saw me sitting half inside the juniper. She studied me for a moment, her face amused.

"Marley. Whatcha doin'?"

"I'm not absolutely sure about this," I said, feeling both of my hands trembling. "But I think there is a dead man around the other side of this juniper."

Tatiana thought about that for a moment. "Huh. Now why do you say that?"

I was having sudden and intense feelings of panic wrapped around a waking nightmare that I had just stumbled across a human victim of the prairie dog plague.

"I say that because there is a man's hand underneath that Stetson. And unless I am confused about human anatomy, I am going to assume that there is a person attached to that hand."

Tatiana looped the reins on the paint's bridle around her saddle horn. She threw a leg over her saddle and dropped to the ground beside her roan. She carefully tied the big roan to a handy sagebrush bush and came over to help me off the ground.

"Why don't I just pop over and take a look?" she asked. "Want to come with me?"

"Ah . . . I can't really feel my legs at the moment," I said.

She gave me a look of pity and skirted the juniper, leaving me standing against the shrub like a statue. She stepped over a branch carefully, and I saw her bend down to retrieve the Stetson.

She stood looking at the ground, holding the hat in her left hand almost as an afterthought. He face twisted up with disgust.

"Yeah. There does indeed appear to be a man attached," she said.

Feeling ashamed of myself, I picked my way around the juniper until I hovered behind her. The branches of the shrub had completely hidden the body. Unless someone was right on top of it, there wasn't any way they could have seen it. As close as we were, I still couldn't see anything but the bottoms of the man's boots.

I stopped a few yards behind Tatiana, feeling my stubborn feet refuse to move another inch.

"Do you have any idea what could have killed him?" I asked.

"I think I have a pretty good idea," she said.

"Does he look like he died of the plague?" I asked, cursing my phobia.

"No, no. I wouldn't say he died of that," she replied.

"If he did, there would be sores on his body, maybe the size of a person's thumb, and they would look black," I told her.

Tatiana leaned down and gently put the Stetson back on the ground beside the body. "I'm thinking this was a bit more sudden than that."

It was a struggle, but I forced myself to move a step closer.

The man's body had been stashed beneath the crowded stand of junipers in haste. That much was plain to see. A broken branch was tossed over him, providing haphazard camouflage and hiding his cobalt blue button-down shirt from a casual glance. His neatly trimmed moustache and manicured gray hair were such a contrast to the gnarled mess of wild juniper branches it was heartbreaking. This man had taken great pains to care for his appearance, and now he had been dumped in the brush like so much trash.

9

"Oh," I said, catching sight of the man's face for the first time. "It's Zane. Isn't it? It looks like Zane."

The man was at least sixty, but still dangerously handsome. I remembered because a man as attractive as him was not easy to forget.

Tatiana let out a sad sound, closed her eyes and nodded. "Zane Ackerson from over to the Bybee ranch. How in hell did he get all the way over here on my place?"

"Bybee ranch is eight miles from here," I said. "I don't see any tire tracks. That's a long walk."

The Bybee ranch had existed since Killdeer had been incorporated. The old family who had started the ranch was called Bybee, and whoever happened to own the ranch these days figured out relatively quickly that it would forever be known by that old family name, no matter how hard the new owners tried to change it.

Tatiana crouched down and studied the man's body. "Well, guess we better go back and call Loy. It looks to me like he was killed sometime early this morning. Can't have been too long ago or else the blowflies would have been at him a lot worse than they are."

I could see a cluster of the black insects buzzing around the body.

"You don't think it was last night?" I asked.

She adjusted her straw hat. "Nope. I don't. Blood still looks a bit wet."

It was not easy, but I swallowed my fear and took another step closer to the body. I could see that Zane's arms were a bloody mess. His crisp blue shirt was in tatters at the elbows, almost as if his arms had been mauled. His right hand was propped up on a branch, and multiple puncture wounds lacerated the palm.

But the wounds to his arms hadn't been fatal. I checked his face and the front of his neck, but I couldn't see any obvious puncture marks. It wasn't until I looked hard at the back of his neck that I could see what had killed Zane.

"Yeah," I said, feeling my stomach flip-flop. "That's not the plague."

The back of Zane's neck was shredded. The flesh had been torn away viciously, exposing bone and tendon. The injuries were so brutal I cringed and had to look away. This had not been a quick, easy death. His neck had been savaged until it was broken. But his chest and the front of his neck were intact. Whatever had killed him had attacked him from behind. He'd obviously tried to fight, using his arms and hands to protect himself, but that hadn't saved him.

I shook my head and tried to look anywhere but back at the body. "It looks like he was run over by a piece of farm equipment."

"Nothing as neat as that," Tatiana said. "This wasn't no human being. And it sure as hell wasn't a tractor."

"You think he was mauled?"

Tatiana nodded and watched me. "What I can't figure out, is why wasn't he fed on? He was mauled, but not eaten. What kind of an animal does that?"

"One that isn't hungry," I said.

We shared a look, and Tatiana's expression was skeptical. "Or one that gets surprised and runs off," she said, her eyes sharp.

I was suddenly very aware of our surroundings, and the emptiness of the sloping foothills seemed much more ominous now than it had a half hour ago.

"You got a gun with you?" I asked.

She jerked her head towards her big roan. "On my saddle."

"Maybe we ought to be closer to your saddle just now," I suggested.

We needed to get away from the area and stop disturbing the ground. I was all too aware of the fact that, as Deputy Nick Wilcox would have put it, we were contaminating the hell out of a crime scene. I started to back away from the body, goose-stepping as I moved.

In spite of the fact that a man's mutilated body was only ten feet away, I still hadn't forgotten that we were only a few dozen yards away from a prairie dog town that had been wiped out by plague. As far as I was concerned, we couldn't get away from the area fast enough.

Tatiana wiped one eye and turned away from the body. She stared at the ground, her disappointment and anger obvious.

"You know what Nick will say when he sees it's been us tramping all over the place," I told her, trying to prod her towards the horses.

She pointed at the dirt beneath our feet. "It's a mess anyway. Look here, nothing but a bunch of coyote tracks."

I knew a little something of coyote tracks, and in spite of the fact that every inch of my skin was puckered with goose bumps, I knelt down to examine them closely.

The tracks weren't quite right. Something about them made me pause.

For starters, they were huge compared to other coyote tracks I had seen. The track was at least four inches long. "Tatiana, these aren't like any coyote tracks I've ever seen."

She squinted and leaned over my shoulder. She studied the indentations in the powder-dry soil. "I see what you mean. That's a damn big coyote."

"Not just the size," I said, laying my palm beside the track. "The shape is all wrong."

"What do you mean, all wrong?" she asked.

"The pads on the front feet are more pointed than usual. And look here, the back feet? They are much smaller than the front feet. This can't be a coyote."

Tatiana rubbed her chin. "What is it then?"

I scanned the ground, searching for anything telling. I wanted to walk all the way around the juniper stand to see if there were any other tracks, but the last thing Sheriff Shucraft and his deputy needed was another set of footprints to sort through.

I was no expert, but something about the entire scene looked strange.

I shrugged and stood up. "I can't think of anything with a paw that big. You don't have any Great Pyrenees dogs on your place to guard your sheep, do you?"

She blinked. "Hell, I can hardly keep Peanut from killin' the border collies the brand inspector brings with him. I can't think what he'd do to a big dog like a Pyrenees."

I looked over at the little paint horse standing beside Tatiana's big roan, his ears swiveling back and forth nervously. "Peanut? He kills dogs?"

"If he can catch them, he stomps them. Peanut hates dogs. I use llamas to protect the flocks when they're grazing. I haven't had dogs guard the sheep for years."

She glanced back at the spot where Zane's body lay partially concealed under the shrub.

Her eyes narrowed and she looked down at the tracks again.

The ranchwoman's face twisted up abruptly and she kicked the ground with the toe of her boot. "Damn ironic, this is."

"What?" I asked, looking back and forth between Zane and the paw prints. "Ironic how?"

Tatiana turned and walked towards the horses without saying another word. I hurried to catch up.

"You thought of something, didn't you," I said.

She stopped beside her big roan and started to untie the reins. The roan reluctantly moved aside, her mouth busy working a wad of prairie grass.

Tatiana shook her head. "Zane always did say it was not right how ranchers have killed off all the top predators. He was all about making the West more like it had been back before the railroads were built."

Her face was set with anger and grief. Tatiana, like most of the women in Killdeer, liked Zane Ackerson. As I remembered him, Zane had been a charming and agreeable man. More often than not when you saw Zane he was smiling or flirting with a woman or cracking a joke with a surly farmer. He had been well liked by almost everyone. That he had come to an early end in such a horrible way didn't seem at all fair to me. But something that Tatiana had concluded was making her noticeably upset.

"He advocated reclamation, didn't he?" I asked.

She fiddled with her stirrup. "Zane didn't just want reclamation. He wanted all the critters that used to be on the prairie to be reintroduced. Buffalo. Ferrets. And the top predators."

I gathered up Peanut's reins, my heart thudding against my chest, and managed to climb into the saddle without falling over the other side. It amazed me how calm Tatiana seemed. She looked angry and sad, but under complete control. I was barely managing to keep my breakfast from coming back up.

The breeze shifted just then, blowing in from the direction of Zane's body. The big roan jerked her head and danced sideways, and both horses froze in place. I looked over at Tatiana and could see that she had noticed it too.

"What's wrong with you, Shiloh?" she asked the big roan. The mare suddenly crow-hopped beneath her, one ear cocked forward and the other pinned back. Something was making them jumpy.

Peanut lifted his head high and blew out an unhappy snort, both ears cocked forward, and stamped his hooves.

Both horses were nervous now. They stamped and blew through their noses, anxious to bolt. I wasn't sure, but I thought that it was possible the horses could smell the body. Or else they could smell whatever it was that had killed Zane. I kept a tight rein on Peanut as we headed back up the draw. The little paint fidgeted and sidestepped. If I let him, he would break and run all the way back to the barn without stopping.

Peanut swiveled beneath me, his ears darting back and forth, and I did what I could to reassure him with a few gentle words, even though I was feeling anything but reassured myself. Peanut's eyes were as wide as silver dollars and he worked his bit between his teeth rapidly. It was almost as if he could sense the violence that had happened here.

"Easy, Peanut. You're alright," I said, giving him a pat on the neck.

"Talking to him won't help," Tatiana said, nodding towards Peanut. "He's deaf as a stone. Can't hear. That's why he hates dogs so much."

"He's deaf?" I asked.

She nodded. "Born that way. We had a few ranch dogs around when he was a colt, and they always got the drop on him. They could nip his heels from behind, 'cause he couldn't hear them coming up on him. Now, whenever Peanut sees a dog he charges. He killed two good sheepdogs before I figured out not to let him around them. He's part of the reason I went to using llamas, but honestly, the only reason I keep Peanut around anymore is on account of my niece. She rescued him from that wild mustang auction down in Wyoming and she loves the little bugger. But me? I think he's a menace."

I frowned and suppressed my urge to disagree. The little paint horse wasn't as big or as fast as the herd of tall quarter horses Tatiana kept on her ranch, but I liked him.

My eyes scanned the lonely landscape. "I'll call Sheriff Shucraft when we get back to your place and let him know what happened to Zane."

I had no idea what I would tell Loy.

Zane had been mauled by some animal, but what kind of animal doesn't feed on a kill? And more to the point, what sort of animal drags a body underneath a bush and then throws a branch over it to hide it?

I glanced over at the ranchwoman and I could see from her determined expression that she wasn't puzzled by the situation.

It looked to me like she had already made up her mind about what had happened to Zane.

It didn't seem that straightforward to me. I took a moment to study the sloping hills around us, searching for anything that might seem out of place.

I wasn't sure what I was looking for, but after the shock of seeing Zane's mutilated body I wouldn't have been surprised to see a pack of timber wolves lined up along the ridge.

Timber wolves . . .

My head jerked towards Tatiana. "You think it was a wolf, don't you?"

"I think it was," Tatiana said, shifting in her saddle. "That's why it's ironic. Zane always did think we should bring wolves back to Killdeer Valley. He was a handsome man, but he was pure crazy. You know what wolves would do to my sheep? Just look what they did to Zane."

"There aren't any wolves this far north of Yellowstone Park." I said.

"This is no mystery, Marley." Her voice was harsh.

"You sure about that?" I asked.

"It's as plain as the nose on yer face. We don't need to be going and reintroducing wolves to Deep Creek Ranch," she said, looking at me with her sharp hazel eyes. "You can't reintroduce something that's already here."

CHAPTER 2

Two hours later, Tatiana's ancient ranch house had become the impromptu base camp for instantaneous and uncontrollable insanity. Sheriff Loy Shucraft stood on the porch facing an angry mob of cowboys. Everyone was yelling at the same time and nobody could understand a word the other was saying.

A dozen men mobbed the stairs leading up to the porch and it was all I could do to keep from being knocked to the ground. I stood halfway up the stairs, behind the sheriff and in front of Tatiana, wishing that I were anyplace else at the moment. The sheriff was holding his ground and Tatiana wasn't moving an inch. I was pinned down.

"Toby, you put your damn thirty-aught-six back in that pickup truck and while you're at it lock your sorry ass inside with it," Loy shouted.

"But Sheriff, there's wolves loose on Deep Creek," Toby said with a whiny teenage voice. The kid was only nineteen and his testosterone was showing.

Loy blistered the kid with a hot glare. "I don't care if there's zombies staggering around the alfalfa fields. You put that thing away before I slap handcuffs on you for disorderly."

"Sheriff, I really think we should go out and just take a look around to see if we can—"

"Shut your mouth, Justin," Loy said, glaring at the man who had spoken. "Let me be clear. If I see anyone going out to the area where the body was found I will arrest them. Got it? This is an investigation, not a posse."

"Loy, we got every right to protect ourselves," said a scruffy, sun-blistered rancher.

The sheriff lifted his heavy fist and stuck out his finger, aiming it straight at the man. "Kevin, you got every right to spend the night in my jail cell if you keep this up."

"This is our livelihood we're talking about here," said a man from the back of the mob.

All this mob was missing were a few pitchforks and a couple of torches.

"This is my county, and I am the sheriff. So what that means is, you-all do what I say, or we go down to the station and have an unpleasant conversation."

Toby shook his rifle. "Our tax dollars pay your salary."

"Where did all these people come from?" I asked.

Tatiana stood behind me with a sour look on her face.

She had just about reached her breaking point.

"I wish God would have never invented the cell phone," she said, her fists clenched.

"Everyone knows wolves never hunt alone," said Justin, suddenly an expert on wolf populations and behavior.

A chorus of agreement rippled through the crowd.

"I don't want anyone searching the Deep Creek Ranch for wolves. If I so much as see someone shoot a ground squirrel I will start hauling people to the station." Loy's face was turning purple with frustration.

"You and Jane Fonda handing out memberships to PETA, Sheriff?"

"Has anybody heard a word I've said?" Loy demanded.

"Alright, that's it," Tatiana said. She spun on her heel and headed inside her modest ranch house, her shoulders squared with determination.

"Loy, I need to talk to you," I said, trying to be heard over the noise.

"I'm a little busy, Marley," he told me over his shoulder. "Can it wait a bit?"

"Hey, Sheriff! Whatcha going to do about it when our cattle start turning up dead?" yelled Kevin.

"And how long do you think it's gonna take them wolves to find our yearling colts?" shouted Toby.

I felt movement beside me and I turned just in time to see Tatiana step off the porch onto the stairs. I almost expected to see her clutching a double-barrel shotgun, but when she lifted her hand I could see she held a fat wad of cash. More than a dozen fifty-dollar bills were grasped in her fist. The sight of so much money in one place instantly sent a hush across the mob.

Tatiana held the money over her head for a moment until she was sure she had everyone's undivided attention. She stared at the men, her weathered face grim.

"I need someone to bring me as many boxes of coyote bait as they can get their hands on. The first man who brings me the bait from Big R over in Killdeer gets this thousand bucks."

For one horrible moment I imagined the men rushing the porch. But after an agonizing pause with no movement and not one sound, the yard exploded with activity as cowboys and ranch hands scrambled for their vehicles and practically climbed over the top of each other to reach the driver's seats of their outfits.

Engines fired and gravel flew in all directions as over half the trucks parked outside the stables ground gears and lurched for the dirt road. A rooster tail of dust blew in the air as nine of the men raced each other towards town.

The three remaining cowboys stood in the yard looking at their boots. The only reason they were still there was because Tatiana signed their paychecks every week and they knew better than to abandon the ranch.

She surveyed her domain with satisfaction. Tatiana was unquestionably the richest woman in the county, but her financial worth had never done anything to change her disposition towards stupidity. She dealt with troublemakers the same way she had handled the sudden appearance of a pair of skunks under her front porch. First, she lured them out into the open and away from her personal property, and then she killed them quick and clean. I'd known her since childhood and not once in all of those years had she ever displayed the slightest bit of fear.

"Do you really think that coyote bait will work if there are wolves on your ranch?" I asked.

Tatiana snorted. "No, but it got rid of the jackrabbit patrol, didn't it?"

Loy turned an impressed smile and looked the ranchwoman up and down. "Not bad. Should keep them out of our hair for a couple hours, at least."

"I can't believe I was dumb enough to tell what I saw," Tatiana told Loy. She crammed the wad of money inside her blue jeans pocket, shoved her straw cowboy hat back and scratched her forehead. "Why do I always think folks will act sensible?"

"Why do I always spend fifty bucks every month on lottery tickets?" Loy asked. "I'm an optimist."

I tugged the sheriff's shirtsleeve. "Can I talk to you now?"

Loy Shucraft and I had gone to high school together, dated briefly our sophomore year, and although we had both graduated with big dreams of leaving our tiny hometown of Killdeer, Montana, and traveling the world, somehow it didn't surprise me we had both ended up living exactly where we had started out. Loy was currently dating my friend Wendy Martinez, but there was a time that he and I had entertained the notion of becoming a couple. For once in my life I had done the sensible thing and kept our relationship platonic. But I never let the fact that we were not sleeping together stop me from leveraging my friendship with Loy. I always seemed to find a way to insert myself into one of his investigations. The only reason I got away with it was because Loy indulged my curiosity for old times' sake.

He fumbled in his shirt pocket for a pair of sunglasses that weren't there. He patted his other pockets and I didn't have the heart to tell him the sunglasses were resting on the top of his baseball cap.

He let his big shoulders drop down when he saw me looking at him expectantly. "Marley, Hun,

I've got to go out and make sure the coroner found Nick and isn't driving around Tatiana's fields going in the wrong direction. Either spit it out, or sit tight until I can get back here."

I smiled hopefully. "Can I go with you? I promise to stay in the truck."

"When have you ever been able to stay in the truck when something was going on?" he asked.

I tried to look as innocent as possible. "You need to take my statement anyway."

His lip curled slightly, but he let his head drop forward and heaved a sigh.

His sunglasses dropped off and fell to the ground. He stared at them for a moment. "This just isn't my day."

I bent down, grabbed his sunglasses and set them in his big hand. "Nick will need someone to show him where Tatiana and I stepped in case he has found any other tracks."

He shoved on the sunglasses and started to argue with me, but after a split second of internal deliberation he rested his palm on the butt of his pistol. "Fine. But, you promised. You will stay in the truck."

"Brian Hix is coming over here," Tatiana said.

"What? How did he find out about . . . ?" Loy started to ask. Then he turned a hostile look in the direction of the three ranch hands still lingering in the yard. Justin, the apparent wolf expert, turned a shade darker when the sheriff caught his eye.

Loy shifted his gun belt impatiently and turned back to Tatiana. "Never mind. Just don't tell Mr. Cellphone over there any other details about what you know, or what you saw. And when Mr. Hix gets here, tell him to wait for me."

"Brian Hix? He owns the Bybee ranch, is that right?" I asked.

"He's Zane's boss. Or, he was," Tatiana said.

"Alright, alright," Loy said, waving a hand and heading towards his sheriff's truck. "If you are coming get a move on." His patience with conversation had come to an abrupt end.

I climbed into the truck beside him and we headed towards the prairie dog town at a slow pace. Out of habit I rolled down the passenger window and leaned out to scan the ground for prickly pear cactus as we drove. A large clump of cactus could blow a tire, and the prairie dog town wasn't exactly at the end of a paved highway.

"Put your seat belt on," Loy told me as we bumped down the cow trail.

"We're in the middle of nowhere," I said.

"It's the law, Marley."

I fumbled with my seat belt and clicked it into place. "Listen, Loy, I noticed something that Tatiana didn't mention to you on the phone."

"Like how there was a juniper branch broken off and thrown over the body?" he asked.

I quit looking out the window and turned towards him. "How did you know about that?"

He smiled curtly. "We're very modern cops. We've got radios and everything."

"And did she mention that Zane's body had been hidden under a bush?"

"When I spoke to Deputy Wilcox he informed me of that, too."

"Why don't you make Nick your undersheriff?" I asked.

Loy grumbled. "Why don't you keep your eyes open for cactus?"

We bounced down the cow trail for a few minutes in silence. I was not surprised that Loy had been in communication with Nick over the radio. I was just disappointed that I couldn't be the one to tell him something that I thought was important.

"Well, did he tell you about the animal tracks?" I asked.

"Nick is from Billings, remember? The only tracks the kid knows anything about are the kind you find on the arms of a junkie."

"They were not coyote tracks. But I am not entirely convinced they were wolf tracks, either," I told him.

"Maybe some kind of a dog?" Loy asked, squinting through the bug-encrusted windshield.

"I don't know. They were too big to be a coyote. There is no doubt about that. But they were the wrong shape for a wolf. The front paws were bigger than the back paws. I would guess it was somebody's Great Dane out on a hall pass or something, roaming around Tatiana's ranch after running off. But that's an awfully long haul for a domestic animal."

Loy jerked the steering wheel hard to the right to avoid a jagged rock and I was suddenly very glad to be wearing a seat belt.

"What makes you think it was a dog and wasn't a wolf?" he asked.

"It's more likely. Besides, the Fish and Wildlife office in Helena never publicly admitted that there are wolves in this part of the state."

I'd quoted the memorized speech we had all been taught to say if the issue ever came up.

"But off the record? There are wolves in this part of the state. Nobody talks about it, but they are here."

"There proof of that?" Loy asked, jerking the wheel to dodge the remnants of a fossilized barbwire fence.

"One of the biologists out of the Missoula office set up a motion-sensing camera on an elk carcass and got three shots of a gray wolf driving off two ravens to feed on it," I told him.

The truck bounced hard over a deep rut.

Loy stared straight ahead, looking perturbed. "Don't tell anyone else about that, would you?"

"I won't."

"Lets stick to the dog theory for now," he said.

"Probably for the best."

"And when are you and Leif Gable getting hitched? I know you set a date but you sure don't seem too keen on sharing it with your friends."

I shot him a perturbed look. "What does that have to do with what happened to Zane?"

He shrugged. "Nothing. I just thought it might do you good to think about something other than the fact that you don't work for the Fish and Wildlife service anymore."

"I was only trying to give you information that might be useful."

"And I am only trying to give you some good advice," he replied.

I stared out the window, feeling the hot breeze suck the moisture from my eyes. "Sometimes it's hard to let go of things."

"But if you don't learn how to do that, you might lose something good that is staring you right in the face," he said.

"Are you telling me that Leif will ditch out on me if I don't marry him?" I asked, feeling defensive. The truth was that I hadn't made up my mind about a date for the wedding yet. I knew Leif was going to want me to sit down and talk it over when he got back into town from his current business trip.

"No I'm not," he said, waving a hand in the air dismissively. "But what I am telling you is that unless you can move on from your old life and find a way to be happy in your new one, you could miss out on some good experiences."

I didn't know what to say, so I didn't say anything. I knew Loy was right. I had been back home in Killdeer for almost two years, and hardly a day went by that I wasn't quoting some hunting regulation or mentioning in passing some experience I had enjoyed back at my old job in Helena. When people asked me what I did for a living, inevitably my response was in reference to the work I used to do. I wasn't employed by the Fish and Wildlife service any longer, but that had not been by choice. I'd been fired after becoming the scapegoat for a botched criminal investigation that I had not been involved with, but had been held responsible for in spite of that fact. Maybe I couldn't let go of the resentment I felt. Maybe it was simply a case of sour grapes. Whatever it was, Loy was right. Unless I figured out a way to put the past behind me and start living my new life, it would be nearly impossible to be truly content.

Nick Wilcox, Loy's deputy, came into view as we bounced over a low hill that flanked the prairie dog town. Much to my relief, Deputy Wilcox was nowhere near the dogtown and had parked his truck at the bottom of the drainage where Tatiana and I had found Zane's body.

A white Suburban was parked beside the deputy's brown sheriff's truck. Nick was standing next to a tall, lanky man with a handlebar moustache so huge I could see it from a hundred yards away. It had to be the county coroner from Parkman. There was no ambulance to transport the body, so I assumed that the coroner had brought his Suburban for that purpose.

"Loy, you know that prairie dog town up above the spot we found Zane has been wiped out by plague," I said.

He grumbled. "Tatiana mentioned it. But I think it's far enough away it won't be an issue for us down here."

"Just keep your eyes open for fleas," I said.

"Okay, Mom."

We stopped behind the deputy's truck and Loy killed the engine. "Remember," he said, giving me a stern look.

"I know, I know. Stay in the truck."

The sheriff climbed out and shut his door, leaving me to sit in the heat. When would I learn to keep my nose out of things?

I watched the three men for a few minutes, thinking that Nick had actually been putting on some muscle since the last time I had seen him. The deputy was so skinny that he barely had enough flesh on his frame to hold up his pants. But today he looked stouter than usual. Maybe Nick had discovered the push-up?

I let my eyes drift out of focus and in no time at all the excitement of being included in an investigation gave way to boredom. There was nothing else to do, so I leaned my head out of the open passenger window and let my eyes roam around the prairie grass while I looked for cactus. Prickly pear cactus was difficult to see, and spotting it was a game, of sorts.

A flicker of movement caught my eye and I focused hard on the spot where I had seen something wriggling through the dry buffalo grass.

For a moment I thought it had only been my imagination. Then the ripple of scales and the flick of a tongue drew my gaze.

A young prairie rattler, no more than a foot long, slithered through the withered vegetation not twenty feet away.

"Would you look at that," I said, surprised by the sight.

The rattlesnake wasn't like anything I had ever seen. Instead of the usual dusty beige with brown splotches that marked the normal pattern of a typical rattlesnake, this little prairie rattler was a dusky green color.

My promise to Loy was forgotten.

I opened the truck door and slid out carefully, placing my feet on the ground gently so I wouldn't betray my presence.

I knew this rattlesnake had terrible eyesight, like most snakes, but vibrations in the ground would give away my location if I wasn't careful.

I wanted to see this little gem close up.

Most snakes in Killdeer were beige or sand-colored. It wasn't every day that a green rattlesnake came along.

The ground was uneven and made walking quietly particularly difficult, but I managed to make my way to the small snake and get a good look at him.

As I stopped a few feet away he sensed my presence and coiled into a tight ball, shaking his small rattle menacingly.

His green color stood out noticibly against the dry grasses.

It had to be some sort of miracle a hungry hawk hadn't made a meal of him yet.

"Aren't you the cutest thing," I said, knowing that the snake was trying with all his might to be anything but cute.

His tongue darted in and out rapidly, betraying his fear, and after I'd gotten a chance to watch him for a moment I knew it was time to stop harassing him.

As I walked back towards the truck I noticed an odd divot in the dry soil. I stopped and looked at the dry soil carefully. Something heavy had sat here recently. Something about the size and shape of a prize-winning watermelon.

I stared at the ground, trying to make sense out of the depression in the dry soil. Then I noticed the remains of a tire tread beside the depression. A few scuff marks drew a messy picture in the soil. It almost looked as if someone had parked a vehicle here, then had kicked out a perfectly round, completely smooth two-hundred-pound sausage next to the rear tire.

I squatted down and carefully lifted a small sprig of buffalo grass that had been underneath the object. The grass was flattened, but it wasn't dead. Aside from looking like it had been squashed recently it was in perfect condition. Whatever it was that had damaged the vegetation here, it had happened only a few hours ago.

I stood up and followed the tire tracks. They were scuffed and windblown, but clearly the vehicle had parked, someone had gotten out and walked around the area in circles, and then left going the opposite direction.

"Loy!" I shouted.

I couldn't see him behind the big juniper bush, but he had to be close enough to hear my call.

I waited until he stomped over from the crime scene and stopped beside me.

He looked at me over the rims of his sunglasses. "Is this waiting in the truck?"

"What is that?" I asked, pointing down.

He clenched his teeth. "What is what?"

"It looks like a Guinness Book of World Records honey-baked ham."

Loy stuffed his sunglasses in his shirt pocket and knelt down to get a closer look. He rubbed his chin and his expression shifted from irritated to intent. "It almost looks like someone got stuck here and tried to put something underneath the back tire to get traction. But that doesn't make any sense. The ground is soft and sandy here, but it's dry and I don't see any place a wheel would lose traction."

"Maybe Nick should take a plaster cast of the tire tracks," I suggested.

He chewed the inside of his cheek, fixing me with a hard stare. "Maybe you could find something better to do with your time than my job."

"I'll, ah, I'll just go wait in the truck."

He forced a smile. "Good idea."

I gave the tracks a wide berth and climbed inside Loy's sheriff's truck to wait. I thought about everything that I had seen, and the more I thought about it the more I doubted that Zane Ackerson had been killed by a wolf.

Animals didn't break off branches from handy shrubbery and use them to hide bodies. Animals didn't typically leave something they had killed without at least eating some of it first. And I was pretty sure that animals didn't drive.

I glanced back to the spot the little rattlesnake had coiled up, but I could see that he was long gone. Most critters don't like to hang around where there is a great deal of human activity.

I looked back towards the stand of junipers and was once again reminded that a substantial prairie dog town just above the shrubs at the top of the drainage had been wiped out by plague. But, before all the prairie dogs had died from disease, I knew that this place was popular with local plinkers, or hunters who liked to practice their shooting skills on something alive rather than a paper target. Maybe my attitude was more practical than humanitarian, but I considered it a waste to kill something and then leave it to rot.

Unless you counted the predators that got a nice meal off of the prairie dog corpses that were left behind after a busy day of plinking, shooting the rodents did little good. Their populations could recover quickly from just about anything other than the plague.

I sat up straighter in the front seat and stared at the dogtown, thinking. What if Tatiana was right and there were wolves here at Deep Creek Ranch? What if Zane had been involved with something crazy, and dangerous, and had tried to do something radical like release a wolf here on Tatiana's place but something had gone wrong and he'd been killed?

I slumped back in the seat and my stomach felt queasy all over again. If Zane had done something so crazy, he certainly wouldn't have tried to do it alone. The fact that a set of fresh tire tracks were only a couple hundred feet from where Zane's body had been found led me to believe that the person who had come out here to help him might have seen what happened.

Loy's radio squawked to life and I jumped in my seat.

"Sheriff, what's your location? Over."

Valerie Newkirk, Loy's dispatcher, was on the radio trying to raise Loy. She waited a moment and tried again.

"Loy. Are you still on location at Deep Creek?"

I wasn't sure I was supposed to be talking to a dispatcher on a law enforcement radio, but I lifted the mike and keyed it before my brain could engage.

"Valerie, this is Marley Dearcorn and Loy is in the bushes with Nick."

I winced. That hadn't come out exactly right.

After a long pause, Valerie replied. "Marley, can you go and get him?"

Her voice sounded odd and I frowned. "What's wrong?"

"The manager over at the Big R hardware store called . . . and, well, just go get Loy and tell him to come in. You won't believe what he says is going on over there."

I keyed the mike again. "Let me guess. There is an unprecedented run on coyote bait."

"How did you know that?" she asked.

I lifted the mike and felt a chill run up the back of my neck. "I'll tell him that a hockey game has broken out down at the Big R."

"Thanks. You better make it quick," she said. "The manager told me the whole lot of them are buying up all the rifle shells in stock, too. It would be a real good idea if the sheriff went down there and threw some cold water on them."

Apparently the yee-haw crowd wasn't anywhere close to letting this wolf thing go.

It was going to be a long summer.

CHAPTER 3

"I hate having that fence walker on my property," Tatiana said as she stared outside the stable door.

I scratched Peanut's nose, letting him lip a handful of sugar cubes from my palm. "Fence walker?"

Tatiana jerked her chin towards the broad dusty lot in front of the stables that served as the parking lot for her ranch. A sleek red pickup truck sat beside Deputy Wilcox's truck. "Brian Hix. The fence walker."

A stocky man in his late fifties with curly blond hair that was slowly turning gray stood beside the red truck. He had his arms folded over his broad chest, his head bent down as he listened to the deputy. Loy had rushed back to Killdeer to deal with the raid currently happening at the Big R store, leaving his deputy to interview Zane's boss.

"Does he trespass a lot, or something?" I asked, not sure I understood her meaning.

Tatiana looked at me like I'd been hit on the head one time too many. "Fence walker. Weenie waggler. You know, Old Man Jenkins."

"Oh, he cheats on his wife." I flattened my palm to let Peanut slurp up the last of the sugar cubes.

"I think he cheats on the women he cheats on his wife with," she said, looping a long lead rope around her elbow to tidy up a snarl of tack that had been left on the ground.

Tatiana and I were hiding in the stables to avoid the unpleasantness outside. Nick had wrapped up the evidence collecting and the coroner had removed Zane's body. Then the deputy had driven me back to the ranch and been confronted by an angry Brian Hix, who was giving every indication he thought the entire process was beneath him. Mrs. Hix had unexpectedly accompanied her husband.

"Is that her?" I asked, catching a glimpse of a very attractive woman loitering beside the red truck. She looked like she was about to expire from boredom.

"Jennifer Hix," Tatiana said. She hung the lead rope on a hook and frowned at Peanut, who was busy mouthing the last of the sugar cubes from my hand. "He hasn't bitten you once."

"Peanut and I are buddies." I gave him a good scratch.

Tatiana grunted. "Want to buy him?"

"Hey," said a woman's voice.

Tatiana and I turned towards the stable door and saw Jennifer Hix standing there, watching us both.

"Howdy, Mrs. Hix," Tatiana said.

At a distance, Jennifer Hix was beautiful. Close up, she was positively striking. Her chestnut hair was so long it brushed the belt loops of her designer blue jeans, and she couldn't have weighed more than 110 pounds, and that included the weight of the diamond ring on her left hand that was visible from outer space. Her blue eyes were wide and perfect. Her complexion was so clear she looked like a magazine cover model. Her riding boots looked English, her red silk blouse fit perfectly, and not one wrinkle creased the smooth fabric. I added up the value of her current outfit and realized that it would have cost me about a month's salary.

"Brian didn't tell me we'd be gone so long. I don't suppose I could trouble you for the use of your ladies'? I've got to piss like a Russian racehorse." She gave us both an easy smile.

I raised my eyebrows. I hadn't expected someone who looked like the wife of a foreign diplomat to talk like a barmaid.

"You just go on in and help yourself, Jennifer," Tatiana said.

"Thanks. The deputy said he needs to get some background information on poor Zane, and they might be a while."

She looked me up and down, her face making an adorable pout. "Aren't you Marry Dearcorn?"

My jeans were stained, as usual. My old flannel shirt had the sleeves cut off and the laces on my hiking boots didn't match. I tried to hold my head up as I addressed Her Majesty.

"It's Marley." I felt about as feminine as a tractor tire.

Jennifer Hix sauntered over and held out her hand. I shook it, trying not to squeeze too tight. She looked so fragile standing next to Tatiana and me. But she would look fragile standing next to a ballerina.

"Pleased to make your acquaintance," she said, gripping my hand with surprising strength.

"Is that a touch of a Southern accent I hear?" I asked.

"Even worse. I'm from Texas." Her smile was more friendly than artificial.

"Jennifer moved up here three years ago," Tatiana said.

"And you-all can't seem to get rid of me," she said, laughing a little.

"I remember hearing about Brian getting married," I said.

Jennifer kept her easy smile. "I'm the new trophy wife. Never thought I'd find myself in Montana, but we seem to get along."

"Well, girl, you've only been married three years. Of course you and Brian get along," Tatiana said.

"No, I meant that Montana and I get along. Brian? That's another story."

The three of us stared at the ground for a moment, and I could see that Jennifer wished she had not let her last comment slip.

But she rallied and flipped a lock of perfect hair over her shoulder. "I'll just nip inside real quick and use your powder room. Thanks, Tatiana."

"Jennifer," I said quickly, stopping her. I wiped the sticky mess from Peanut's sugar cubes off on my jeans. "How well did you know Zane?"

She kept her smile, but the light from her eyes faded instantly. "Zane was my friend. I can't tell you how awful this is. God, if only I had been there. Or if Logan had been there, then maybe this wouldn't have happened."

"Been where?" I asked.

"Well, out where he got killed. If he hadn't been alone, if someone had been there with him, he'd still be alive."

Tatiana moved a step closer, folding her arms.

"What was he doing on my place, anyway?"

37

Jennifer blinked and looked at us both with surprise. "He was looking for ferrets. Didn't you know that?"

I kept my expression even, but my tone must not have matched. "Looking for ferrets? The sheriff never said a thing about that."

Jennifer's eyes regained their twinkle. "I know, it sounds nuts. But Zane knew all about the efforts by the local wildlife management agencies to get a black-footed ferret population going again. He always wanted to see one, and sometimes he would ride out to prairie dog towns around Killdeer at sunrise and try to spot them. It was sort of a game for him."

"Guess he didn't know about the plague," Tatiana said.

Jennifer's eyes widened. "What plague?"

"That dogtown was wiped out by plague. There won't be any black-footed ferrets there for a very long time," I said.

Deep frown lines marred her expression and she glanced over her shoulder towards the deputy and her husband. "Is it dangerous for people to be around here?"

"Not unless you are standing in the middle of the dogtown," Tatiana said.

Jennifer relaxed and gave a relieved chuckle. "I won't be doing that anytime soon. I don't think I even know where the prairie dog town is."

She turned to me with a faint smile. "Marley, if you don't mind me asking, how is it that you know the sheriff wasn't in the loop about Zane looking for ferrets?"

"Marley and Loy have an understanding," Tatiana said with a smirk.

Jennifer cocked her head to the side. "Pardon?"

"We went to high school together," I said hastily. "He's sort of an old boyfriend and we never really outgrew each other."

"So you too are . . . ?" Jennifer waggled her eyebrows suggestively.

"No, God no," I said. "Loy and I are only friends. Let's just say he sometimes bounces his case notes off me to see what I think. Never anything critical, of course."

"Of course," Jennifer said, eyeing me with a speculative expression.

A man's voice bellowed from the front of the stables. "Jenny, let's roll!"

"Deputy Wilcox must be done," Jennifer said. "Oh, Tatiana. Brian wanted me to ask your permission to look for Zane's horse."

"You think it's around here?" Tatiana asked.

"He never did like to drive up on a prairie dog town," Jennifer said wistfully. "He said the engine noise would scare off the ferrets. He always parked a trailer a few miles away and rode in. But since you-all are neighbors I'll bet he just rode over here from our place sometime this morning, right before he . . . right before he died. I'm certain his horse must have bolted when Zane was . . ." she trailed off miserably.

"Look all you like." Tatiana waved a hand in the general direction of the entire ranch. "If I see an animal come in with a saddle but nobody on him, I'll figure it's Zane's horse."

Jennifer thanked Tatiana and went straight to the red truck parked outside the stables. She hopped inside and slammed the door, giving her husband a pained look. Brian gave a hasty response to Nick's last question and practically bolted for the driver's seat.

"I guess she didn't have to use your bathroom all that bad after all," I said, watching as the couple roared down the road in a cloud of dust.

"Explains why we didn't see any vehicle tracks around the body," Tatiana told me.

I swallowed my reply and decided not to divulge the fact that there actually had been a vehicle there. The last thing Loy needed was for me to be describing the murder scene in intimate detail to folks not involved in the case.

Tatiana shook her head and hung up the lead rope. "Wish folks would tell me when they are out messing around on my property. You know how many times I catch kids from town out there plinking dogs without my say-so? And now I find out Zane Ackerson was stalking ferrets on my land. I ain't running no damn petting zoo out here."

I gave Peanut one last scratch before following Tatiana outside the stables. Deputy Nick Wilcox had his nose buried in his signature notebook. Nick's notebook contained extensive notes about every aspect of any case he was currently working on.

He looked up when he saw us come from the stables. "Marley Dearcorn. You know, someday I am going to get called to an incident and you won't be involved somehow. Boy, that'll be the day."

"Good to see you too, Nick."

Tatiana stood beside the deputy for a moment, staring at his shirt. Her face was twisted up with disgust.

Nick looked down at his lapel. "What? Is my badge on upside down or something?"

"You've got ticks," Tatiana said.

She reached out to snag the tiny brown bug creeping up the deputy's shirt.

"It's a bit late in the year for ticks, isn't it?" Nick asked. "Well, get it off me."

He held still while Tatiana tried to scrape the tick from his shirt, but her fingernails were too short to get a grip on it.

I barely had enough in the way of fingernails to peel a price tag off the bottom of a cast-iron skillet, but I had enough of a nail to catch a bug. I reached for the deputy's shirt and scooped the tick into the palm of my hand. It rolled onto its back, and I flipped it over to see what sort of tick was still active in August. I didn't recognize it though, and the more I studied it the more I realized I had never seen one quite like it before.

Tatiana knelt down and peered at the ground, toeing the soil with her boots. "There's a rock here someplace. Let me get one and we can smash him."

As I looked at the markings on the back more closely, it seemed wrong somehow. "Hey, Tatiana, have you ever seen a tick like this before?"

The ranchwoman gave a grunt as she stood up to squint into my palm. She tilted her head. "It does look a little funny, don't it?"

I gave the deputy what I hoped was an endearing smile. "I don't suppose you would let me borrow one of your evidence containers?"

"For a tick? Go get an envelope or something if you want to start bug collecting. I've got to get back to Killdeer."

"I've got an old Kodak film canister in the kitchen, Marley. Bring him inside and we can stick him in that," Tatiana told me. She gave Nick a sour look.

I wasn't the only one who got irritated with the surly deputy from time to time.

"Hey, Dearcorn, you ever see that Finn character anymore?" Nick asked.

I felt my face darken with a hot blush. "No."

The deputy studied me for a moment. "That's not what Loy said. Anyway, when you talk to him again, ask him to come by the station for me, would you? He's so damn hard to get in touch with."

"Why don't you go talk to him yourself?" I asked.

I had dated Finn very briefly a few months before Leif Gable had managed to convince me to marry him. Finn and I had ended our relationship badly. I still saw him occasionally, much to my chagrin, and he seemed to have a knack for turning up in my life when I was in the middle of some sort of catastrophe. Finn had always kept me at arm's length, never giving us a chance to be a genuine couple, and at the same time had been so overly protective it bordered on dysfunctional. I hated to admit it to myself, but I still harbored unresolved feelings about him.

"It's personal," Nick told me. "It doesn't have anything to do with work. How hard will it be for you to give him a stupid message?"

"If I see Finn," I said reluctantly, "I'll mention it to him."

He climbed inside his brown sheriff's truck and drove off without another word. Not even a thank you to Tatiana for her cooperation.

"He's not ever going to run for sheriff, is he?" she asked.

I grimaced. "Not as long as Loy is still around."

She nodded, looking relieved. "Come on, girl. Let's get you a jar for your bug."

We sat at the stained kitchen table and Tatiana handed me an old aluminum film canister from a drawer beside the sink. The canister was ancient. It seemed that Tatiana was one of those people who never threw anything useful away.

I never could figure out the ranchwoman's habit of holding on to things. She was by far the wealthiest woman in the county, and yet she still used the same stained pine table that had come with the ranch when she had purchased it thirty-five years ago.

"I haven't seen a film container like this for years," I said, tipping the tick inside and screwing the lid on tight. I slipped it inside my shirt pocket, knowing that I really didn't care one way or the other what sort of tick it was, only that I could use it as an excuse to go tie up some loose ends back at my old job. The tick was less important to me than the access it would give me to the branch office I had once worked for. I was going to use it as a prop, more than anything. Loy had been right when he told me it was time for me to move on and let go of the past. There was just one thing I had to do first.

"How's your dad?" Tatiana asked, easing herself into the wooden chair beside me.

"He's gone nuts and went out and bought a brand-new truck," I said.

"With all that money he got from selling the dinosaur you folks found on your ranch?"

"You know he got a Silverado king cab with heated leather seats? Whoever heard of using a truck with leather seats to go pull an old baler into town?"

"Oh, let him be, Marley. He deserves it. You Dearcorns have had enough bad luck for two lifetimes, and it's about damn time something good happened to you for a change."

We shared a somber look across the table. Tatiana had been my mother's best friend. When I was seven years old, my mother had been killed by a drunk driver. Tatiana had never been close to my father, but she respected him and she kept her friendship intact with us both even after my mother had died. I thought about how hard it must have been for her to see me from time to time, and to notice just how much I looked like my mother. Tatiana had never let her personal pain over the loss of her friend mar her genuine affection for me. I considered myself lucky to have such a strong woman in my life.

"Leif and I are getting married and I'm not sure it's such a great idea," I said quietly.

"Leif Gable ain't at all like your Allen," she said.

I rubbed both eyes with the heels of my hands. "I think the Space Shuttle has more in common with a hammer than Allen does with Leif Gable."

My ex-husband, a randy game warden working in Missoula, had been my first serious relationship out of college and I'd made the mistake of marrying him even though I knew he had problems with fidelity. Like all young women, I had convinced myself that I could change him. It shouldn't have been a surprise to me when I'd figured out he was cheating on me with a cocktail waitress.

Tatiana laughed. "But you still don't trust yourself."

"Trust myself?"

Tatiana peered at me intently, and then regained her smile as I tried to cover up the panic in my voice with a shaky laugh.

"Allen cheated on you so you think you have trust problems with men. But the truth of it is, you don't trust yourself yet to pick a good man out of the pile of bad ones."

I traced a crack in the old pine tabletop with my finger. "I suppose I still have some demons to conquer."

She put her hand on my arm and patted it a few times. "It's none of my business, but I imagine that Finn fella the deputy was talking about didn't help matters much."

I felt my face flush again at the mere mention of his name. "Finn wasn't the easiest man to be with."

"I never heard anything bad about him. Come to think of it, I don't think I ever heard anything about him. What's he do, again?" she asked.

"He's the security chief at the weather station up in Fable." It wasn't really a weather station, but that was the story Finn always told and so I was going to stick to it.

"Law enforcement. That can make a man funny," she said speculatively.

"You have no idea," I told her.

"But that's all over and done with. Isn't it?" She waved a hand as if waving away a bothersome horsefly. "It's time for you to think about Leif and what you want to do about him."

"I don't have any doubts about what I want," I said.

"So, you and Leif are happy together?"

"I have never met a man as wonderful as he is. Sure, his life is a bit . . . unconventional. But that's only because his job is so tough."

"How many companies does he own?"

45

"Only one, at the moment. But he works for the government sometimes, too. He's a forensic accountant."

She leaned back in her chair. "I don't suppose he would take a look at my tax returns, would he?"

I chuckled and shook my head. "Not that kind of accountant. At least, not anymore. Now he tracks down people who hide money from the government in other countries and use it to fund illegal activities."

"Like, drug dealers?" she asked, her eyebrows arched.

"More like tax-evaders setting up shell companies they use to cheat folks out of their retirement money," I said.

"Well, see? He's got a good job, then. Nobody in Killdeer knows what he really does for a living, so whenever I hear someone mention Leif Gable, the other person always says something about the nice secret agent man who lives up above the Dearcorn ranch."

It was my turn to laugh. "Do they really say that? You know, someday I'm going to start a rumor that the quarterback for the Denver Broncos is going to buy a ranch in Killdeer Valley and see how much traction that story gets."

"But in the meantime," Tatiana said, giving me a stern look, "why do I get the feeling you ain't totally sure about Leif?"

I shrank back a little. "I take marriage seriously. It's not something that I want to jump into. He would get married tomorrow on the front porch with an owl and a squirrel as the witnesses. He doesn't have a bit of hesitation when it comes to us tying the knot."

Tatiana took my hand and squeezed it hard. "Marley, that's a good thing. You want a man who knows what he wants and isn't afraid to go get it."

"Do I deserve it?" I asked.

"Do you deserve what?" she demanded.

"Do I deserve a man like Leif? He's practically perfect in every way. I have a hard time finding a pair of shoes that match when I go to work."

"Does he love you just the way you are?" she asked, looking me in the eye.

"He sure seems too." I was ashamed of my own doubts.

"Listen to me," Tatiana said, giving my hand a quick shake. "There is only one thing that I can say that I think might do you any good in this situation."

"What's that?" I asked.

"You just have to ask yourself one question. The answer to that question will tell you all you need to know."

"What's the question?" I asked, hoping that it really was that simple.

Tatiana released my hand and tapped her finger on my forehead. "Forget about your head. Sometimes it can lead us off in crazy directions. Ask yourself what is in your heart, instead. When you know what that is, then you will know what to do."

CHAPTER 4

Irene Baker slammed the telephone down on the café counter and gave me a pointed look. "So, make the call."

I felt a bead of sweat roll down between my shoulder blades. Maybe this wasn't such a brilliant plan after all.

"Are you sure you don't mind me using the café's phone?" I asked, hoping she would change her mind.

I sat in my usual spot at the counter of Lil's, the busiest diner in Killdeer.

Irene, my best friend and confidante, who just happened to own the café and was dating my father, pinned me down with her fierce blue eyes. "Don't be chicken. Call him. If you think this will put an end to all of your self-flatulating, then do it."

"Uh, I think it's self-flagellating," I said. "Flatulence is something else altogether."

"Marley," she said, ignoring my comment, "you should have put this whole issue to bed a long time ago."

"Could we please not talk about putting things to bed when we discuss my cheating ex-husband?"

Irene pulled a small stool out from underneath the counter and propped one hip on the seat. She swept her busy café with a stern gaze and let her sharp eyes drift back to me. "Call him. I think it is a great idea. You have let your past get in the way of living your life for long enough, and it's time you confronted Allen about a lot of things, not just what happened with the cocktail waitress."

"Irene, I don't want to dredge up that awful deal again. Particularly with him."

To say that what had happened two years ago was an awful deal was the understatement of the year. I had been fired from my job at the Montana Fish and Wildlife branch office in Helena because I stuck my nose into a criminal investigation that had turned sour. A poacher our office investigator had been pursuing had a thriving illegal elk velvet business going, and we were about to put him out of business permanently. But something had gone terribly wrong, and the poacher had pulled up stakes and disappeared days before the investigator planned to make an arrest.

The case had been a total loss. Since the lead investigator in the branch office was my friend, and I had occasionally overstepped my official duties by collaborating with him while he worked a case, the investigator assumed that I had made a mistake and somehow said something that had tipped the poacher off. I was convinced it was actually the investigator himself who had made some sort of mistake, but either way, someone had to get fired because of it, and that someone turned out to be me.

Our branch office was tiny compared to the huge main office in Helena, and because of our small size we were perhaps a bit too familiar with each other. The investigator, Bruce Duvekot, had a wife and kids to support, and at the time I only had a car payment and rent. Maybe I should have fought harder to keep my job because I hadn't done anything wrong, but I knew someone was going to get fired and since I didn't have a family it made more sense for me to take responsibility. I took the fall for the botched investigation, left the office under a cloud, and never looked back.

It was a mistake that I regretted almost every single day.

It hadn't helped matters that I had divorced my husband Allen, who was also a game warden, six months before the botched investigation.

After I was gone he'd invested a great deal of energy in daily Marley-bashing with his coworkers, who in turn gossiped with the staff from my old office. The truth of it was that I couldn't stand the thought that everyone back at my old job thought I would have made such a catistrophic mistake. My hope at the time had been that most of my friends and coworkers would make the assumption that I had simply made an awful mistake.

It hadn't quite worked out that way.

Even though I hadn't been responsible for the poacher fleeing and the case falling apart, Allen took great delight in telling me it would have been a terrible mistake to ever show my face in Helena again. He informed me shortly after I'd moved back to Killdeer that I was persona non grata in Helena, and particularly with the Fish and Wildlife service.

I couldn't stand the thought that my ex-husband had spent so much time trying to convince everyone that I had set out to sabotage an investigation, which simply wasn't true at all, and that he didn't know I'd actually taken the blame to protect Bruce.

The way things had unfolded still hung over my head like a black cloud, even now.

These old feelings were even now getting in the way of my potential happiness with Leif. My confidence was shot. Irene was right, I had to confront Allen about his awful behavior and put it behind me at last.

I picked up the phone, cradled the receiver in the crook of my neck and dialed the number.

Irene gave me a curt nod, her short blonde hair bouncing with the gesture. I could see by her expression that she approved of what I was doing, even though I was not at all certain that my actions would have the desired outcome.

He answered on the fourth ring. "This is Allen Hunter."

I tried to say something but my throat was so dry nothing came out. I squeaked out a cough, cleared my throat and tried again. "Allen, it's Marley."

Total silence.

"Allen?"

"I heard you the first time," he said.

"Listen, I know it's sudden, me calling like this. But I need to ask you a favor."

"Oh? You didn't call to gloat?" he asked.

"Gloat about what?"

"Never mind. What do you want?" he asked.

I could hear the roar of a truck engine in the background. He was driving somewhere and that meant he was on his cell phone in the middle of nowhere. I needed to talk fast in case his signal cut out suddenly.

"Allen, I need to meet you in Three Forks. I need your help with something."

I could hear him shifting gears. "You want my help with what?"

His tone was harsh, which I had expected. Allen could be charming to the nth degree, but he could also be as abrasive as a hornet.

"Can you meet me or not?" I asked. "This isn't something I want to talk about over the telephone."

The engine noise abated and I could hear that he had pulled over and parked. He sighed. "When?"

"Tomorrow. Can you meet me at the Sacajawea Hotel?"

"I suppose. What time?"

I did some quick mathematical gymnastics. "About four. I'll be in Pompey's Grill in the hotel."

"Fine."

The line went dead. I stared at the receiver for a moment before hanging up the phone.

Irene leaned both elbows on the counter. "He say he would be there?"

"He'll be there," I told her.

Irene set a glass of iced tea in front of me and placed a white paper napkin beside it. "Okay, spill it. What is this meeting really all about?"

I sipped the tea and tried to find a way to tell her without telling her everything. I had made a promise to Bruce that I would never talk about what had really happened during the investigation, at least, not in any great detail. But Irene was my best friend and she deserved to know at least part of the story.

"The reason I called Allen is mostly so that I can clear the air about what happened when I got fired. But the excuse I am going to use is this."

I pulled out the film canister Tatiana had given me and I unscrewed the lid.

Irene peered inside and saw the small brown tick crawling around on the bottom of the aluminum canister. "A blood-sucking insect. Is this some sort of esoteric comment on the nature of the relationship between men and women that I just don't quite get?"

I replaced the lid on the canister and shoved it inside my shirt pocket. "Ticks are arachnids, not insects. And it's just an excuse I'm using to go talk to him. I want him to take it to the biologist up at the Missoula office and have her identify it for me."

"And while you're at it, just happen to bring up all the nightmares from your past together," she said.

"And get a little bit of information about wolves if possible," I said.

"Wolves? What do they have to do with anything?" she asked.

I stared at her. "Irene, haven't you heard about Zane Ackerson?"

She kicked the stool out from under her hip and shoved it back under the counter. "What about Zane Ackerson?"

"He's dead," I said, incredulous. It was the first time I could remember telling Irene news that she didn't already know.

"What? When did this happen?" she asked, her mouth gaping. "And when in the bloody blue blazes were you planning on telling me?"

"It happened this morning, early. Over at Deep Creek Ranch."

"Did a jealous husband finally put an end to him?" she asked.

"It looked like he was attacked and mauled by an animal." I rubbed my tired eyes.

"Tell me you were not smack in the middle of this."

"More like I was on the periphery."

"And just how periphery are we talking here?" she demanded.

"Tatiana called me to come over and determine if the plague wiped out a prairie dog town on her ranch. We found Zane not too far from the dogtown. It looked like he had only been dead a couple of hours."

"Mauled, huh? So every idiot with two brain cells to rub together is going to jump to the conclusion that Zane was killed by a wolf. No wonder you want to go see Allen out of the blue like this."

I suppressed a yawn. It was already four in the afternoon and I hadn't eaten since breakfast. I was starting to fade fast. "I know he might be able to tell me a little bit about what a wild animal attack looks like. Although mostly, I think the attacks he has seen are bear-related. But, it's a place to start."

"Does Loy have anything to go on?" she asked.

"Not anything specific. Deputy Nick interviewed Brian Hix while we were there. Tatiana found out that people trespass on her land from time to time when she isn't looking, and I found out that Jennifer Hix may or may not be very happy being married to Brian."

"I can't imagine anyone could be happy being married to Brian Hix. That crew over on the Bybee ranch could give Italian gigolos a bad name."

"Gigolos?" I asked.

"Everyone is sleeping with everybody over at the Bybee. It's Peyton Place, with bits and spurs."

"I'm not sure that was why Zane got killed, at least in this case. I guess Zane was a conservationist at heart. Jennifer told us that Zane was riding alone out to the dogtown hoping he could see a black-footed ferret. He sort of had a passion for them and always wanted to see one in the wild."

I noticed for the first time how much dirt was collected underneath my fingernails.

"That's a shame," Irene said. "And right before rodeo weekend. Zane won't get to have one last hurrah. I didn't know him all that well, but I know he loved rodeo weekend."

"Name me one cowboy who doesn't. Can I have a bowl of minestrone?"

"You are having the buffalo burger," she said.

"Since when have you served buffalo?"

Irene glanced back through the portal leading to the kitchen and gave her pale, plump cook a nod. Andy nodded back and started preparing something.

"I'm only putting buffalo burgers on the menu for the weekend. But you are my taste tester, so tell me if you like it or not."

I rarely actually ordered my own food in Lil's, Irene's busy café. Inevitably whenever I sat down at the counter, on the center stool, which may as well have had my name on it, food arrived shortly thereafter whether I had requested it or not. Since Irene seldom accepted my money, I felt like I had no right to complain.

"Well, for once it is clear that you didn't discover a murder victim," Irene said with relief in her voice. "This sounds more like some kind of accident."

She snapped her fingers at a new waitress and pointed toward the door. Four lost and tired-looking tourists were heading across the parking lot and they wouldn't know about Lil's seat-yourself policy. Tourists usually stood in the doorway awkwardly until staff led them like sheep to a comfortable booth.

"I don't think it was an accident," I said.

Irene turned away from the door and gave me a glare that could wilt flowers. "Please tell me you are not mixed up in some sort of suspicious something-or-other."

"I'm not mixed up in anything. I have nothing to do with it," I said.

"And you plan to keep it that way, right?" she said, eyeing me.

"All I did was point out to Loy that I thought a few things looked out of place around Zane's body."

"Holy fitted sheets, Marley. Why don't you just apply for Nick's job while you are at it?"

"Don't worry. I won't have anything to do with this. I intend to leave it alone from now on."

"Promise me," Irene said, her arms folded.

"Look, just because I got a little carried away in the past and ended up involved in a couple criminal investigations doesn't mean that I shouldn't at least point it out when I see something that might help Loy solve a case he is working on."

Irene slapped one hand on the counter. "Promise."

I leaned back, spent a few moments fiddling with my ponytail, tying and retying it, so that I wouldn't have to answer right away.

"Marley," Irene said, her tone dangerous.

"Alright, alright. I promise. I won't get involved. Satisfied?"

Irene turned when she heard the order-up bell behind her and scooped up my buffalo burger deftly from the cook's window. She plunked the plate on the counter in front of me and slid a bottle of ketchup next to my elbow. "I'm satisfied for now.

But I've got my eye on you. And if I think you are getting too curious, like you sometimes have a habit of doing, I'm pulling out the big guns."

"You'll buy me a puppy so that I won't have time to snoop around anymore?" I asked.

"No. I'll tell your father," she said, her expression smug.

My lips pressed together. "You wouldn't."

"Bet me."

"Just because you are dating my father doesn't mean you are not bound by the best-friend confidentiality agreement."

"Maybe I am getting tired of visiting you in the hospital?" she asked.

I clamped my mouth shut and stared down at my plate. I couldn't argue with her about that. In the past I had pushed my curiosity to the breaking point while trying to uncover the secrets of my fellow small-town citizens in Killdeer, and on more than one occasion it had almost gotten me killed.

"Alright, I will stay out of it. There really isn't that much to stay out of anyway. Loy will probably find out it was nothing more than a horrible accident."

"The key here being that Loy will find this out," she told me.

Irene topped off my iced tea and I tore into the burger with both hands wrapped around the huge bun. With my mouth mostly full I gave the burger a thumbs-up. "This is really good."

"Now, back to Allen," she said, pulling her stool back out and propping herself up with one hip.

"While I'm eating?" I said with a groan.

"I just want to know what you intend to talk about with him, that's all."

"The blood-sucking bug."

57

"Not to be confused with the cocktail waitress from Kalispell," she said.

"And I want to discuss the wolf issue," I said, taking another bite of the burger and ignoring her comment.

"There are no wolves in this part of Montana," she said.

"That's what I keep telling everyone."

Irene poured herself a cup of strong black coffee. "Except that everyone knows that there really are wolves in this part of Montana."

"And I want to confront him about what happened three years ago," I told her.

"And by confront you mean kick him in the balls."

"I mean sort out what happened and try to put it all behind me."

She patted my arm sympathetically. "You know, men don't need both testicles. If he was to rupture one while walking to his truck . . . "

I waved my arms. "It's not going to be like that."

"Honey, it's not you who should be apologizing, or explaining anything. It's Allen who should be apologizing to you."

"Maybe that's true," I said, feeling my appetite slow down.

"But if you need to do this in order to move on so that you and Leif can settle down without any baggage, then you need to do it."

"Thanks, Irene. I knew you would understand," I said, giving her a genuine smile.

I heard the café door open behind me, and Irene's eyes bulged when she looked up. She smoothed the lapel of her bright yellow blouse, then pasted on her cheeriest customer service smile and hastily slid her stool back under the counter.

"Sit anywhere you like." She beamed like a Dallas Cowboys cheerleader at the Super Bowl. "Anywhere here at the counter is fine."

I spun around to see what, or who, was making her act so girlish and saw a man standing directly behind me, staring right at me.

"I'm looking for Marley Dearcorn." His voice was like a tiger growl, and he spoke with a slight accent.

I looked him up and down, and then dropped my burger back on my plate and wiped my hands quickly on my napkin.

"I'm Marley," I said, getting to my feet.

He immediately reminded me of someone, but I couldn't imagine who. He didn't look like anyone I had ever seen in Killdeer.

His long golden hair was sun-bleached, tied with a leather strap in a loose ponytail that trailed down his back, and his skin was so tan he looked like he'd been baked in a brick oven.

He wore khakis from head to toe, a thick leather belt with a long knife dangled from his hip, and a faded oilcloth cutback hat was pulled low over his eyes. His boots were laced up almost to his knees, and I could see at a glance they were incredibly expensive Danner snake boots. They weren't made out of snakeskin, although their price would lead one to believe that. Danner snake boots were impervious to snake bites. And they were practically indestructible.

"I'm told to bring you to see Brian at the Bybee ranch," he said. "He's got questions about Zane. I heard you were there when they found him. We should go. Now."

Irene looked like she was about to cry. "Why don't you stay and have a little lunch first?"

"Sorry, Miss. Can't do that. Got to keep the boss happy." A half-smile played at his lips.

My ear strained to pin down his accent. It was very familiar.

"Can I finish my buffalo burger first?" I asked.

He frowned, looking at me like he was trying to judge how much I weighed, and determining whether or not it would be practical to simply carry me outside. Patience won out over duty.

He smiled. "Not a problem. You see that black Humvee in the lot? That's mine. I'll give you a lift when you are ready."

He turned and walked out without another word, leaving Irene staring after him with obvious frustration painted on her face.

"Wow," Irene said, breaking the silence. "That's Logan Hiser. He works for Brian at the Bybee ranch. Logan is their gamekeeper. I heard about him, but I've never seen him before."

"Gamekeeper," I said. "Why do I feel like I know him from somewhere?"

"Eat! You don't want to make him wait. And as soon as you get back tell me everything." Irene shoved my plate forward so hard it hit my elbows.

"You know what my father would say about me climbing inside a vehicle with a total stranger?" I asked.

"He's not a total stranger. Everyone knows who Logan Hiser is, but nobody knows anything about him. You like doing investigations, so get out there, and investigate him."

"Why do Brian and Jennifer Hix need a gamekeeper?" I asked, before cramming another bite of burger into my mouth.

Irene smiled and leaned over the counter until we were eye to eye. "Half the women in Killdeer think Logan is a keeper, but what they really want to know is, is he game?"

"Have I mentioned you are a dirty old woman?"

"Come on, Marley. You are off the market, but take one for the team and make the dreams come true for all the single gals down at the bank. Go find out if he is single. It will give you something to talk about on the ride."

CHAPTER 5

Logan Hiser turned out to be as talkative as a New York City hairdresser.

I didn't say two words the entire drive, but he chatted away like we were best friends.

"I understand concrete," he said, one hand on the wheel of the black Humvee and the other dangling out the window.

We tore down the dirt road like a stagecoach being chased by bandits.

Every single horse underneath the hood was going for all she was worth.

I tugged my seat belt to make sure it was tight.

"Concrete?"

"That's what he said. Rick, I mean. You know that he and Holly have been going at it for over fifteen years?"

"Rick. He works for Brian Hix, like you?" I asked.

"Rick is the ranch foreman, and Holly is the cook out there. They fight all the time, even though they aren't even married. One day, Rick says to me, he says he understands concrete. You put water on it, you pour it, smooth it out. Simple. It makes sense. But women? He says he never will understand them."

"Okay," I said, staring at him shamelessly. I was still trying to place his accent. Not exactly British, but not that different.

Logan glanced over and saw me watching him. His eyes were such a familiar steel blue color, I couldn't shake the feeling that I had met him before. But that was impossible. Who could forget a character like him?

"I told him, Rick, I says, you can't think about women like you think about concrete. Or horses, or vehicles for that matter. Makes me a wee bit spikey when blokes say things like that. Like women are that difficult to understand."

"Okay . . ."

His foot smashed the gas pedal to the floor. "I say that if you really want to get to know a woman, go camping with her."

I clutched the armrest and braced my knee on the dashboard. "Camping?" He didn't seem to notice the abject terror in my voice.

"Right. Camping. In the middle of nowhere. Preferably in the rain. You can learn more about a woman in twenty-four hours spent inside a soggy tent with nothing hot to eat and no dry socks than you could after five years of comfortable marriage."

I suppressed a yelp as he swerved around a tight corner, dust flying up behind us like smoke from a forest fire.

"Have you ever been married?" I asked, secure in the knowledge we would roll the vehicle at any moment.

"Me? Sure. Twice. Probably would have worked out except for that little problem I always seem to have with my pants."

"Pants?"

He gave me a wink.

"I couldn't seem to keep them on."

"Ah . . ."

"Now, if I had gone camping with my second wife before we'd gotten married, I would have known beforehand that she can dress out a fresh deer carcass in half an hour with nothing but a sharp boot knife."

"You think that would have made a difference?" I asked, watching him drive with a mixture of horror and admiration.

"I might have been more careful about where I left my pants." He tilted his head to the side speculatively. "I can tell you one thing, though. I understand women a lot better these days."

"You understand women?" I asked, my eyebrows in a permanent state of surprise. If he had a nasty rash somewhere personal, I was certain Logan was the type of man who would proudly strip down to show it off no matter who was watching.

He waved one hand, temporarily taking both hands off the wheel. "Sure I do. Women and men aren't that different. Take you, for instance. You probably want the same things that I want. A good job. Personal freedom. A happy relationship. Are you in a happy relationship at the moment?"

"I'm sorry," I said, interrupting his flow completely. "But do I know you from somewhere? I mean have you and I met before?"

Logan turned to look at me slowly, letting his eyes drift from the road for an alarming amount of time. "You don't know me, Cookie. But I know you."

"You do?"

He chuckled and turned the wheel sharply, miraculously managing to corner the speeding Humvee down a long driveway without killing us both. "Looks like we made it. Listen, a hunting party is just wrapping up their tour. If any of those blokes bother you, just smile and nod and walk away. When the fellas Brian brings up here from Texas see a pretty woman they go about half crackers."

A massive stone and timber house stood on the crest of a perfectly manicured ridge like it had been plucked straight off an Alaskan hunting resort and dropped in the middle of Montana. Tall pine trees protected the house from sun and wind on the east side. A grand view of the mountains came into view towards the southwest, showing off a spectacular vista of rolling hills dotted with clusters of aspens and massive cottonwood trees. A deep pond, swimming with ducks, graced the area at the base of the house and a redwood boardwalk snaked the entire perimeter of the blue water, giving the place a theme-park appearance.

A huge stable could just be seen poking out from the tree line behind the house, and from the looks of the roof, the stable was twice the size of Killdeer High School.

"I know, it's a bit overwhelming when you first see the place. But, it's boss, isn't it?" Logan said.

"I almost expect to see John Wayne walk out on the porch," I replied.

"John who?" he asked.

I laughed. "You're kidding, right?"

We pulled up the long driveway and Logan slammed on the brakes, grinding the Humvee to a halt in the massive courtyard beside the house. He threw the vehicle in park and kicked open his door, slamming it behind him with so much force I jumped.

I got a good look at the long stables behind the house and realized that all of the barns and sheds on my father's ranch could easily fit inside.

Further down the slope from the stables sat a smaller building that looked like it was constructed of cinder blocks. The cinder block building was squat, square and painted industrial beige. A long row of fans lined the roof, and it looked like a warehouse of some sort. All of the fans on the roof were running full-blast.

Logan saw me looking at the cinder block building and jerked his chin towards it. "We keep the meat in there. After a hunt, it saves time for us to have our own refrigerated storage house."

"This is some operation," I said.

As we headed across the compound I saw a cluster of a half a dozen men gathered on the wide porch watching us. They looked to be in their forties, and most of them were fatter and paler than the average ranch hand. They stood with their legs spread far apart, wearing haughty grins on their faces. Each one of them held either a cigar or a bourbon glass.

I'd been around Leif Gable long enough to recognize a wealthy businessman when I saw one. But where Leif held himself with self-assurance, these men seemed to have an aura of entitlement about them.

Logan nodded towards a side door. "This way. Brian said you were to wait in the library."

Logan took one step for every two of mine, and I trailed after him, hurrying to keep up as he bounded up the stairs two at a time. All of the men on the porch leaned over the railing to get a good look at us as we went by.

I couldn't hear the comments, but a chorus of laughter erupted from the group as we disappeared inside the massive house. One of the men leaned over the railing and called out to Logan.

"Is she for dessert tonight?"

Logan muttered something under his breath. He gave me a sideways glance. "Sorry about that, Marley. They are crude, but the bastards help pay the bills "

We went through the heavy side door and instantly a cool wave of air-conditioning washed over us. We tromped through a big utility room and I could see that we had just come through what was probably considered the servants entrance.

Logan led me out of the utility room, down a wide hallway and into the main part of the house. I actually missed a step when I saw the huge entryway.

The ceiling was thirty feet tall, at least, and supported by massive beams that were less like boards and more like whole trees. A single one of the long beams could have supplied enough lumber for an average-sized toolshed. The floors were hardwood, polished, and gleamed from the reflected light of the elk horn chandelier dangling over the center of the room like some huge floating antler graveyard.

Logan didn't even glance up as we went through the entryway and down another long hallway. I couldn't take my eyes off it.

"Here we go," he said, stepping aside and making a sweeping gesture towards a huge room just off of the hallway.

As he lifted his hand it exposed his right tricep, and I could see a row of old white scars trailing across the skin. They looked like claw marks. Big claw marks.

Logan dropped his arm and stepped aside. I walked inside the library and I swore my footsteps echoed in the enormous space.

I turned a slow circle around the room, staring at the walls with confusion. "Where are the books?"

Logan glanced at the bookcases as if seeing them for the first time. "Huh. Guess I've never actually been in here before. Couldn't tell ya."

The tall cases were constructed of polished oak, with shelves that went from floor to ceiling, but not one book sat on the empty shelves. The furniture was oversized, leather, and looked like it had been brought in on a forklift.

I heard the sound of high heels on hardwood and turned to see Jennifer Hix striding around the doorway. She smiled when she saw me, spared a quick, disapproving glance towards Logan and swept to a stop in front of me with a gracious smile and her hand extended.

"So good of you to come, Marley."

I shook her hand, noticing that she had ditched the jeans she'd worn to Tatiana's ranch and was now dressed in a black linen skirt, white sleeveless crushed velvet top and enough turquoise jewelry to open a pawn shop in Arizona.

My hand stuck to hers ever so slightly, and I realized Peanut's sugar cube slobber was crusted all over my palm. Had I eaten my buffalo burger with horse spit all over my hands?

"Not a problem," I said, trying to casually wipe off my hands on my tattered jeans.

Jennifer turned towards Logan with a brittle smile. "That'll be all for now, Mr. Hiser. Don't worry about taking Miss Dearcorn back to town, I can give her a lift when she is ready to go."

He was staring at me with a lazy grin. "I don't mind."

"I said, I will give her a lift," Jennifer told him, her tone indicating that there would be absolutely no negotiations on the subject.

I felt the hairs on the back of my neck rise up as Logan swept me with his gaze one last time before backing out of the room. Before he turned away he gave me a sly wink.

"Why don't we have a seat?" Jennifer said, motioning with a perfectly manicured hand towards the massive leather sofa.

I looked down at my grungy jeans and mumbled, "I might be covered with hayseeds."

"Nonsense, darlin'. You should see the men who come in here after a hunt and get blood all over the carpets."

Jennifer eased onto the sofa and I perched at the other end, doing my best not to touch too much of the fabric.

"Logan told me that your husband wanted to ask me a few questions about Zane," I said, not entirely sure what I could possibly add. Surely Nick had gone over all of the important details with Brian when he had interviewed the man earlier?

Jennifer's eyes glittered mischievously as she watched me. "Listen, Marley. I've got to level with you. It wasn't Brian who wanted to talk to you. It was me."

The afternoon's events had been so surprising up till now that this was mild compared to what I'd already seen. "Really."

"You see, I think that I spend too much time out here at the ranch with nobody to talk to, and well, I liked you when we met over at Tatiana's. So I thought maybe we could be friends."

She tossed her hair and rested her arm on the back of the sofa.

"There does seem to be a shortage of women on this ranch," I said.

She caught me staring at her velvet top and twenty pounds of hammered silver jewelry and a slow smile spread across her face. "It's obscene, isn't it?"

"Excuse me?" I asked, not entirely certain what she was talking about.

What was going on here? I'd met her six hours ago, but apparently that was long enough for us to be cozy.

"This," she said, running a hand over her expensive top. "And this." She waved one arm, generally taking in the house, the decorations and the ranch itself.

"This place. These clothes. They really are over the top, don't you think?" she asked.

"This is a lovely ranch," I said, knowing my tone sounded forced.

"It's all for show. I mean, for Brian and his clients."

"Is this some sort of a hunting lodge, then?" I asked.

Jennifer's face stiffened. "Something like that. You know we raise buffalo, and we have access to fifteen miles of the Snowy River with some of the best trout fishing in Montana. God almighty, I sound like one of Brian's brochures."

I was beginning to think there was a lot more going on underneath the surface of Jennifer Hix than even her husband knew about. But was she so desperate for company she would reach out to a total stranger? Well, being lonely and locked in total isolation surrounded by crude businessmen at all times would make any woman desperate.

"So, I take it that you didn't always live like this?" I asked.

"Not even close," she said. "I'm from Austin and most of my life I've spent wondering if I'd be able to pay the rent or if I'd starve to death. I met Brian three and a half years ago at a fund-raising event for a sportsmen's organization."

"So you like to hunt?" I asked.

Jennifer laughed. "I don't even know which end of a gun to point where. I was only there because I was one of the items up for bid."

"You were up for bid?" I asked with a laugh. "I guess Texas isn't such a stick-in-the-mud state after all."

"See? This is why I wanted Logan to bring you out here. You don't take things so damn seriously."

"I don't think I've got it in me to take things too seriously," I told her.

"I was one of the prizes, but more like my time was the prize. I'm a painter, an artist. I'm really good, too. I donated my time to the auction and the one who bid the highest would be able to sit for a portrait that I would paint for them. That's how I met Brian. He saw me on the auction block and bid twelve hundred bucks for me before anyone else could raise their hand. Six months later . . ." she held up her hands and her bright expression faded.

For the first time I noticed an oil painting hanging above the fireplace. It was a spectacular close-up of an African lion, and the detail was so stunning it almost looked like a photograph.

"Is that one of yours?"

She beamed. "I did that one six months after we moved up here permanently. You like it?"

I studied the bright golds, intense yellows and the striking eyes of the lion. "It's amazing, actually."

"I never expected to be able to paint full-time, but here I am."

"Married and living in Montana," I finished for her.

"I can't complain," she said, shrugging. "I mean, look at this place. It's sort of like something out of an architectural magazine. And the vistas? I never run out of things to paint. And I sure as hell don't have to worry about my dental plan."

"Are you trying to convince me, or you?" I asked.

Jennifer closed her mouth and gave me a steady look. "I love my husband. I do. Don't misunderstand me. But being married to Brian is really difficult sometimes. He is always so busy with his clients. The hunters, I mean. The men he flies up here from Texas to take on fishing trips, or guided hunting trips. He charges a fortune, but it's more of the Wild West experience than most of these guys would ever have otherwise, so they pay the fee. They can all afford it, too. But they are terrible shots. That's why Brian hired Logan."

"Where did Logan come from, Jennifer?" I asked, genuinely curious about the man. I was certain I had never met him before, but he apparently knew who I was.

"That's the thing," she said, frowning. "Logan just showed up one day. He said he heard we needed a gamekeeper and after twenty minutes alone with Brian he was all of a sudden on the payroll."

"What do you think of Logan?" I asked.

"What do I think of him? He gives me the creeps, that's what," she said. "One minute you are sitting on the patio minding your own business and then there's Logan, leering at you from behind a shrub and who knows how long he has been standing there. He doesn't make a sound when he walks. He wears this big knife strapped to his belt like Tarzan. Marley, he's genuinely odd."

"I know what you mean," I said.

Jennifer was so forthright, so disarming, that talking to her was as natural as if we had known each other for years.

Either that, or she was going to extraordinary lengths to make it feel that way.

She rolled her eyes. "Not that I think Logan is dangerous, or anything. He's just so . . ."

"Strange," I said.

"Do you know that I once opened up the big freezer out in the garage and there was a live rattlesnake inside?"

"You're kidding." I tried to remember if my own father had ever done that before. Probably.

She rested her forehead against her hand. "Logan said he was saving it for later. It was still alive, just so cold it couldn't move very fast. Talk about giving a girl a heart attack."

"What was he going to do with a live rattlesnake?" I asked.

"That's nothing," she said with a laugh. "I went into the kitchen once and there was this huge—"

A man's voice boomed from the hallway. "Jenny, what in the hell are you doing?"

We glanced up and saw Jennifer's husband Brian, standing in the doorway of the library, glowering. His hands were balled into fists and his wide frame blocked out most of the light.

"I've got a half-dozen hunters for dinner tonight. Rick said the generator is on the fritz and nobody knows what happened to Holly. And who's this?" he asked, glaring at me suspiciously.

"Marley is a friend. She and I were just visiting." Jennifer's voice was suddenly demure and placating.

"You aren't some waitress or shopgirl from Killdeer, are you?" Brian asked me. "You look like you should be cooling down the horses in the stables."

I blinked with my mouth hanging open before I realized that he was actually serious. "Excuse me?"

"Marley is engaged to Leif Gable, remember, dear?" Jennifer said quickly. "You know, the CEO over in Killdeer?"

Brian's eyes narrowed as he studied me. He lifted his chin and grunted. "Right. I remember Gable. Well, don't get too carried away in here, girls. We have cocktails starting up in the dining room and we men need our privacy."

Jennifer smiled with perfect teeth. "I was just running her back to town. I'll be home in time to wish them all goodnight."

Brian turned and walked away without another word, leaving us staring after him.

I turned back to Jennifer and whispered, "What was that all about?"

She leaned towards me, her voice conspiratorial and low. "Brian doesn't like it when I associate with girls who are beneath my status." She laughed and covered her mouth to stifle the sound.

"Honestly?"

She rolled her eyes and squeezed my arm with one hand. "He won't even let me be friends with Holly, can you believe it? She's our cook. He says that you don't associate socially with people who bring you your food."

"Do you like Holly?" I asked, shocked that some husbands had that sort of power over their wives. If Leif had ever tried to tell me who to be friends with I would have reevaluated the relationship. Not that Leif would ever have done such a thing in the first place.

Jennifer let her disappointment show. "I love Holly. She's the best. But the only time I ever get to spend with her is when Brian is on a business trip."

We both turned towards the doorway as the raucous sound of restless hunters erupted from the front of the house.

The horde was descending on the dining room and they were so loud the windows were rattling. Jennifer jerked her chin towards the door and the two of us made a break for it.

We slipped out the back through the kitchen, down the steps and trotted across the vast courtyard, leaving the group of men behind. Jennifer pointed at a white sporty SUV with sleek lines and tinted windows parked behind Logan's black Humvee. The little white vehicle was some sort of an Audi. Not cheap, that was for certain.

"That's mine. I'll take you home now, because trust me, you won't want to be around when those hunters start drinking."

"Amen to that," I said.

We climbed inside the little SUV, the heat from summer making the seats hot to touch, and shut the doors. Jennifer reached over and hit the start button on the dash and immediately cranked on the air-conditioning. I noticed that the key fob that allowed the engine to start was nestled inside the cup holder.

"You leave your keys in your car?" I asked.

"Who's gonna steal it out here?" she replied.

"I could," said a woman's voice.

Jennifer screamed, I spun around and each of us had one hand on our door as we frantically looked behind us.

"Holly Koltiska!" Jennifer said, clutching her chest. "You scared the life out of me."

A woman sat in the backseat of the SUV, crouched down, her face wet with tears. A half empty beer bottle was clutched in her right hand. The interior of the car was scalding hot, but she didn't seem to notice it.

"Oh, darlin'. You and Rick have another scrap?" Jennifer asked, looking at her tear-stained face.

"Why do men have to be so stupid?" Holly asked, wiping at her cheeks. "Rick went ballistic about it being rodeo weekend and he says he doesn't want me to leave the ranch until after Sunday afternoon. Like I'm going to stay locked up inside while everyone else gets to party."

She looked to be about my age, maybe a little older, and even though my life hadn't always been smooth, this woman wore an expression that said she expected trouble at any moment. Her long auburn hair was braided in a tight weave, but strands had come loose and framed her face like a halo. She was dressed more like me than like Jennifer. Jeans, clean button-down white shirt. She couldn't be described as pretty, but she was attractive in a strong way. She looked like a woman who could handle herself, and yet here she was, crouching out of sight like a wounded animal.

"Why do you always hide out in my car whenever you and Rick have an argument?" Jennifer asked.

"Because your car has tinted windows and the idiot never thinks to look in here," Holly replied. "It's the only smart thing I've done all day."

76

"Now, Holly. Stop it," Jennifer told her.

"Jen, why do I put up with him?" Holly asked. She took a long swig from her beer.

Jennifer's expression softened. "Why do any of us put up with them?"

"I need a drink," Holly said, staring at her beer.

"You've got a drink," Jennifer pointed out.

"I need something stronger," she said.

I looked back and forth between the two women and decided that perhaps now was the time to give in to circumstance. It seemed that my night was destined to be hijacked and the best course of action was to just go with it.

"Well, rodeo is here this weekend," I said, watching them both. "Anyone up for a round of butt-darts?"

Jennifer's face squinched up. "Butt-darts?"

"God, that's perfect," Holly said, sitting up and pulling her seat belt on. "Take us to the fairgrounds, Jen."

"What is a butt-dart, exactly?" Jennifer asked as we peeled out of the courtyard.

We bounced down the road away from the house, and as we rounded the first turn beside the pond I noticed that Logan Hiser was standing on the redwood boardwalk, watching us as we zipped by.

"Jennifer, you just have to see it for yourself," I told her.

We drove around the pond and started down the road towards Killdeer, and when I turned back and looked behind us at the boardwalk, Logan was nowhere in sight.

CHAPTER 6

"I'll bet you've never seen so many belt buckles in your entire life," Holly said to Jennifer, her voice straining over the crowd noise.

Jennifer took a swig off a Mike's hard lemonade. "Are you kidding? I'm from Texas, remember?"

"Okay, they are getting ready to start." I took a sip from my bottled water. It had already been firmly established that I didn't plan on drinking, so Jennifer and Holly were taking it upon themselves to make up my deficit between them. Holly was furiously slurping down a Long Island iced tea.

"Explain the rules to me again?" Jennifer asked, leaning forward on the bench so she could see the arena below.

We sat in the front row of the fairgrounds bull and livestock auction pen. The pen was surrounded with a tight circle of benches like a typical arena, but the pen was much smaller than a sports complex. Its only purpose was to accommodate up to seventy ranchers who were contemplating purchasing that million-dollar bull they had always wanted. But tonight the pen was being used for an entirely different spectacle. More than a hundred spectators crammed the benches, hooting and catcalling the butt-dart contestants shamelessly, and violating six or seven county fire codes simultaneously.

"First, it helps a lot if you have no sense of shame," Holly explained.

"And if you have good clenching abilities." I pointed to the row of contestants.

Six mostly sober cowboys were lined up at the start of a hastily fabricated obstacle course, their boots polished and their hats brushed clean.

"Is this like that game where you toss pennies onto dishes at the carnival?" Jennifer asked, pointing at a tray filled with several shot glasses sitting on a small table.

"Not exactly," I said, trying to find a way to explain it.

Holly took a long pull on her drink and gestured at the obstacle course. "It's like this, Jen. You see those six guys standing around like they are about to win the Nobel Prize? They are the butt-dart contestants. They take a quarter, you know. A regular quarter, not a fifty-cent piece because those are too big. Well, they stick that quarter between their cheeks, and I'm talking the ones holding up their Wranglers and not the ones they use to hold their chewing tobacco. They clench it tight, and then they have to walk through that obstacle course without dropping that quarter."

"Seriously?" Jennifer asked.

"It's not as easy as it looks," I said. "The average cowboy wears jeans that are so tight it's a miracle they can hold on to the quarter for six seconds, let alone keep it clenched there through an obstacle course."

Jennifer made an adorable pout while she thought about it.

"And what do they get if they make it clear to the end of the course?"

"Oh, it's not over yet," I said. "When they get to the end, they have to straddle a shot glass that is sitting on the ground. Then they let go of the quarter and try to make it drop right into that shot glass. If the quarter hits it and stays in, then they win."

"The guy on the end can barely stand up," Jennifer pointed out.

"You know, your degree of intoxication isn't really a factor in how well you will do," I said. "The only time being drunk seems to get in the way of these guys is if they are not able to stand up anymore."

"Sort of reminds me of my wedding," Jennifer remarked.

"Let's hear it for Randy Newman!" shouted the man running the show. The emcee was tall, dressed in his best black jeans and sported a spotless white Stetson cowboy hat. His perfect white button-down shirt looked like it had been pressed five minutes ago. He positively gleamed.

"Randy was second runner-up last year, and might have won the entire competition if we hadn't had that unfortunate incident of spectator interference," the emcee said.

"Randy got hit in the head by a beer bottle," Holly explained. She shrugged. "I wasn't throwing it at him."

The emcee lifted his hat, signaling off to his right, and I saw a tight little guitar band hunched together in the stock chute off to the side. They started playing a Charlie Daniels Band song.

"Drinkin' My Baby Goodbye?" I asked.

Jennifer nodded. "I love that song."

"Amen to that!" Holly said, lifting her drink and sucking down another swig.

"She doesn't mean it," Jennifer said, leaning in and talking low in my ear. "Rick will beg and plead and they will be back together by lunch tomorrow."

"Do Rick and Holly fight like this all the time?" I asked, giving Holly a worried look. She was digging in her pocket for more cash to refill her glass.

"They go on benders. Sometimes it's quiet for weeks, and then all of a sudden Rick decides Holly doesn't love him enough, or she hasn't shown him enough affection, whatever. He starts in on the demands and the yelling is so bad you can hear it all the way from the stables."

"Ready, Randy? On your mark," said the emcee.

Randy, the enthusiastic cowboy wearing a garish purple plaid shirt, shoved the quarter between his butt cheeks and pinched it hard. It slipped once and he used his right hand to position it higher, using his thighs more than his cheeks to hold the quarter in place. The entire process was hysterical to watch and everyone hooted uproariously. Once the quarter was firmly clenched, Randy grinned and gave the ready signal.

"Set, and go!"

Another man, apparently the official timekeeper, also wearing a spotless white cowboy hat, clicked a digital stopwatch and Randy set off for glory.

His purple shirt making me cross-eyed from its loud colors, Randy wiggled his way over the tiny rocking bridge, walking very much like a penguin, hopped skillfully over a balance beam laying on the ground, successfully picked up and rode a handlebar skateboard, then walked backwards twelve paces until he was near the finish line. The man in the gleaming hat pointed him towards a shot glass resting on the ground.

The emcee handed Randy a shot of whisky, which the cowboy downed with one gulp, and stepped aside.

"You know what to do, Randy," he said, nodding towards the glass on the ground.

The crowd was clapping and hollering like crazy. I felt a splash of beer dribble down the back of my neck as the folks behind me jumped to their feet.

Randy slowly and carefully straddled the shot glass.

The crowd went still.

Randy bowed his knees out and held his breath so hard he turned red.

The quarter fell, clanged loudly on the edge of the glass, hopped once and then settled inside with a final chink.

Everyone cheered.

"That was . . . amazing," Jennifer said, her voice barely able to project over the noise. "Can we go?"

"Had enough?" I asked, smirking.

"Maybe we could go someplace with actual chairs," she said, getting to her feet and rubbing her back. The benches were probably more comfortable when you were so intoxicated you couldn't feel your legs.

"Where are you going?" Holly demanded. She was snatching her second drink from a harassed waitress who was doing her best to keep up with the demand. I had no idea where the bar was located. Probably in the animal holding pen.

"Let's go to the Scape Goat," I suggested.

Jennifer gave me another worried look.

"It's a saloon here at the fairgrounds. We can sit down, if we can find a table."

"Holly, we're going to the Scape Goat," Jennifer said loudly, tugging Holly's arm.

The three of us shoved and stumbled our way out of the arena and I led them both towards the saloon that had been built, conveniently enough, beneath the fairground stands.

As we crossed the dusty track heading towards the Scape Goat, a huge black horse stormed by, trailing its reins and kicking and bucking like it had just broken out of a chute. An angry wrangler sprinted after it, waving his arms and shouting for people to get out of his way.

"You-all have a different idea about bad traffic here in Montana," Jennifer said as we pushed our way through the crowd.

We managed to squeeze through a loud bunch of PRC bareback riders who were loitering by the door of the Scape Goat, sipping beer and keeping a sharp eye out for the sheriff. I could tell from looking that at least two of them were considerably underage.

Jennifer got us a table. When her smile, charm and good looks didn't manage to move the hostess, a fifty-dollar bill did the trick. We were hastily seated at a small table at the end of the bar, with a good view of the action and within earshot of a loud group of seriously intoxicated bull riders. A trio of plump rodeo committee members shot us dirty looks from the crowded doorway, obviously incensed that we had gotten a seat before them.

"It's only Tuesday," Jennifer said, marveling at the crowd of energized patrons crammed inside the little saloon.

"It's Friday-o'clock somewhere!" Holly shouted.

The table of bull riders lifted their drinks towards her in solidarity and cheered with approval.

A four-top table of Crow Indian bareback relay racers sat quietly with their backs to the noisy bull riders. They turned and glared at the rowdy men who were shouting and saluting Holly with mostly empty bottles. One of the Crow men muttered something hostile, shaking his head and glaring towards the drunk cowboys with disgust. The bull riders ignored them, or they were so intoxicated they simply didn't notice the comment.

Cowboy hats bobbed, boots stomped on the wood floor, and dust drifted down from the rafters.

"What can I get you?" asked a pert waitress, wearing jeans so tight it hurt just to look at them. Her red hair was piled on the top of her head and bolted in place with at least twenty hairpins. She popped her chewing gum and watched us expectantly.

"I'll have a lemonade," I said.

"You want a shot on the side?" she asked.

"No. I'm driving."

She looked at me with a vapid expression. "Uh-huh. And how about you, honey?"

Jennifer smiled. "Oh. Give me a chardonnay."

The waitress stopped chewing her gum and stared.

Holly nudged Jennifer hard in the ribs with her elbow. "She means tequila."

"Sure," the waitress said, her face relaxing.

"And I'll take another Long Island," Holly said, slugging down the last gulp of her second drink.

The waitress sped off and we did our best not to rest our elbows on the top of the small round table. It probably hadn't been wiped off since January.

"Jen, look. It's Logan," Holly said, pointing to the door.

I turned and saw Logan Hiser waltzing to the front of the line. He had a shameless grin plastered across his face and a fat wad of caramel kettle corn clutched in one hand, and he strolled inside the saloon scanning the crowd until he saw us. He completely ignored the protests of the irate hostess and shoved his way through the pack like a rugby player.

He sauntered over to our table and pulled a chair next to mine, sat down and gave us all a happy grin. "Ladies."

"What are you doing here, Logan?" Jennifer asked, her eyes blazing with anger.

"Brian asked me to give you a lift home." He smiled at her with a full set of perfect teeth.

I almost expected to see a set of fangs.

"He did no such thing," she said.

"How did you find us?" I asked suspiciously. Was he following us?

"This is a bar, yes?" he said around a mouthful of kettle corn. He cast a meaningful look at Holly and rolled one shoulder in a casual shrug, as if that was explanation enough.

Apparently this was not the first time Logan had been sent to retrieve the women of the Bybee ranch.

He set his bag on the floor, all business now. "Anyway, I've never seen a Montana rodeo before. When do the bull riders go on?"

"Friday," Holly said, gushing and sighing as she glanced over at the table of noisy men. "They are so bad ass."

Holly tipped her glass as high as it would go and slurped the dregs of her drink. I found myself watching her with utter fascination. I'd never seen someone who liked to drink this much.

One of the bull riders had caught sight of Holly watching him, and he was doing his level best to focus his bloodshot eyes enough to determine if she was attractive or not.

Jennifer rolled her eyes and nudged Holly with an elbow. "Her problem is that she doesn't know when to quit."

"So, Mrs. Hix. How about we settle up with your server and get you home?" Logan stared at Jennifer like an irritated bird of prey.

Her face was red with anger. "I just got here, Logan."

I glanced over at the table of bull riders as the biggest member of the bunch stood up and announced to the saloon that drinks were on him. Then he lifted the last swig of beer from his bottle and poured it on his own head, laughing hysterically at his own bad joke.

The Crow relay-racers sitting at the table beside them kept shooting angry looks at the bunch. As the beer-soaked cowboy moved to sit back down, one of the Indians hooked the leg of his chair with his toe and pulled it sideways. The cowboy sat down into thin air and fell to the floor with a thud like a side of beef. He swore the air blue and tried to regain his footing, but only managed to hit his head on the bottom of the table during his struggles. The Crow Indians were laughing with delight.

The least drunk member of the wild bunch was pointing at the Indian who had moved the chair and was shouting accusations.

I wasn't sure how much longer the peace would hold.

The bull rider who had crashed to the floor managed to get to his feet and was searching for someone to blame for his sudden fall from grace. He turned to the Crow Indian man behind him and said something I couldn't understand.

"Hey, I'm talking to you," he said loud enough for the entire saloon to hear.

One of the younger Crow men gave the bull riders a smug look. He said something in his native tongue and the entire table of Indians laughed appreciatively at the joke. Obviously he'd said something derogatory.

"Hey, this is America," said the weaving cowboy. He held up one finger, making a proclamation. "And we talk American here."

A few of the other patrons of the Scape Goat were casting worried glances back and forth between the relay-racers and the bull riders, and one or two of the more sensible and sober customers were inching towards the door.

"Logan, I think leaving is not such a bad idea," I said. "Let's forget our drinks. We need to start heading for the car."

"No we won't," Holly said, pounding a fist on the table. "Rick thinks he can order me around, tell me what to do, make me stay home instead of going out and having a good time. I'm my own woman, dammit."

"So why don't you head on back to the ranch without us, Mr. Hiser?" Jennifer's lip curled up with obvious contempt.

"Don't tune me any cack, Mrs. Hix. We're going."

Tune me cack?

I felt my mouth drop open. I'd heard that expression before, many times, and I suddenly knew exactly where he was from. "Logan, you are from South Africa."

Logan waggled his eyebrows with a sly expression. He leaned in, his voice low. "Let's keep that between us, right?"

The bull rider who had crashed to the floor turned his full attention to the table of relay-racers. He weaved as he spoke. "I think you owe us a round. By way of apologizing."

"You wouldn't like our beer," said the young Crow man.

"Why's that?"

"It's 3.2 and probably too strong for you," he said, laughing.

The other relay-racers laughed right along with him.

"Yeah? Well, I'll bet your sister's not too strong for me."

At that moment the Crow Indian relay-racers' obnoxious meter went off, and they, as a group, stood up.

Jennifer and Holly seemed oblivious to what was about to happen.

I kicked Logan beneath the table and nodded towards Holly and Jennifer. "You take one. I'll take the other."

The bull riders, taking a cue from the irate relay-racers, were pushing their chairs back and doing their best to stand up without falling over.

Logan shot to his feet and grabbed Jennifer's elbow. "Right. We're leaving."

"I'm right behind you," I said, snagging Holly's arm.

The relay-racers burst into song and began pounding on their table with their bottles.

You didn't have to be a linguist to know what it was. It was a Crow war song.

The bull riders shouted at the relay-racers to shut up. The relay-racers shouted something back, and I saw Jennifer and Logan shoot out the front door.

"You spilled my beer!" yelled the weaving bull rider.

"You've had enough to drink, Cracker!"

And then the fight started.

A half dozen bottles sailed through the air, some striking their targets and some veering off in wild directions and hitting random patrons packed in the saloon.

Someone screamed.

Holly's arm slipped from my hand, she ducked sideways and ran, and in an instant the crowd swallowed her.

"Holly!"

I searched for her but she was darting through the press of bodies so fast I lost sight of her almost at once.

The bull riders rushed the Indians like a squad of offensive linemen. Tables, chairs and bodies crashed in all directions.

I hit the floor.

People started running madly, and it was clear that most of the patrons were too shocked to remember where the door was. I started crawling for the exit, trying to keep my hands from getting stepped on and stopping only when the legs were too crowded together to squeeze through.

Two men with handlebar moustaches and tall roper cowboy boots carefully set their beers down on their table and slowly got to their feet. They were older, wiser, and both of them were built like bomb shelters. They were true cowhands from the L Bar T Ranch, and had seen enough bar fights in their time to know how to deal with a mess. They waded into the fray feet first, kicking kneecaps and stomping insteps. It was turning into an every man for himself situation in a hurry.

I crawled under tables, using the furniture that was still upright as a shield. I slowly worked my way across the floor, and was halfway to the door before the fight spilled across the saloon and crashed into my shelter. My cover was blown and I was kneeling in the middle of the fight with nowhere to hide.

Just as a bull rider took a hard punch to the face and started to topple towards me, I felt a strong pair of hands grip me underneath my arms and hurl me to the side. The bull rider hit the floor in front of me with a sickening thud.

"Keep your head down!"

I couldn't see who was talking, but I obeyed desperately.

It was all I could do to keep my feet moving. I dodged chairs and weaved between bodies, trying to get to the door as fast as I could.

Someone held onto me from behind, steering me through the mess like I was a runaway wagon.

I was shoved forward and before my feet could slow down I crashed into two delighted oil-rig workers who were standing back-to-back, swinging their fists gleefully.

Before I could react one of the rig workers, caught up in the joy of fight frenzy, aimed a wild punch straight for my face.

I squeezed my eyes shut and braced for impact but the punch never reached me.

When I opened my eyes the worker was sprawled on his side, laid out on the dusty floor looking dazed.

I felt a hand underneath my arm and before I could stop I was shoved forward right towards the second frantic oil-rig worker. His glazed eyes locked on me and he lifted one fist almost in slow motion. Before he could blink, a hand quicker than a snake strike broke his nose and he toppled sideways.

With both men on the floor a hole appeared in the crowd, just big enough to break through, and I tumbled out the front door of the saloon and landed facedown on the ground. My palms skidded across the gravel as I slid to a stop.

The last thing I wanted was to be trampled by a mob rushing out of the front door and I tried to scramble to my feet.

Before I could even push off with my knees I was lifted off the ground and tossed bodily into the backseat of Logan's black Humvee.

I was facedown on the seat, but I heard someone shouting and the door slammed shut behind me. When I managed to sit up I saw Jennifer in the front seat, her face covered with smeared makeup and her hair sticking up.

"Marley, are you alright?" she asked. Her voice was oddly calm.

"Drive," said a voice beside me.

Logan was sitting in the driver's seat. He hit the gas, steering us deftly out of the fairgrounds and managing not to kill anyone in the process. Bodies lunged aside as Logan drove us across the fairgrounds.

I leaned back in the seat and looked over.

Finn sat beside me, scanning the parking lot with laser intensity. He quickly locked the door.

"Hey, Finn," I said, rubbing my hands.

He spared me a quick glance. "Are you injured?" His ice-blue eyes were flashing.

I winced as my palms started to sting. I looked at my hands. "Just a little road rash from the gravel."

He nodded once and continued to scan the crowd. His hands were up and ready.

"Where's Holly?" I asked. "We got separated."

"I saw her heading for the dustbins behind the saloon," Logan said. He spun the wheel hard, veering us toward the rear of the chaos.

Finn leaned forward. "Do not take us back there."

"Give it a rest, Finn. It's not a nuclear summit meeting. It's just a little bar fight."

Logan dodged and weaved through the bodies. People leapt out of our way as we headed for the rows and rows of covered garbage cans behind the saloon.

As Logan screeched to a halt, something heavy bounced from underneath the seat and landed on top of my foot. I rummaged around the floorboard and my hands found something cold and metal. My fingers wrapped around a pistol grip and I sat up abruptly.

"Logan, there's a gun on the floor back here," I said.

"It's a tranquilizer pistol," he said. "If Holly gives you any trouble we can dart her."

He chuckled and I glanced over at Finn to see if Logan was kidding. Finn shook his head with an expression of irritated disgust.

"There she is," Jennifer said, pointing at the last garbage can in the row behind the saloon.

I threw open my door and stepped out. My stomach did a flip-flop when I saw what she was doing.

"Jesus, Holly," I said.

She was standing beside a big green garbage can, and I could see that the entire lid was covered with discarded beer cups, some half empty, some with cigarette butts floating in the leftover beer, and some almost full.

Holly was picking up the cups that held the most beer and drinking them, one by one.

"Holly Koliska, you get in this car," I said, doing my best to snap her out of her stupor.

She looked up with a blurred expression, seemed to register the Humvee and reluctantly staggered towards me. I shoved her inside the backseat and climbed in after her.

As soon as my door was shut, Logan wheeled us around and we drove out of the fairgrounds at a furious clip, passing both sheriffs' trucks as we darted down the road towards Killdeer.

Loy's siren blared and his truck was lit up like a calliope. He and Nick raced towards the saloon, swerving through the running mob in tandem.

Jennifer sat back in her seat, shaking her head and muttering. "Butt-darts."

Holly was crying and saying that she was sorry, over and over again. I caught Rick's name muddled in with the sobs.

After a moment I turned towards Finn and stared at him until he noticed. "So," I said, flicking my eyes towards Logan, "which one of you is the oldest?"

CHAPTER 7

We screeched to a halt beside my vehicle in the parking lot of Lil's café. Finn stepped out of the Humvee and made a point of holding his door open.

I finally got the hint and climbed out after him, noticing with immense relief that the café was closed and there were no other cars in sight. At least Irene wouldn't be pestering me with questions after this. It would be the holy grail of gossip to see me get out of a vehicle containing a peeved-looking Finn, a laughing Logan Hiser, as well as a very drunk Holly and a furious Jennifer Hix.

It was like a bad sitcom joke waiting for a punch line.

Holly was curled in a ball on the backseat of the Humvee and Finn slammed the door. She didn't even twitch at the sound and it was obvious she was in a stupor, and for her, the night was officially over.

Logan rolled down his window and nodded at Finn. "What about your Jeep?"

Finn was clearly still in bodyguard mode. "I will retrieve it tomorrow. Marley cannot drive. Go home, Logan."

"I can drive." I fumbled in my jeans pocket for my car keys, wincing from the small cuts and scrapes on my palms. I'd hit the ground harder than I'd thought. Blood had dried on my hands and using them to handle a steering wheel would be a real problem.

Finn gave me a perturbed look and snatched the keys away from me. "No, you can't."

Jennifer pulled herself half out of the open passenger's window and poked her head over the top of the Humvee, her right butt cheek propped on the door's armrest. "Marley, I want you to come out to the ranch. We'll go riding."

"I don't own a horse anymore," I said.

"I'll get you one," she said. "Tonight was a wreck. But come out to the ranch and I'll make it up to you. I promise."

Logan started rolling up the passenger window, squeezing Jennifer's torso as he did. She struggled to free herself and slid back inside the Humvee, practically snarling at him.

"Seat belts fastened, Mrs. Hix," Logan said.

Jennifer slumped down and said something harsh to Logan, her face rigid. It was painfully obvious that the two of them hated each other.

Logan grinned at me and jerked his chin towards Finn. "He's older."

The Humvee squealed all four tires as it tore out of the parking lot.

Finn was already unlocking my SUV and climbing into the driver's seat. I scrambled to hop in as the engine fired up.

We drove south out of Killdeer and headed down the deserted dirt road that led to my father's ranch.

Our ranch had been in the Dearcorn family for four generations, and I lived at the very end of the road with Leif in his beautiful custom-built home on a secluded section of land that was, literally, the very end of the line. Thick pines and tall aspens surrounded Leif's home, and unless you knew it was there, it was practically invisible.

Finn wordlessly drove me past my father's ranch and headed down the rough dirt road, keeping his eyes fixed ahead, deliberately not looking at me until he pulled into my driveway.

"Ask Leif if he will take me back to the weather station," Finn said as I started to climb out.

"He's in Panama."

Finn grimaced. "You should not tell people when your man is not at home."

"You just pulled me out of a riot," I pointed out. "I think you can be trusted. And, how did you know where I was, anyway?"

He seemed to consider the question. "I was not looking for you. I was trying to find Logan."

"Lucky for me," I said.

"If I bandage your hands, do you think you can drive me back?" he asked.

It didn't take long until we were sitting at the black granite-topped counter in the kitchen with a bottle of hydrogen peroxide, swabs, bandages, ointment, tape and medical scissors.

"Leif keeps a very respectable complement of medical supplies," Finn said, deftly cleaning and dressing my palms.

I could tell from his curt responses and stern expression that he was still on duty in his mind.

He moved so quickly I hardly had time to wince. "Thanks for saving my hide tonight."

"It was nothing," he said.

To him, that statement was absolutely true.

For anyone else the events at the fairgrounds would be a story to tell again and again in perpetuity.

But to Finn, it was just another day at the office.

"Did you take first aid classes when you were studying to become a bodyguard?" I asked, half-joking.

"I am trained on a level equivalent to what you call EMT's here in the States," he said, snipping off the last bit of tape and securing my bandages.

"You'll make somebody a good wife someday," I told him, teasing.

Finn's hands froze and he looked up at me. "That isn't very funny."

"Husband?" I ventured.

"You know how I feel about you getting married to Leif Gable." He sealed up the first aid kit.

"I really have no idea," I said, starting to get a bad feeling in the pit of my stomach.

Finn and I had only dated for six months, if it could be called dating, and it had ended badly as far as I was concerned. Finn's problem had been that he could never allow himself to be in a relationship completely, but had always hovered around the periphery, keeping his distance. Because of his turbulent past, when he wasn't busy keeping his distance emotionally he was practically neurotic about protecting me. Finn sometimes had a difficult time switching off his bodyguard training and his way of dealing with problems could be described as . . . physical. On more than one occasion he'd embarrassed us both by overreacting to a situation and elbowing people aside he considered a potential threat to me, but at the same time he maintained his lack of emotional commitment. To say it had been difficult to know where I stood was putting it mildly. The only option left to me was to sever our relationship and move on.

When word started making it around Killdeer that Leif Gable had proposed to me, Finn confronted me in a panic and practically ordered me not to get married. That confrontation had happened almost a year ago, and Finn and I had still not broached the subject. We had managed a tacit friendship, but nothing more. I hadn't ever brought it up because something told me I would not like his explanation for why he was so adamant that I shouldn't marry Leif.

I could feel the conversation spinning in a direction I sorely didn't want to go, and changed the subject.

"Don't be angry at Logan. He didn't tell me that you are brothers. I figured it out all on my own."

He folded his arms across his chest and stared at the countertop. "I asked him to leave after I discovered he had come to Killdeer. I was looking for him tonight to see why he had not used the plane ticket back to South Africa I purchased for him."

"The fact that he is still here makes me think that Logan doesn't really listen to you, even though you are the older brother," I said.

"Logan is everything I am not. He is sloppy, unprofessional, obnoxious and a bully."

"And he thinks that you are a boring, straight-laced know-it-all?" I asked.

"That is not too far from the truth."

"So, what's he doing here? And why the whole show with tracking me down over at Lil's and dropping hints that he knew who I was before we had even met?" I asked.

Finn's face darkened with embarrassment. "I may have mentioned you to him in a phone conversation."

"You may have mentioned me?" I asked. "He talked like he knew my third grade teacher's first name."

If possible, Finn's face colored even more. "Ah, I may have mentioned you on more than one occasion."

I felt a pang of surprise. "I see. Does he do this often? Show up unannounced?"

Finn leaned both elbows on the countertop and rubbed his eyes. "It's all he ever does. Logan never sends a letter or Christmas cards. He won't ever tell me where he is, and his way of checking in is by taking a job in whatever city I am currently working in and arranging it so that we run into one another in a public place. He likes the drama, I imagine."

"Working out at the Bybee ranch, he'll get plenty of that," I said.

Finn turned slightly to look at me. "Marley, what do you know about the body they found on Tatiana Phelps' ranch this morning?"

My face must have fallen into a deep frown, because Finn put a hand on my arm and shook it slightly. "I didn't want to upset you. I apologize."

"No, it's not that. I just thought of something. Something that happened today that really bothered me. Is it alright if I run this by you? I could sure use your perspective."

Finn's jaw clenched. "I won't help you get yourself involved in another washout, Marley."

"I'm not involved in anything. I was just curious about something, that's it. I swear."

Finn gave me a suspicious look. "That's what you told me the last time."

"Loy and Nick are dealing with the murder investigation and they don't need any help from me," I said.

"The sheriff and his deputy are currently scraping vomit and blood off of their boots while

JESSICA McCLELLAND

they process fifteen wankers who beat each other senseless out at the fairgrounds tonight. They are unable to devote their full attention to a suspicious death, and I know that you have always been very eager to fill in the gaps."

I shrugged dismissively. "By Thursday we will get six cops from Bozeman on loan for the duration of rodeo weekend. Sheriff Shucraft will be on tap for giving orders, but the muscle will be taken care of. He and Nick can handle investigating a suspicious death, as you call it. He can walk and chew gum at the same time, Finn."

"But given the opportunity, you may decide there is no harm in asking a few simple questions. Something tells me you do not think that Zane Ackerson's death was an accident."

I dropped my gaze. "It wasn't too hard to see from the way he was left that Zane was murdered."

Finn's eyes bulged. "You were present?"

"Only because I was there to see if the plague had killed Tatiana's prairie dog town."

His face twisted up. "You were examining a possible plague kill and discovered a homicide victim?"

I sighed and leaned back. I could see he was about to overload all of his circuits. "Finn. Take a deep breath. It's fine."

"How is any of this even remotely close to fine?" he demanded, his voice rising.

I gave him a pleading look. "Can I get this out, please?"

He composed his expression and took in a gulp of air. "Alright. I'm listening."

"When Tatiana and I found Zane's body, we could see immediately that he had been mauled by an animal. She thinks it was a wolf, and I hate to admit it, but that is a possibility. However," I said before he could interrupt me again, "I could see there was a lot more to it than a mauling. There was a person involved in this, somehow."

"I don't suppose there was a big hunting knife sticking out of his neck," Finn remarked.

"Doesn't your brother carry a big hunting knife?" I asked.

He looked away. "I was joking. Why couldn't it have simply been a wolf? Why do you think there was someone involved?"

"Zane's body was dragged underneath a juniper bush and a broken branch was thrown on top of him, like camouflage or something."

Finn was quiet for a moment. "Not really what wolves are known for, is it?"

"And the body hadn't been fed on."

I felt squeamish saying it, but it was a fact that needed to be pointed out.

He seemed to be considering it. "Describe the wounds that you saw."

I swallowed a bad taste in my mouth and did the best I could.

"His arms were punctured from bite marks, or what looked like bite marks. And the back of his neck was mauled so badly that had to be what killed him. We could see the bone."

"I'm not very good with things like this. Logan is much better than I am at distinguishing the difference between a mauling from a canine or a feline." His expression clouded up. "You have cougars here, yes?"

"We have cougars. I suppose it could have been that."

"You said that something was bothering you," Finn said, prompting me.

I was jolted back to the thought that had started this.

"It's about the way all of the folks out at the Bybee ranch behaved when I was there this afternoon."

"Some of the things that they said?" Finn asked.

"Just the opposite," I told him, replaying the day's events in my mind.

His eyes narrowed. "Something they didn't say?"

"Exactly. You know, I drove all the way out to the Bybee ranch with Logan, sat with Jennifer Hix at her house and chatted away for half an hour, and then the two of us road into town with Holly, the gal who cooks out there, and during that entire time, not one of them said a word about what happened to Zane. They never brought it up, not even once. Don't you think that's a bit odd?"

He didn't say anything, and I was starting to get the impression that he was not happy about what I had just said.

"If it had been me, I would have wanted to know what had happened to Zane," I insisted. "You know, share in the grief with my coworkers and talk about what a great guy he had been. But nobody at the Bybee ranch said a single thing about it. The closest they came to showing any concern was what Jennifer said about him back at Tatiana's place."

"What did she say?" Finn asked. He had taken on the thousand-mile stare and was looking straight ahead.

"Jennifer told Tatiana and me that Zane had a soft spot for black-footed ferrets. She said he always wanted to see one in the wild and that is why he was out at the prairie dog town so early in the morning. But, as far as I could see when I was out at the Bybee ranch, nobody was even speculating about what had happened to him. Don't you think that's strange?"

"In what way?" he asked, frowning.

"It was almost like they already knew what had happened to him and they didn't want to talk about it," I said.

"That's a big maybe," he said.

"Well, what do you think?"

His eyes were hard. "I think you should assume they didn't talk about it because it was difficult for them, and they wanted to put on a brave face in front of company."

"Now that just sounds silly," I said.

Finn shot me a sour look. "Why is that silly? A bloke like this Zane, works a tough job as a ranch hand, and his buddies hear that he gets mauled because he's sneaking out to look for ferrets? Not very manly, right? So maybe they were more embarrassed than anything else."

"So embarrassed they wouldn't want to find out what had killed him? I just don't think so, Finn."

He waved a hand. "This doesn't seem like too much of a mystery to me. He got killed by a wolf, or a mountain lion, and his friends tried to cover it up because he was trespassing."

I gave him a doubtful look. "It can't be that simple."

"You want it to be more difficult than it really is, because you would rather worry about other people's problems than face your own," he told me.

"I don't have any problems," I said, trying not to sound too bitter.

"You don't?" he asked doubtfully.

I shrugged one shoulder.

"What did Logan say to you when he drove you out to the ranch?" he asked.

"Nothing important. Rick and Holly, and their disagreements. He asked me some personal questions, like if I was in a happy relationship, that sort of thing."

"That sort of thing." His tone was flippant.

"Don't try to say it sideways, Finn. If you've got something to tell me, spit it out."

He ran a hand through his thick blond hair and avoided my eyes. "Logan was fishing when he talked to you about whether or not you were in a happy relationship. He's here in Killdeer because he knows, based on some conversations we had, that you mean something to me and he came all the way to Montana to check you out."

"I mean something to you?" I asked.

He started to look desperate. "That we were a couple. Once. That we had been a couple. The death of that ranch hand was probably just an accident, but it looks like Logan is using it as an excuse to get a chance to talk to you about me. Well, about how you might feel about me. He's a meddler."

I had to hide my smile. My first thought was that Finn's evaluation of the situation was about as self-centered as a person could get. I wasn't about to argue with him, though. I just knew that I wasn't going to get anything else helpful out of him.

Finn stood up and turned his back on me. "Take me back up to the weather station."

He walked out of the kitchen without another word and I had to scramble to catch up. He was already sitting in the passenger's seat of my SUV by the time I found my keys.

"You want to explain what has gotten you so worked up?" I asked.

He buckled his seat belt. "No."

I knew better than to push him when he shut down, and instead of playing twenty questions, I figured that if it was important enough, eventually he would get around to telling me what he was really thinking. Truthfully, it was almost a relief to get him out of the house at last. With Leif out of town I felt uncomfortable having an ex-boyfriend around. Even if the ex-boyfriend was someone I trusted.

I drove him back to the weather station that wasn't really a weather station and stopped when my bumper was a few feet from the heavy security gate surrounding the squat, gray buildings. I could see the rows of satellite dishes on the other side of the compound, and I shook my head over the fact that Killdeer had been chosen as the spot for the monitoring station.

Leif had some friends with connections in high places, so to speak, and he'd explained to me a few months ago what was really going on at the little weather station. According to Leif, back in 1977 Ohio State University had been using a radio telescope to listen for signals from space. It was part of the SETI institute's effort to locate signals that could possibly be the product of an intelligent race other than our own. And, on the afternoon of August 15th, they heard something. Something amazing. A narrow-band radio signal was picked up by the University's Big Ear radio telescope, and the signal lasted for seventy-two seconds before cutting out. Nobody ever managed to fully explain what had caused the signal, and to this day it was still a complete mystery.

Some in the scientific community speculated that if the signal had been heard once coming from that location, it might be heard again someday. So a private firm had decided to invest in building a new facility to do nothing but scan that section of sky in case the signal came back. What better place to hide a SETI monitoring facility than in-the-middle-of-nowhere Montana?

The station had been built on a lonely hillside above Killdeer Valley more than three years ago, and it had been listening to the sky, at the exact same point from which the original radio signal had been heard back in 1977, ever since. Obviously, they hadn't found anything, or everyone would have heard about it by now. Still, it gave me a smug feeling to be one of only six people in Killdeer who knew what really went on inside the gated compound.

Finn opened his door and paused before shutting it behind him. He leaned back and I could see his fingers drumming nervously on the door as he scanned the thick tree line surrounding the station. He hadn't spoken once on the drive, and his expression was pensive. Something was making him extremely jumpy, but I had no idea what it could possibly be.

"Listen, Doll. For what it's worth to ya, it sounds like it was just an accident, what happened to this Zane fella, and someone tried to cover it up. I wouldn't put a lot of thought into it if I was you. It'd be best not to get yourself involved."

"Okay, but I wasn't planning on getting involved."

"You never do," he told me.

Then he sighed and dropped his head. Before he shut the door he looked over at me, and his expression could only be described as pleading.

"Marley. Do something for me, would you?" he asked.

"Sure, Finn."

He drew in a long breath before he spoke, and he stared at the ground. "Stay away from Logan. He's nothing but a pirate."

He slammed the door and walked towards the security gate, thumbed a keypad and pushed it open, making certain to lock the gate behind him before going inside the compound.

I sat in the running vehicle for a full minute before finally backing out of the narrow driveway and heading for home.

The conversation had me irritated. It wasn't as if I had sought out all this trouble. I certainly hadn't wanted to get involved with Zane's death. That had been a simple case of bad luck. And it wasn't exactly like I had hitchhiked out to the Bybee ranch in order to pump Jennifer Hix for information. She had sent Logan after me.

And what exactly was the reason behind all of the friction between Finn and his little brother, anyway?

Whatever it was, I could tell that Finn and Logan had some old, tender wounds that they each had inflicted on the other. But how was that my problem? Well, it wasn't.

I should stay away from Logan Hiser?

Maybe Logan Hiser should think about staying away from me.

CHAPTER 8

The Sacajawea Hotel was just opening the bar and grill for early dinner when I drove into the parking lot and pulled up beside Allen's Fish and Wildlife truck. The familiar gold letters and official seal of the Fish, Wildlife and Parks division on the door of the black truck gave me a small shudder of regret when I saw the logo. I had expected to feel nervous about seeing Allen again. I hadn't expected to feel so much sadness.

I got out of my black BMW and saw that Allen was sitting in his truck waiting for me. He stepped out and adjusted his gun belt, his beige uniform shirt so wrinkled he looked like an unmade bed, as usual.

He gave my BMW a careful examination. "Nice wheels, Marley. The old man give that to you?"

"My fiancé," I told him, with a bit more smugness in my voice than I had intended.

"Can we just get to what it was you wanted?" he asked.

I forced myself to take a deep breath. "Let me at least buy you lunch."

He wiped a line of sweat from his upper lip and nodded. He looked too tired to argue with me. "Yeah, sure. What the hell."

We found a table inside the cool bar and in no time had a couple of iced teas and two menus. Since lunch was on me Allen ordered a smothered chicken burrito with everything. I had a salad.

I could feel Allen watching me as I stirred a packet of sugar into my tea, and suddenly I didn't feel so silly about the fact that I had taken a page out of the Jennifer Hix style manual. My strawberry blonde hair was up in a high twist and I'd spent an hour doing my makeup and carefully choosing an outfit. I'd decided on a white sleeveless crocheted top with a silk shell underneath, and a flowing midnight blue linen skirt. I kicked them off when I drove, but outside the car I wore a pair of wedge sandals that gave me at least a four-inch boost. A pair of sterling silver earrings shaped like hawk feathers dangled against my neck. Except for the road rash on my hands, I looked pretty darn spectacular.

My palms were still sore, but I'd been able to take off the bandages. When I sat down I kept my hands in my lap.

Allen stared at me, his face unreadable.

"How have you been?" I asked, finally mustering the courage to dive in.

"Fine."

"How is work going these days?"

"Fine."

I swallowed my impatience.

"Are you still friends with Tammy?" I asked.

He leaned back in his chair, his stocky frame making the armrest creak. "Tammy still talks to me."

His dark hair looked greasy. He hadn't showered yet today and I wondered what sort of night he had endured to meet me at this halfway point. I'd gone to bed early the night before and had a leisurely breakfast of blueberry muffins and freshly brewed coffee. Allen looked like he hadn't seen a toothbrush for thirty-six hours.

I pulled the aluminum film canister from my little purse and set it on the table.

Allen looked at it, one eyebrow askew. "It's not a bomb, is it?"

"It's a tick. You know, the creepy-crawly kind?" I said.

"Divorcing me wasn't enough for you? You want to give me Lyme disease too?"

"I want you to give it to Tammy and have her take a look at it."

"Why?" he asked.

"Because she is a biologist." I sipped my tea diplomatically instead of uttering a snide retort.

"You want me to go all the way over to Helena for a tick," he said, giving me a hard look.

"It may be important."

Allen snatched the canister and unscrewed the lid. He shook the tick around inside until he could see it clearly. "What's so special about it?"

"I don't know what species it is and I'd like to find out," I told him.

He snapped the lid on and screwed it back in place. He shoved the canister back across the table. "So look it up on the Internet."

I shoved the canister back. "Try not to be a wanker, Allen."

His eyes shot to my face and he stared at me for a moment. "Wanker?"

I watched him speculatively. "You know, I'll bet that's the term they always put on your performance evaluations that keeps you from getting promoted."

I thought he would stand up and walk out of the bar and not look back. But to my astonishment, Allen curved a smile across his tan face and actually laughed. "If you'd had that kind of a sense of humor four years ago, we might still be married."

"If I'd known the term wanker eight years ago we might never have gotten married."

We stared each other down, neither of us willing to break our stance. When the waitress slid plates of food between us, we relaxed enough to eat and took a break from the sniping.

After a few bites of a smothered chicken burrito, Allen started to act more like a human being again.

He chewed a few times, swallowed and reached for the film canister. He slid it inside his shirt pocket and wiped his mouth with the back of his hand. "I'll have Tammy take a look at it. Did you come all the way to Three Forks just to give me a stupid bug?"

"No."

He gulped more tea, and as I watched him devour his food and chew with his mouth open I realized that Leif would have never been so crass when eating.

"So?" he asked, shrugging.

I wasn't sure how to proceed. I needed to find a way to tell him how I felt without dredging up too much of the past.

I poked at my salad. "On the phone, you said something."

"That's why it's called a conversation," he told me around another mouthful.

It was all I could do to keep my temper under control. I had actually been married to this man?

"You asked me if I had called to gloat. What did you mean by that?"

Allen stopped chewing and his hand froze halfway to his glass. "I would have thought you'd have that found out by now."

"That's why I asked you about it," I said. "I have no idea what you were talking about."

He dropped his fork on his plate. "Word is, you and the stockbroker are getting married pretty soon."

"That's the plan," I said, watching his stony face. "And he's not a stockbroker. He's . . . never mind. Found out about what?"

Allen slumped in his chair, tracing the tabletop with a stray finger like he was trying to organize his thoughts.

"Funny how you seem to know things about me, but I never hear very much about you," I told him, trying to prompt the conversation forward.

"You didn't know about me and Caitlyn having a baby?" he asked.

If I'd been drinking my tea I would have sprayed it all over him. "You and the cocktail waitress?"

"Caitlyn is going to school to be a radiologist," he said, defensive. "Don't sound so surprised. I'm sure somebody told you about it already."

"How could I have known?" I demanded. "You poisoned everyone at my office after I left to the point that nobody will even talk to me anymore."

"I think that's your imagination getting carried away, Marley," he said, throwing his napkin on the table. He crossed his arms like an angry six-year-old and pouted.

It took all of my strength, but I forced a smile. "Congratulations?" I managed.

He started in on his burrito again. "Maybe," he said, shrugging.

"You don't sound all that thrilled about becoming a father." I could feel my upper lip sweating and I dabbed it with my napkin.

"No, I think that's swell. But I'm not sure I really understand Caitlyn at all."

"Oh, for the love of Pete," I said, leaning back and rubbing my temples. "Seriously? You are having a baby with this woman and now you decide you don't understand her? That's like enlisting in the navy and then deciding you don't like boats."

"Don't say it like that. It makes it sound so—"

"Accurate?"

"How come you are being so damn judgmental?" he asked.

I thought about the phrase Logan had used. "I don't know. Could it have something to do with you losing your pants at key moments during our marriage?"

"Can't a guy make a mistake once in a while?"

"A mistake," I said, my lips pressed tight. "So now the cocktail waitress was just a simple little mistake. You promised to love and cherish, till death do us part, you putz."

"It's not exactly easy being married to Wonder Woman, alright?" He waved his hands with frustration.

"What does that mean?" My voice was louder than I'd intended.

"For crying out loud. You chased a badger off the porch with a shovel."

"What was I supposed to do?" I said. "Let him come right inside the kitchen to help himself to the fried chicken?"

Allen's left eye started twitching. "Women are supposed to wait for their husbands to deal with situations like that. You never, ever let me handle things. You just ran off and dealt with problems all on your own."

"So you had an affair because I know how to change a gasket in the bathroom faucet?"

He had the decency to look contrite. "It wasn't like that, not exactly. But to tell you the truth, it was sort of nice to be needed by someone for a change."

This meeting was supposed to be about my feelings, but that plan was coming apart quicker than a beaver dam on the Yellowstone during flood season.

I leaned my forehead in my palm and tried to slow down my heartbeat. "So you found someone who needs you. I'm happy for you."

He sighed and shifted awkwardly in his chair. "I think she does. Hell, sometimes I don't know what she is thinking."

"Like when you say something to her and she looks at you like you have lobsters crawling out of both ears?" I asked.

"What?" His face screwed up in confusion. "No. More like when she is throwing her high heels at me and yelling that she wished I would listen to her more often."

I couldn't believe it, but I was actually counseling my ex-husband about his new girlfriend. Being caught in a bar fight the night before was looking better and better every minute.

"Okay, Allen. What is it about her you don't understand?"

He toyed with his fork, a pained look spreading across his face. "Everything?"

"Now come on, it can't be that bad."

"Only sometimes. There are bad days, I guess," he admitted.

I scooted my plate aside, the salad hardly touched. "You have to realize all couples have bad days. It doesn't mean you give up, or hope that the problems just magically go away. You have to face your troubles together. That's why it's important to know what kind of a person your partner is before you hitch your wagon to their star."

He glanced up at me, his chin propped on his knuckles. "I thought I understood you pretty well when we got married."

I wasn't going to get a better chance to confront him about what had happened back at my old job. I hadn't meant for the conversation to turn into an exploration of our failed marriage, but at least now I had an opening so I could start looking at all the old baggage from the past.

I folded my arms and gave him a stern look. "And I thought I knew you enough to be able to count on you even after I got fired from the Helena branch office."

His eyes flashed and he sat up straight. "That was different."

I pointed at him. "You didn't know all the details about why I got fired, but that never stopped you from dragging my name through the mud every chance you could get."

Down went the fork and Allen propped both elbows on the table so that he could lean in and look me directly in the eye. "And maybe I was sick of the fact that every time you had a problem, no matter how small it was, you always went to Bruce."

"What does that have to do with anything?"

"Marley, it wasn't even like you were married to me. It was more like you were married to Bruce. Dammit, you didn't go on a lunch break without checking with him first."

"There were only five of us in that branch office, Allen. We were close." I felt my face burn.

"Close. Is that what they are calling it these days?"

It took me a moment to register what he was implying. "You think that Bruce and I were sleeping together?"

"Weren't you?" he snapped. "Working late? Eating supper together at night while you were supposedly going over files? I think it's pretty obvious what you were doing."

My jaw actually ached from clenching it shut. There was no way I could tell Allen what we had really been doing all that time. We'd been talking over cases, investigations and timelines. Bruce had used me for a sounding board for his logistical problems concerning investigations, and I'd gone right along with him and openly talked about things that I had no right to be involved with. But I could never tell that to Allen. If anyone knew just how deeply he had confided in me during his investigations he would certainly lose his job.

"We were friends, Allen. There was never anything more to it than that. I would never have crossed that line. I took our marriage seriously."

"Sure, until you clocked in every day."

There it was. That same, self-righteous look that he always had when he was about to pin someone to the corkboard like a butterfly specimen. I looked at his smug, taut expression and thought hard about everything that had happened to me since we had gotten divorced. I thought about all that I had endured over the past four years, from the gunshot wound to the broken ankle to the moment when I had looked into the eyes of the person who had killed my grandfather.

I wasn't the same person I had been when Allen had decided to bring our marriage to a screeching halt.

I wasn't the same person, but he still was.

"You know, I don't think I really care anymore what you believe," I said, meaning every word. "Bruce and I were never anything more than friends and if you don't believe that, it's not my problem anymore."

I could almost see his thoughts play across his face. His mouth opened, then it shut, then it opened again and he glared at me like I had threatened to slash the tires on his truck.

Something else dawned on me, watching his angry expression. "You told everyone that we had an affair, didn't you?"

"I may have let it slip," he said, looking at me with a nasty glare.

"That's why everyone in the office was so distant to me when I left. They thought I was cheating with Bruce. It didn't have anything to do with an investigation he was working on that went wrong. It was because they thought I was a home-wrecker."

"You were a home-wrecker," Allen said. "But it was our home that you busted up, not his."

I stood up and pushed my chair away from the table. I felt the blood rushing up to my ears and I was so angry I could barely manage to keep my voice level.

"And it never occurred to you that I may have simply wanted to be around people who seemed like they wanted to actually talk to me? You were gone all the time, Allen. When you were home it looked like it was such a chore to be around me. Maybe I had to be so resourceful because you were never there for me to lean on."

Allen's chest puffed up and he stammered. "That's . . . that's not the way it happened."

"And maybe I know a few things about why I got fired that you don't, and maybe I prefer to keep that information to myself because the last thing I want to do is hurt someone else," I told him quietly.

I pulled a fifty-dollar bill out of my wallet and carefully set it under my plate. "And nothing I say is ever going to get you to think about it differently."

He stared at me blankly. "What are you talking about? The real reason you got fired? I don't understand."

I leaned one hand on the edge of the table and gave him a searing look. "How could I have wasted so much time and energy on you?"

"What people could get hurt?" he asked, grabbing my hand. "Maybe you should calm down. People are looking at us."

I glanced down at his hand, my voice hostile. "Allen, go back to Missoula. Tell everyone over and over again what a horrible, evil person I was and how you can't believe you put up with me as long as you did."

"Marley, babe, keep your voice down."

"And in the same exact breath, tell them that I never did one single unselfish thing in my entire life that helped out a friend, even when it cost me everything."

He pushed his chair back and got to his feet. "Maybe we should go outside."

I was beyond mad. Now I just felt numb. "You know what? I finally figured you out. You didn't tell everyone I had betrayed the job, you told them I had betrayed you. You didn't spend all that time and energy telling everyone what a terrible employee I had been. You told them that I was a bad wife. Didn't you? Well, that was a really rotten thing to do."

I turned and walked out of the bar, leaving him standing alone by the table.

I made it to my car before I felt his hand on my shoulder.

"Wait," he said, his tan face a shade paler. "Just wait, would you?"

I shoved his hand aside. "I should have confronted you about this a long time ago. But all of a sudden it just doesn't seem that important anymore."

"You've got this all sideways," he said.

"No, I think I finally have it all straight, for once."

"I never set out to turn everyone against you," he said, leaning against my car door so that I couldn't open it.

My throat felt so raw it was hard to speak without my voice cracking. "I don't think I give a good goddamn anymore what you did or didn't do."

He seemed to be struggling to find the right words to say. "Maybe I was angry and said some things that were a bit over the top. But I never did anything criminal."

"Neither did I." There wasn't a hint of apology in my voice.

"What did you mean that you knew things that could get people hurt?" he asked. "Nobody even knew in the beginning that you got fired. The

Bureau Chief said you resigned. It all happened so fast."

"He said I resigned?" I asked. That wasn't how it had gone down at all.

"That's what everyone thought, until you got back to Killdeer and I talked to your dad."

"You called my father?" I asked, stunned.

"It took you ten hours to close your bank account, get out of the lease on the house, pack and leave town. Nobody had a clue where you went. What the hell was I supposed to do?"

"I got fired," I said.

"Not according to Bruce."

"Well, he was probably just being kind." I said quietly.

There wasn't anything left to say. It didn't matter one way or the other if I was fired or if the record showed that I had quit. It was over, and there was no going back.

"Just leave it alone, Allen. There is nothing you need to know anyway. I left and that's all there is to it."

Allen held up his hands like he was making an offering. "I know that Caitlyn was a mistake. I know I shouldn't have been so hard on you after you left Helena. What can I do?"

"What can you do? You can be a man, Allen. For once in your life, be a man and do the right thing."

"Tell me what that is," he said, standing in front of me, his eyes pleading.

I put one hand on his chest and gently pushed him away from my car. "Let me go."

His face fell and he backed away from me, rocking his head from side to side. "I did that a long time ago, Marley. And, to tell you the truth, even when we were together I wasn't really sure I ever had you in the first place."

All I could do was stare at him.

He held up a hand. "I don't think I ever felt like you really gave yourself to me. It was like you always held something back, just in case, you know? Like you were always waiting for the other shoe to drop."

"Waiting for the other . . . ?" I said, my chest feeling so tight I thought I was having a heart attack.

He took a couple steps away from my door so that I was free to leave. "Maybe you think you didn't, but I could see it. You always seemed to be waiting for me to let you down. You never believed in me. I always felt like you were just waiting for the day I would ditch out on you."

"Maybe I knew you would ditch out someday and I was just bracing for impact," I told him.

"Do you know what it's like to see that look on your wife's face, day after day? That look that says she doesn't trust you?"

"It turns out I had a pretty darn good reason not to," I said, digging in my bag for my keys.

Allen watched as I opened my car door and slid into the driver's seat.

He put one hand on the door before I could pull it shut. His voice was strained. "Marley. She's having my baby."

I had both hands wrapped around the steering wheel so tight my knuckles were bone white. A hot breeze drifted through, bringing the smell of dry sagebrush and thirsty cottonwood trees. Sweat trickled down my back, making my shirt stick to the seat. Everything felt like it was slowly melting.

When I managed to look back at Allen he was watching me with a look of desperation.

"A baby," he repeated. "It's not so bad when it's just two grown-ups who can't seem to get along and end up going their separate ways. But a baby? That changes everything."

"Changes everything?" I asked with a sigh. My anger was all worn out and all I had left was pity.

"A little baby doesn't understand it when his parents can't work things out. Grown-ups can move on and start their lives over. But for him, it's about a thousand times worse when his mother leaves his father. I don't want that to happen to Caitlyn and me. I don't understand what it is she wants from me. Hell, I'm not sure I know what she needs. How am I going to keep us together?"

His fear was genuine, even if his point of view was almost childlike. For the first time that day, I could see that Allen wasn't the villain I'd imagined him to be. He was just an average man, dealing with everyday problems, and doing the best he knew.

Maybe I would never be able to repair my reputation with my old coworkers from the Helena branch office. Maybe I would never really be able to understand what it was that ultimately had destroyed my marriage to Allen. But at the very least, what I could do at this point was to try and do no more harm.

"Take her camping."

He blinked and shook his head once. "What?"

"Take her camping. In the rain. Might not be a bad idea to forget to take along the matches, and bring a sleeping bag that has a hole in it."

He looked at me like I had gone slightly crazy. "And what good is that going to do?"

"It's going to show you who she really is. I guarantee it. If you don't know what she's thinking by the end of a soggy weekend camping with no fire or hot food, you never will. Thanks for taking that tick to the biologist for me. And Allen?"

"Yeah?"

"Good luck. I really mean that."

I shut my door and started the engine, gave him one last look and tried my best to smile as I backed out of the parking lot. When I drove away from the hotel I caught a last glimpse of Allen in my mirror and saw him standing beside his truck. He didn't look desperate. He didn't look angry. He looked determined.

I hoped the best for him. But I also knew that it wasn't my concern any longer whether or not he stopped talking bad about me, and whether or not my former coworkers chose to believe what he said.

I'd muddled through my problems for the past two years, encumbered by the whisper campaign I'd imagined going on all around me, and allowed myself to believe it actually had bearing on my day-to-day life. But now it was obvious to me that I'd been wrong all this time.

It hadn't been the rumors and lies circulating around the grapevine of former friends that had defeated me.

I'd done that all on my own.

I rolled down the window, letting my arm dangle outside, and I let the hot wind dry my tears. The guilt and shame I'd invented for myself had gotten too heavy, and I decided then and there that I didn't need to carry them anymore.

CHAPTER 9

Loy pulled me over going eighty-five just outside Killdeer city limits. Thankfully, it wasn't Deputy Nick Wilcox, or I'd be looking at a two-hundred-dollar ticket. I killed the engine and waited while he parked sideways behind me, shutting off his own engine as he did. The only sound was a soft whisper from a light breeze blowing through the dry buffalo grass and the metallic ping from the hot engine.

I heard the sheriff's truck door slam and boots on asphalt.

When he stood beside my door, he leaned an elbow on the open window and looked at me over the top of his sunglasses.

"Do you know why I stopped you today, Miss?"

"I'm guessing it wasn't 'cause I was playing my radio too loud," I said.

"Don't you miss the days of reasonable and prudent?"

Loy was referring to the glorious days of fall, 1995, to the spring of 1999 when the posted speed limit for the entire state of Montana had been open to interpretation. In fact, on the interstate there hadn't really been a speed limit at all, and the signs had simply said reasonable and prudent. Those days were long gone, and I had been booking it twenty miles per hour over the legal limit for about eighteen miles now.

"Would you believe that I have to go to the bathroom really, really bad?' I asked.

"There better not be any empty beer bottles on the floorboards." He pulled off his sunglasses and rubbed his tired eyes.

The road was deserted in both directions. The mad stampede of trailers and trucks would begin at sunrise the following morning, but for the moment Killdeer was still just a quiet little town.

Aside from the occasional riot at the fairgrounds.

I patted his arm. "Get much sleep last night?"

"Wendy wants me to go back to school and become a chiropractor," he said, yawning.

"One more night and you will have six probies from Bozeman to keep the peace."

"They're only sending five," he told me.
"Maybe you should deputize a couple ranch hands from the L Bar T. They seem to know their way around a redneck boxing match."

He gave me a sharp look. "I don't even want to know how you know that."

I set my sunglasses on the seat beside me and rolled my tired neck around until it cracked.

Loy leaned both elbows on the window. "You okay, Hun?" His expression was worried.

"I went and saw Allen this afternoon up in Three Forks," I said, pulling down the visor to shade my eyes.

The air looked choked with dust and a few wispy clouds crept across the horizon, picking up the last golden fingers of light from the setting sun.

A meadowlark landed on the old, bug-eaten fence post beside my SUV and started to sing.

"Irene told me," he said, letting his hands dangle half inside my vehicle.

"Who needs CNN News with her around?"

He smirked. "So, how did it go?"

I didn't answer right away. It was easier to watch the huge orange orb melt behind the distant pasture. Finally I looked back at Loy and shrugged. "Not so bad. I think you were right, after all."

He chuckled. "I was right about something? For God's sake, what? We need to make a note of it."

He stopped smiling and waited for me to answer.

"I do need to forget about Helena, and the whole deal that happened up there. Allen and the cocktail waitress—I mean, Caitlyn—are having a baby, and if that isn't a reason for me to let go of the past and move on, I don't know what is."

"You don't regret getting divorced, do you?" he asked, looking concerned.

I shook my head. "Not at all. But if Allen is moving on with his life, why can't I? It's time to quit thinking about the past and start looking ahead."

Loy smiled slowly and put his sunglasses back on with a flourish. "I'm really glad you said that. There is another reason I pulled you over. I've got some news you might want to hear."

"Don't tell me the road grader hit our mailbox again."

"Leif is back from Panama," he said, backing away from my door. "And you might want to be heading home. Right about now. Put on some lipstick."

He was back in his sheriff's truck and pulling away before I could ask him what he meant, and I heard his truck engine rev as he flipped a U-turn and sped off in the opposite direction.

"Put on lipstick?"

As usual, the other denizens of my little town knew more than I did about the goings-on around Killdeer. I drove through town and took it easy heading south.

When I turned down the rutted gravel driveway leading home, I hit the brakes.

"Son of a . . ."

Multiple cars lined the road. There had to have been at least twenty vehicles crammed nose to bumper down the lane.

I snaked my way through the parked cars until I squeezed my BMW into the garage. As soon as I was out of the car and walking up the back steps Irene threw open the door, reached out and grabbed me by my shoulders.

"There you are! Get in here right this minute, Missy. And for heaven's sake, put on some lipstick!"

"Irene, what is all this?" I asked. "Is Leif having a barbeque he forgot to tell me about?"

"Everyone is in the backyard. Hurry up! We all thought you'd be home an hour ago."

She pulled me inside and ushered me upstairs at a sprint. I had time to comb my hair, dab on blush and fix my mascara before she was pulling me back down the stairs.

"At least you wore something nice," she said, dragging me along behind her.

I felt my pulse speed up. "This isn't a barbeque, is it?" I asked.

I could see through the dining room patio doors that the backyard was alive with activity. Our patio was full of chairs. A long table covered with plates, food, candlesticks and vases of white flowers crowded the space.

When I stepped through the double doors onto the patio Irene snatched my hands and shoved a bouquet of calla lilies into them.

"Hold these. Don't pass out. And smile."

My heart caught in my throat. "Ohmygosh is this what I think it is?"

"This is your wedding, Marley. You are getting married. Leif said he wanted to surprise you. So . . . surprise!"

"He said what?" I asked, my knees ready to buckle.

"Here's your father. Now, hold his arm and walk over to the white arch over there."

Music started playing, coming from somewhere, and my mouth fell open when I saw a string quartet, sitting just off the patio, charging into a formal version of the wedding march.

My father hurried to my side and gripped my arm. "Are you alright, Kiddo? You look a little pale."

"Holy jumping weasel critters," I said, feeling my mouth go dry and my hands start to shake. There wasn't time to panic.

My father squeezed my arm reassuringly. "One foot in front of the other, here we go."

He was wearing a navy sport coat, and Irene was dressed in a powder blue crepe dress and heels. Both of them looked slightly terrified that I would fall over, or worse, bolt.

Irene walked ahead of us, leading the way across the vast expanse of yard behind the house and towards a white arch set at the base of a huge ponderosa pine.

A horde of faces stared back at me.

"Dad, I think I'm gonna be sick."

"Remember that time you fell out of the bucket of the tractor and split open your forehead and had to get seven stitches?" he asked.

"Um . . ."

He grinned at me and shook my arm. "This isn't nearly as bad as that was. Just nod and say 'I do' and it'll all be over in a few minutes."

My father half carried, half dragged me across the lawn. When I saw the crowd of onlookers part down the middle to allow us to pass, I felt the rest of the blood drain from my. Face. Finn was watching me from the back. When I caught his eye he looked straight at me intently.

As I walked up the crest of the sloped yard, I saw Leif waiting for me at the base of the arch and the panic eased back slightly.

He was smiling at me with fearless contentment, his stance relaxed and his expression confident. Leif could inspire courage in other people when he wanted to, and I locked my eyes on his relaxed face and held on to it like a lifeline.

He wore a simple charcoal gray suit with a ruby red satin shirt. I'd always thought Leif looked a little like Yul Brynner, and wearing such a sharp suit made the similarity even more pronounced.

His shaved head gleamed under the ornamental lights that were strung over the arch, and he held a small pink box in his left hand.

David Jordan, the mayor of Killdeer, stood directly under the arch wearing an ancient black tux, holding a Bible, watching me expectantly. "Who gives this woman to be married to this man?"

My father looked confused. "It's me, Mayor. Nathan."

The mayor cleared his throat. "I know it's you, but you have to say the words."

"Oh. I do," my father said, handing my arm over to Leif with a happy bob of his head.

Leif stepped up beside me and squeezed my arm reassuringly. "Hi, sweetheart."

"Hi," I said, leaning on his arm to steady myself. "Got tired of waiting for me to make up my mind about the date?"

He gave me a quick kiss on the cheek. "It just seemed like a good day to get married."

The crowd hushed behind us, and David Jordan lifted his head so that everyone could hear his words.

"We are gathered here today to see the joining of Marley Sarah Dearcorn and Leif Alexander Gable in holy matrimony. If there is anyone present here today who has just cause why these two should not be wed, let them speak now or forever hold their peace."

I swore I heard Irene mutter the words "don't even think about it" from somewhere behind me, but the mayor hardly paused before plunging ahead. If anyone did have just cause why Leif and I shouldn't be married they wouldn't stand a chance of getting a word in edgewise. The train was already pulling out of the station.

David Jordan turned to Leif and held up one hand.

"Do you, Leif, take Marley to be your lawfully wedded wife?"

Leif glanced over at me, his eyes twinkling. "I do."

Apparently we were getting the short, short version of the ceremony.

"And do you, Marley, take Leif to be your lawfully wedded husband?"

For one frantic moment I was certain that the words about to come out of my mouth were not

"I do," but "can we think about this for a minute?" Before I answered I turned to Leif and looked at his serene expression, hoping for all of my fears to evaporate.

Nothing evaporated, and if anything the fears I harbored shrugged off with little effort my attempt to shut them down. Did I really deserve this man? What about all of the things we hadn't been able to learn about each other yet? What if this was a mistake?

I mustered my courage and thought about what Tatiana had told me sitting around her kitchen table.

Forget about your head. Sometimes it can lead us off in crazy directions. Ask yourself what is in your heart, instead. When you know what that is, then you will know what to do.

There wasn't a doubt in my mind that Leif Gable was the most wonderful man I had ever met. And I might not have had all of the answers to many of my questions about what a future with him would bring, but I did know that I truly loved him, and that was all I really needed to know.

My voice came out stronger and louder than I'd expected. "I do."

"The ring?" David asked.

Leif lifted the lid from the pink box he held in his hand and carefully slipped out a simple platinum band, circled all around with perfect diamonds. He let me slide it on my finger, and to my astonishment it was a perfect fit.

"I now pronounce you husband and wife," David said, holding up his arms. "You may now kiss the bride."

Leif cupped my face with both hands and kissed me, crushing the bouquet of flowers between us. Our friends and my father clapped and whistled, and when I turned to face everyone Irene was wiping away tears.

My boss from the library, Rose, was standing beside Deputy Wilcox, elbowing him excitedly in the ribs. My friend Dean Tisdale was sandwiched between Wendy Martinez and Valerie Newkirk. Valerie, Loy's dispatcher, must have somehow finagled a couple of hours off from the sheriff's station to come to the wedding. Three other librarians stood together, hooting and whistling like teenagers. I caught sight of Tatiana at last, waving at me from the center of the crowd, wearing a broad smile and dressed in her best pair of Levis and a cheerful yellow button-down shirt.

A smattering of people I didn't know came forward to pump Leif's hand and offer him congratulations.

A slender man with a shock of red hair and piercing blue eyes offered Leif a simple handshake and a soft murmur of congratulations. Then a group of men who looked completely out of place moved in to mob him. There were four of them, looking uncomfortable in their snug JC Penney matching beige sport jackets. I noticed that a price tag still dangled from the sleeve of one of the men's jackets. They certainly were not business associates of his. That was plain to see. The men had accents I couldn't quite place. Eastern Europe? That didn't seem right. They talked loudly and waved their hands with animated expressions and gave me the impression they were here as a group to support Leif on his wedding day, but that dressing in suits was something terribly unfamiliar to them all. One of them had a terrible scar across his chin. The others wore scruffy beards, and to the man, they positively reeked of vodka.

Leif beckoned to me and gestured towards the group.

"Marley, sweetheart, I'd like you to meet some friends of mine."

I shook hands with each of the four men in turn, and they traded comments back and forth in their native tongue, beaming at me and slapping Leif on the back.

After the four men had offered their blessings in English, the accent finally hit home.

They were Polish. And from the clumsy way they handled English, it was obvious they were native Poles. English was barely a second language for them.

I was so flabbergasted I forgot their names as soon as Leif said them, but it would be impossible to forget that the men all referred to Leif as "brother" whenever they addressed him.

As far as I could see there wasn't a family resemblance at all, but whatever their relationship, it was clear that the four men were truly fond of him.

David Jordan nudged me towards a small table set up beside the arch and handed me a pen.

"Sign here, and we need two witnesses," he said.

Irene practically knocked one of the Polish men to the ground to get to my side. "I'll do it. Nathan, sign your daughter's marriage license."

My father was surveying the four men chatting with Leif, his expression bemused. "What? Oh, right. Where do I make my X?"

"David, I didn't know you were a minister," I said, my hand still trembling slightly as I signed my name.

"I registered over the Internet. Universal Life Church. Can't say I hold with their support of gay marriage, but the certificate was free, so, what the hell, right?"

"Irene, stop crying on the license," my father said, patting her on the back.

She was trying not to sob, failing miserably, and managing to smile and cry at the same time. "It's all so beautiful," she said, burying her face in a napkin and honking her nose loudly.

Standing behind the crowd, I caught sight of Finn lingering alone, hands laced behind his back and his face forlorn.

"Miss Marley, I hope you and Mr. Gable have a happy marriage."

I turned and saw my friend Dean Tisdale standing at my left elbow. He held out his hand, offering to shake mine, but I surprised him with a grateful hug.

"Thank you, Dean. How have you been?"

He looked the same. Half-wild. Hands covered in calluses. But his blue eyes were just as sharp as always.

"Got a job doing animal control up at the airport," he said, beaming. "Your dad helped me set up a bank account."

"Good for you. They are lucky to have you," I told him.

Irene started herding the rest of the guests towards the patio and urged everyone to sit, stand or lean, whatever they preferred, and I heard the clink of glasses and the scrape of silverware on china.

Nothing was proceeding with anything remotely resembling usual formality. People chatted, laughed and ate while propping themselves on chairs or standing in the grass holding a plate with one hand.

Starting with the incredibly brief ceremony, the rest of the evening promised to break with tradition on every front. I didn't expect anyone would be making speeches.

The calla lilies were threatening to wilt, and I headed for a table to pour a glass of water for them.

"Congratulations, Marley."

I looked up from the table and Finn was watching me from a few paces away, his hands still laced behind his back like he didn't know what to do with them.

"Thank you," I said, trying not to notice his pained expression.

"Your new husband keeps some very interesting company," he told me, nodding towards the four men still swarming around Leif. They were all doing shots of something from a bottle with Russian writing on the label, and toasting each other loudly.

"I have no idea who those men are," I said smiling, "but they seem to love him like he was family."

"Are you sure this is what you want?" he asked abruptly. His gaze was so intense he looked like a man about to land on the beach at Normandy on D-day.

I felt my mouth drop open and all I could do was stare at him incredulously.

"Am I sure?" I asked weakly.

He took a step toward me. "It is never too late to do the right thing, Marley."

"You really want to ask me this question now?"

I felt my heart stutter when I saw the look of total sincerity on his face.

He really meant it.

He wanted me to say the words.

135

I squared my shoulders. "Yes, it is. He really is the most wonderful man I have ever met."

Finn blinked and wiped his palms on his black shirt. "If you are certain."

"I'm certain," I said, even though a tiny part of me was still stunned from the shock of it all.

It was like a vortex of wind blew through my chest, and my life had suddenly been neatly divided into two distinct paths. One path taken, and one path left behind.

Finn's eyes shimmered as he took in my words. "Alright then."

Once again, he wore black head to toe. Not exactly fitting attire for a wedding, but it was Finn, after all. I knew he had at least one pistol hidden somewhere on his person at all times. But, this being Montana, half the wedding party probably had a hunting knife or a pistol somewhere on their person.

"I wish you nothing but happiness," he said.

He stepped forward, reached across the table, took my hand and kissed my fingers lightly.

He tried to smile but it was beyond him to muster it.

"Thank you," I said.

He let my hand fall and started to back away. "See you around, Mrs. Gable."

"Dearcorn," I said.

He stopped. "Excuse me?"

"I'm keeping my maiden name. Leif said it would mean less paperwork."

"Is that so?" His head tilted to the side ever so slightly. "Well—"

"I see you found my girl," Leif said suddenly, wrapping one arm around my shoulder.

I squeezed Leif's hand. "Finn was offering us his congratulations."

"But I should chuck." Finn managed a rigid smile. "Got lots left to do tonight," he said, backing away another step.

His South African accent and slang terms always did get more pronounced when he was nervous, and he was almost unintelligible at the moment.

Leif gave me a quick hug. "I'll walk Finn out. Back in a moment."

Finn's face twisted up with surprise, but he shrugged one shoulder and stepped in time with Leif as the two of them walked side by side across the yard.

I finished squeezing the bouquet of flowers into the water glass and watched the two of them as they strode away from the bustle of the other guests.

I could see at once that Leif wanted to put distance between them and the rest of the group, that he was practically leading Finn away, and instantly my curiosity was piqued. I found myself trailing after them.

I stopped when I got to the crest of the yard and I peered towards the tree-lined driveway hoping to spot them. It was nearly dark, the sun casting nothing more than a faint pink glow over the tops of the cliffs surrounding the house, but someone leaving the party early was starting their car on the lane, and the headlights beamed a bright spotlight along the driveway.

I saw them suddenly silhouetted in the headlights standing next to Finn's black Jeep.

They were too far away for me to understand what they were saying, and Leif's back was to me, but I could see Finn's head bent forward and he was listening intently. His expression was somber.

To my astonishment, Leif deftly pulled a white envelope from his inside jacket pocket and handed it to Finn with a subtle move, and when Finn looked up at Leif's face I could clearly see that he was in utter shock. Finn asked a question, his eyes wide.

Leif put one hand on Finn's shoulder, speaking quietly.

Finn nodded, his mouth hanging open and his face a blur of expressions. He was clearly stunned by what Leif had just said.

Leif gave Finn's shoulder a hard shake, perhaps asking a question?

Finn shook his head rapidly with denial. But when Leif pressed him, Finn dropped his face and nodded, muttering something I couldn't see.

Leif took a step back and gripped Finn's hand firmly. He shook once, hard, not a handshake of farewell, but more like a handshake to seal a pact, or an agreement.

Abruptly the conversation ended and Leif pivoted away and headed back up the slope towards the patio.

I spun around and trotted back to the patio, darted to the table and snatched a plate of food someone had left sitting on the edge.

As Leif came back up the yard towards the patio I scooped up a fork. I was shoving cucumber salad in my mouth when Leif appeared at my side and gave me a sideways squeeze.

"How is my wife?" he asked.

I mumbled around a mouthful of cucumbers, "I'm perfectly perfect."

"Yes you are," he said.

Leif poured himself a glass of white wine and poured one for me. He handed me the glass and lifted his in a toast. "To us. And to finally being able to get on with our lives."

I clinked his glass with mine and took a sip of wine. I hardly ever drank, but tonight one celebratory glass was definitely in order.

The four Polish men had broken up their vodka shot competition and were chatting up the three librarians who had come to the celebration. Or, from the look of it, the librarians were chatting up the men. If possible, the Poles looked slightly flustered and the librarians looked like they were moving in for the kill.

My father and Irene sat together on the deck swing, both of them smiling and content not to speak, but simply taking in the evening.

I looked down at the simple, yet elegant platinum and diamond band circling my finger and I broke into a childlike grin. "I'm married. We are married. Just like that."

"Just like that," Leif said. "I know it was a rush, but I have absolutely no patience for ceremony and I wanted this to get wrapped up with as little fuss as possible."

"It's a wonderful surprise." I was thankful that I hadn't had time to fret about it and that Leif had arranged this ambush ceremony. The initial shock wave had passed and I felt less like a car crash victim and more like someone who had just climbed out of a white-water raft.

But more than that, I truly felt happy.

It had happened so fast, but the impromptu ceremony hadn't given me time to be too nervous and now I felt relieved.

One dark cloud crept across my blue sky when I thought about what had just happened between Leif and Finn. What had they talked about?

What in the world could have been in that envelope? And, more to the point, did I really want to know the answers to those questions?

Whatever had just occurred, it couldn't have been that important. My torrid relationship with Finn had never developed past infatuation, and even though we could have shared a much deeper commitment, I knew that he was still chained to his past and probably always would be. If he had been able to settle down, things might have been different between us.

But Leif? He was a genuine, truly open and straightforward man who made no secret of the fact that he was devoted to me. And I had always felt as comfortable with him as it was possible to be with a man. Whatever doubts I had about a future with Leif would fade with time. As would my nagging "what if" questions about Angus Finn.

The envelope that Leif had given to Finn puzzled me, but I shook it off and told myself that it was nothing. If it was important, Leif would tell me all about it when he was ready. Right now I had more important things to worry about. After all, I had a new life to start.

CHAPTER 10

I wandered into the kitchen the next morning and could see that Leif was already hard at work in his downstairs office.

Fresh coffee had been made, filling the house with a rich aroma. I went to the top of the stairs that led down to his office and could hear him talking, could hear the crack of a cue against the balls on the pool table, and I knew that he was in the middle of a telephone conference. If he was playing pool at seven in the morning, he was already up to his armpits in alligators. Playing pool relaxed him when he had work issues.

I poured coffee and padded down the stairs, marveling at the ring on my finger, and sat on the bottom step outside his office door so that I could eavesdrop on his phone conversation.

Normally I felt uncomfortable listening in on his telephone conferences, but I wanted to tell him good morning before heading off to work, and I knew that it was better to wait for an opening in his conversations before knocking.

"I realize that their stated borrowing base is thirty million, Tom. That's not the point. It's understated. Their true borrowing base is closer to thirty-five million. What? No, I'd have to disagree with that assessment. Wait a second, would you? I'm getting another call."

There was a pause.

"Leif Gable," he said. "Oh. Good evening, Mr. Ambassador. No, no, this is a perfect time to call. What can I do for you?"

Good evening? He had to be talking to someone literally on the other side of the planet if it was their evening. When he started talking about currency exchange rates, and the likelihood that China would manage to corner the Brazilian soybean trade, the conversation went way over my head.

I sipped coffee, listening to him bounce back and forth between two phone calls for a while. It didn't sound like he was in a place where he could break free at the moment, so I went back upstairs and showered.

I was just stepping out of the shower when the house phone rang. Since Leif's office line was separated from the house line, I always answered the house line when it rang. I dripped water across the white carpet in the bedroom as I rushed to grab the phone beside the bed.

"Hello?"

"Marley, why haven't you called me?"

It took me a moment to recognize the voice. "Jennifer? I've been a little busy," I said, digging the corner of the towel into my ear.

"You have got to come over to the ranch today."

"I'm sorry, Jennifer, I can't. I have to work. And, I don't own a horse anymore. I haven't had one for years."

She blew out a sigh. "I'll get you a horse to ride. And what do you mean you have to work? Aren't you engaged to Leif Gable?"

"Well, married to Leif Gable now. He surprised me last night and we had a very small wedding ceremony."

"Oh my God! You didn't invite me?" she said.

"I didn't know about it until five minutes before we were standing in front of the JP," I told her, wrapping up in the towel.

"Well, come out tomorrow, then. You don't have to work tomorrow, do you? I miss you, Marley. Rick and Holly are back together and she is ignoring me again. Brian is in town for the day. The Texas hunters are still here and driving me nuts and I don't have anyone to hang out with. So, will you? Please? No more Long Island iced tea. I promise." Her tone was a mixture of mock desperation and teasing.

I fiddled with my towel, trying not to drip any more on the carpet, and felt torn. I wanted to spend the week with Leif, but he had warned me the night before that we wouldn't be able to see much of each other over the next few days, during business hours at any rate. He was in the middle of a project that would require most of his focus. He had also let me know we would be taking a honeymoon at some point, but that it would have to wait until Christmas or New Year's. He assured me the project he was working on would be over in about ten days and then we could take a long weekend and fly his plane down to Santa Fe for a break.

"Please?" Jennifer said again, plaintively.

"Well, I suppose. What time?"

"Yes! We will have a blast. Why don't you come out about one and we can have lunch and then go riding."

My enthusiasm waned considerably. It would be hot as hell by one in the afternoon, but I had to admit spending time with Jennifer wasn't boring.

"Sure. I will be there. See you tomorrow, Jennifer."

She hung up and I finished getting ready, slipping into a cream skirt and sandals, and topped it off with a white half-sleeve blazer. I was picking out a set of earrings when I felt Leif wrap his hands around me from behind.

"Good morning," he said, giving me a tight squeeze.

"How did you sleep?" I asked.

"I think you know the answer to that question."

We hadn't gotten rid of all the guests until close to midnight, and even then we had stayed up until past two consummating the marriage.

"Jennifer Hix wants me to go out to the Bybee ranch tomorrow and go riding," I told him, fiddling with my earrings.

"It's going to be too hot," he said.

"I would imagine she wants to chat more than ride, but I can be home for an early dinner."

"I have conference calls all day, so it might not be a bad idea to go spend time with a girlfriend tomorrow. I'm sorry, sweetie. Panama is not the best place in the world to do business if you want things done quickly. Once this deal is pushed through I will have a lot more time for us."

He gave me a kiss on the forehead and we shuffled down to the kitchen for breakfast. We were newlyweds, but the morning felt as normal as it ever did. If anything, I felt as if nothing had really changed at all.

He went back down to his office, I went to work and spent an uneventful morning opening up the small branch library in Fable, the small town just east of Killdeer. The morning was for shelving leftover books from the night before, looking up reference questions that had come in at the last minute before we had closed last night, and generally tidying the place up.

When Loy Shucraft pushed through the door and plopped down in the chair across from my desk, I wasn't too surprised.

"Mrs. Gable," he said, nodding.

"Ms. Dearcorn," I said. "I'm keeping my maiden name. Less paperwork. And why didn't you warn me what was going on last night?"

"Irene told me if I ruined the surprise she would gut me like a pig." He leaned back in the chair, smug. "You were pretty damn surprised, huh?"

"You seem awfully relaxed today," I remarked, taking in his slump.

"The probies showed up today. I'm back to being sheriff and Nick is busy taking them on the grand tour of Killdeer Valley, showing them all of the hot spots."

"Speaking of hot spots," I said, "Jennifer Hix wants me to go riding with her tomorrow out at the Bybee ranch. You and Nick are all finished interviewing them, aren't you?"

Loy's face darkened. "What's she so interested in you for all of a sudden?"

"I don't know, maybe she is lonely. I don't imagine she gets a lot of female company out at that deer hunters boot camp."

"That crew is a mess," Loy said. "Everyone's sleeping with everybody else."

"I thought Rick and Holly were the only ones sleeping with anybody out there."

He smirked. "Not the way Irene tells it."

"I should ask her who's hopping in and out of each other's beds on the Bybee ranch," I remarked. "That might be why Zane got killed in the first place."

"Maybe you should stick to being a librarian."

"Maybe I should," I said. "But sometimes I just hear things and it gets in the way of me minding my own business. Like, Jennifer told me that Rick is crazy jealous of Holly."

He grimaced. "Rick is just plain crazy. I know he hits her. But I haven't been able to catch him at it or I would arrest him. Are you going out there, then?"

"Yes. Have you met Logan Hiser? The gamekeeper out there?"

Loy's eyebrows worked across his forehead. "The Australian?"

"He's South African," I said.

"I've heard about him. Not exactly the type of man you want moving into your fair city."

"I think he's mostly harmless," I said, debating as to whether or not I should tell the sheriff about Logan's relationship to Finn. It might make Loy feel even worse.

"Right. The way a hibernating bear is mostly harmless."

I laughed. "You worry too much."

"Yeah? Read the police blotter in the paper sometime." He got to his feet.

"Have you been able to find out anything else about what happened to Zane that I don't know?" I asked.

He stopped and looked down at me. "No comment."

I pressed him. "Does everyone in the valley still think it was a wolf?"

He rubbed the back of his neck with one broad hand. "I was just about to ask you that same question. You seem to get information before I do."

"If anyone brings it up I will let you know," I told him.

He leaned across my desk and tweaked my nose. "I'm happy for you, Hun. Leif is a good man and I wish nothing but the best for you."

"Thanks, Loy. He is a good man. It happened so fast, but honestly, today I just feel on top of the world."

The sheriff headed out and I spent a very quiet day catching up on work that had been put off during busier times. After eleven, hardly a soul came into the library for the rest of the day. It wasn't too much of a surprise. Everyone was busy in Killdeer cruising the fairgrounds and wearing out the bar stools down at the Broken Spoke Saloon while they gathered steam for the rodeo. At exactly 4:59 the phone rang, and, even though I didn't want to answer it so that I could finish locking the front door, I sprinted to the phone and snatched up the receiver.

"Fable County Library." I cradled the receiver under my chin and fumbled with the keys to the front door.

Rose, my boss, was on the line. "Hey, it's me. I'm so glad I caught you. Listen, the director at the main library said we are supposed to be closed on Saturday, so you don't have to cover for me. Take the day off. We all decided that circulation will be practically nonexistent during rodeo weekend anyway so we are both shutting down. Call it employee appreciation day."

"That's great news," I said, frowning as I saw a vehicle pull into the tiny parking lot. I hadn't been able to get the open sign turned around, and I could see that someone was about to come inside. "Have a great weekend and I'll see you on Tuesday."

Rose hung up the phone, and as I was setting the receiver back in the cradle the front door burst open. I forced a smile and turned to greet my last patrons of the day.

"Oh. It's my two favorite nuclear physicists," I said.

Will and Seth, the two scientists who monitored the listening equipment over at the weather station, stopped in front of my desk, glaring.

Seth, his long blond hair as scruffy and unkempt at usual, shoved his glasses back up on his nose indignantly. "Astrophysicist. And, what the hell did you do to Finn last night?"

Will, his neatly groomed companion, folded his arms as well, affecting a stance of irritation. "Yeah. What did you do?"

"Why? Was he moping around the office today listening to My Chemical Romance CD's or something?"

"Don't joke about this, Marley," Will said hotly.

His neatly trimmed beard made him look more like a university professor than a coal bed methane roustabout, which was the cover story they worked under in order to keep a low profile.

The financial backers of the monitoring facility wanted it to be a secret. Which was, in itself, ridiculous. Particularly in a town this size.

Will and Seth drove a beat-up truck with a made-up name for some pretend coal bed methane company decaled on the side door. Neither one of them had ever seen the inside of a methane gas pump station, much less ever turned the bolt on so much as a spare tire. Still, they were the two most brilliant scientific minds the likes of Killdeer Valley had ever seen, and they were my friends. I couldn't be too hard on them.

"Okay, I'm sorry," I said, softening my tone. "What happened?"

"Finn put in his two weeks' notice this morning," Seth said.

I sat down hard in my chair. "What? Why did he do that?"

"We were sort of hoping you might be able to tell us," Will said.

"So, spill it, Marley. What happened between the two of you last night?" Seth demanded.

"I . . . I have no idea. I mean, well I got married last night."

"Oh, swell," Seth said, letting his arms flop to his sides. "You got married? What did you want to go and do a stupid thing like that for?"

"I don't know Seth, maybe because I love my new husband and I want to have a happy life?"

"Did you stop to think for one minute about what it might do to us?" Will said.

"What it would do to you?" I asked.

Seth waved his arms. "We just got Finn broken in. He even tells a joke once in a while. We didn't even think he could talk for the first five days he worked there, and now that we finally have him the way we want him, you are ruining it for both of us."

"Ruining it," Will echoed.

"Did he say why he was quitting?" I asked, dumbfounded.

"All we know is that he put in his notice and he will be gone in fourteen days. He said he couldn't talk about it."

My thoughts raced to the memory of the exchange between Finn and Leif the night before. There had to be a reason Finn would quit his job so abruptly, and it was no coincidence that he had done it right after talking to Leif in private. But I could not remotely imagine what Leif could have said that would make Finn want to leave Killdeer and never come back.

All I could do was shake my head at the two physicists. "Well, did you try to change his mind?"

Seth ran a hand through his mass of tangled hair. "Of course we did. He flat refused to discuss it. He said he had some unfinished business to take care of, and that was all we could get out of him. He pretty much stopped talking after that and he spends all of his spare time on the Internet looking at maps."

I dropped my head and felt slightly queasy. The news shook me to the core and the feeling surprised me. "Would you two do me a favor?"

Seth gave me a suspicious look. "You want us to bug his cell phone or something?"

"No. But could you tell him to at least come and talk to me before he leaves? I'd like to say goodbye."

And find out what the hell he was really thinking.

Will had lost most of his bluster. "Sure. I think we can do that."

The two of them left, climbed into their beat-up roustabout truck, and I turned the sign around to show that we were closed. I locked up the tiny library and headed home, my spirits low.

What had Leif said to Finn that would make him want to leave like this?

I had no idea what they could have possibly talked about. The more I thought about it, the more

I realized that if I let myself worry the issue to death, the only thing I would accomplish would be inventing a slew of crazy explanations that probably had nothing whatsoever to do with reality. The best thing would be to simply talk to Finn myself.

But that presented its own set of problems. What would I say? Please don't go? Stay here because I would miss you?

No, I couldn't say that. Finn would do whatever he wanted to do. I considered him my friend but I had no right to ask him to stay in Killdeer. He had to do what was best for him.

And maybe, just maybe, this really was what was best for everyone.

CHAPTER 11

Leif was gone when I wandered down to the kitchen the next morning. I was a little disappointed when I read the note stuck to the coffee machine.

"Good morning Wife. Had to dash to Billings for a few hours. Be home late. Have fun riding! L."

He had at least one attorney in Billings, so I guessed that his quick trip involved some sort of corporate paperwork.

Leif often parked himself up at the tiny Killdeer airport and flew his Baron Beechcraft airplane to meetings or on quick trips to visit attorneys. Lately, I dropped him off and picked him up myself, unless it was a trip he wasn't expecting to make. Probably, that was the case with this impromptu flight. Being a pilot made Leif's travel arrangements a lot easier.

I spent the morning cleaning house, since it was much easier to do when the place was empty. I was a bit surprised when the knob on Leif's downstairs office door turned and the door opened. Normally it was locked up tight. Since I was cleaning, I wanted to be thorough. The garbage can would be full of shredded paper and I wanted to clean it out for him. Going into his office when he wasn't at home felt a bit like trespassing, but we were

152

married now, so I tiptoed in and started dumping the full trash can into a garbage bag.

The massive oak desk faced the wall, and the only thing that sat on top was the telephone. His papers and notes were all neatly stowed away in one of the drawers, I guessed. I'd never met a man as tidy as Leif.

In the center of the office his pool table dominated the space. It was so large it looked more like it had been constructed in place, and not simply installed. As I ran a hand over the cover on the pool table to check for dust, I really looked around the shelves and cabinets. Not one photograph sat on the shelves. Not one picture hung anywhere on the walls. It was as if the room was nothing more than rented space. Not one personal memento could be seen anywhere.

For the first time since I'd moved in with Leif, that realization hit me. There was nothing, anywhere, about Leif that was a part of his history. No pictures of his deceased parents. Not even a photo of his stepson, Scott. Nothing.

Curious, I went to the row of closed wooden cabinets that sat on the other side of the pool table. Maybe he had a picture or two inside? None of them looked like they were locked, so I peeked inside the closest one just to see what sort of knickknacks or mementoes he kept inside. The first cabinet was empty. The shelves were arranged like bookshelves, and I thought he might have a photo album, some books, maybe even a Navajo ceramic bowl or two. But it was completely empty.

Frowning, I pulled open the next cabinet door and nearly dropped the garbage sack.

Resting in a tall gun rack inside the cabinet was the biggest rifle I had ever seen. I could tell in an instant that this gun was not used for hunting deer. Drab green, the rifle had a long barrel and complex vent on the end of the muzzle. A flat-black heavy scope was attached to the stock, and the writing on the surface of the scope was in a language I didn't recognize. The body of the rifle looked more like a praying mantis than a weapon, and I resisted the urge to run my finger along the barrel to see what it felt like.

I'd grown up around guns. My father routinely propped a twenty-gauge shotgun by the door at the ranch. But this? This was like something from a military hardware catalog. The only writing I could decipher was a series of letters stamped on the stock: SAKO-TRG. The first thing that popped into my head when I saw the rifle was that this gun was used to kill people. The stock was scratched and worn. The barrel gleamed like it had recently been cleaned, but it was not uniform in color and had signs of wear. There wasn't a strap. This obviously wasn't the sort of rifle that you would sling over your shoulder and walk around with. Under the stock were two folding arms, and I could see that they were designed to click down underneath the barrel and form a bipod. This rifle was built to be set on the ground when fired.

Then a word popped into mind, and as soon as I thought it, I closed the cabinet as quickly as I could.

That word was sniper.

I was no expert, but I knew enough about rifles to recognize one that was designed to shoot great distances.

Leif and I had talked a little about his past involvement with the military. He'd never been an active duty member of the armed forces. Everyone who knew him in Killdeer assumed he had been involved with the army in some capacity, but that simply wasn't the case. Leif had spent a summer in Iraq during the first war, but he'd told me his role had been as a civilian contractor, and his job had been to oversee the transfer of State Department money to our allies to assist them with financial expenses.

He'd said that during the first Iraq war, he had basically been a glorified accountant.

If that was the case, what the hell was he doing with a sniper rifle?

I fiddled with the garbage sack in my hands and after a moment's thought, I took the sack back over to the garbage can underneath the desk and put the shredded paper back inside. I didn't want Leif to know I had even been inside his office.

I stood with my back to the door for a moment, thinking about what I had just seen. Maybe it was a gift? Maybe Leif had worked with someone in Iraq who had become a close friend and as a gesture they had given him the rifle?

"Yeah, right."

I thought about all of the cowboys and ranchers I knew, and the likelihood that they would give away their favorite gun to a friend as a gesture of camaraderie. In my experience, that hardly ever happened.

Where could he have possibly gotten a military sniper rifle?

Then I recalled the four men who had come to our wedding. It was a short walk to reach the conclusion those four guys were some sort of military. They had obviously been uncomfortable wearing cheap, store-bought suits. And they were Polish, not American.

Polish soldiers? At my wedding?

155

I stopped my spiraling thoughts then and there. The more I thought about it, the less I wanted to know the answers to my questions. Some things were better left in the past, and since Leif had never volunteered any information about those men, and had never discussed the strange rifle sitting in his office, it might be a good idea if I gave him his privacy and never mentioned it.

I went back upstairs to finish cleaning the house, and I told myself to forget about the rifle. It was obviously a relic of Leif's past, and it had nothing to do with our lives going forward. I vowed then and there to simply forget I'd even seen the thing.

It was only eleven-thirty when I finished cleaning the house, and I had time to take a long shower. If Jennifer wanted to go riding, long light-colored pants and a long-sleeve white shirt were the best wardrobe idea for the day. It would be hot, but with a long-sleeve shirt I wouldn't have to worry about getting scorched.

I pulled on a worn pair of cowboy boots, dropped a straw cowboy hat on my head and wondered what sort of horses Jennifer kept on the ranch. It would be just my luck to get a squirrelly young gelding that would make it his mission to throw me off the first chance he got.

It was noon by the time I left the house, and as I drove down the rutted dirt road I found myself slowing down as the car came to the straight stretch heading north towards Killdeer. I pulled over, not exactly sure what I was thinking, and parked my vehicle on the side of the road not far from the place I had parked the first time I had met Finn.

I got out next to the ditch and stood beside my SUV, shaking my head at myself.

Finn had introduced himself to me on this same stretch of road on a warm fall day two years ago. I'd pulled over when I had seen a wounded deer hiding in the tall grass of the barrow ditch, and Finn had arrived a scant fifteen minutes later, willing and able to euthanize the badly wounded animal. It was illegal to euthanize a game animal unless you were a game warden or a law enforcement officer, but it would have taken a full day for a warden to reach the deer and Finn had given me every impression he was capable, and authorized, to handle it.

I hadn't known at the time that he was technically not law enforcement, because he gave every indication otherwise with his mannerisms. It wasn't until later I found out he was a security chief.

We had dated, if you could call it that, for six months. He had never given me a phone number to reach him. I had learned his first name by finagling it from his coworkers. He was the most secretive man I had ever met.

Since he was impossible to get in touch with, and he had gone out of his way to make sure I could never really get into contact with him, the only way I'd ever reliably been able to reach him was by coming to this stretch of road, parking beside the ditch, and waiting.

I didn't know how, or why, but I'd always been able to get his attention by doing it and typically it never took him more than twenty minutes to arrive. Whether he could see the road from the weather station, or if the surveillance equipment at the station let him see who was parked on the road below the compound, I didn't know. But somehow, he always came.

I waited.

The sun was already blazing hot, baking the dusty road and making the tall buffalo grass dry as straw.

Nothing.

I listened intently for the familiar sound of Jeep tires on gravel, but I realized after a half an hour I would be waiting all day long if I expected Finn to make an appearance.

I climbed back in my SUV and headed for the Bybee ranch.

Granted, our relationship had ended abruptly, and maybe I had underestimated what getting married to Leif would do to him emotionally, but it seemed pretty childish to me that Finn would simply disappear without at least saying goodbye.

I felt a pang of regret as I drove through Killdeer. I would be late getting there, but Jennifer was such a flibbertigibbet I didn't think she would notice.

As much as I hated to think it, there really was nothing that I could do about Finn leaving Killdeer. He'd made his choice, and he had decided that it was time for him to move on.

"Look where you're going, not where you've been," I said out loud as I drove to Jennifer's ranch.

When I finally pulled into the parking area in front of the huge house, Jennifer bounded down the wide front steps and practically skipped to the door of my SUV.

"Come and see what I got for you," she said, beaming.

We walked to the stables together, Jennifer looking self-satisfied, and when I saw Logan Hiser walking through the big double doors of the stable, leading a horse, I stopped in my tracks.

"Peanut!"

The little mustang lifted his head when he saw me and gave a snort. In Peanut's mind I was probably equated with sugar cubes. He looked happy to see me.

"I talked to Tatiana, and she said Peanut and you were buddies," Jennifer told me proudly.

I went to his side and gave his neck a good scratch. He nosed my palm, slobbering all over it. I didn't mind

"Did you buy him?" I asked.

"Tatiana said he wasn't for sale. But she said that I could borrow him for a couple weeks if we wanted to go riding," Jennifer told me.

I took in Jennifer's outfit and tried not to roll my eyes. She was dressed in a striking white cotton blouse encrusted with intricate beadwork that looked more detailed than a Sioux Indian ceremonial dance vest. Her jeans were brand-new and looked expensive. Her boots still had a showroom gleam, and it was clear that she had just pulled them out of the box.

At least she had a sensible hat on. Her long chestnut hair was gathered up in a ponytail and she'd stuffed some of it underneath her wide-brimmed hat. The hat was a basic canvas outdoor fly-fishing hat, and it looked like she'd swiped it from her husband for the day.

Peanut was saddled, ready to go, and I could see a canteen of water looped over the saddle horn.

After Logan handed me the reins, a man I didn't recognize came out of the stable leading a tall buckskin mare.

"You must be Rick," I said politely. I didn't step forward to offer my hand, as I normally would have done. It was possible I knew just a little too much about all the people working out here.

"I'm Rick Lee. Pleased to meet you, ma'am."

He certainly was a long cool drink of water.

Rick Lee stood an easy six feet tall, had broad shoulders and narrow hips, and a pair of big brown eyes that could charm a nun. It was no surprise that Holly was smitten with him, in spite of his rogue reputation. Rick was a looker, no question about it.

I was reminded of Zane Ackerson almost instantly.

Both men were prizewinners in the handsome department. I wondered if Jennifer had taken part in the hiring process when it came to the ranch hands. She claimed that Logan gave her the creeps, but he was certainly easy on the eyes, too. The entire crew for the Bybee ranch easily landed in the top ten percent in terms of sex appeal. What sort of ranch were they running out here?

Logan gave me a wink, right on cue, and offered his hand to give me a leg up into the saddle.

"I've got it," I said, swinging up easily without his help. I hadn't needed a hand getting onto the back of a horse since I was nine years old, and I wasn't about to backslide.

Jennifer accepted a boost from Rick, and it might have been my imagination but she seemed to linger beside him with one hand pressed against his shoulder for a bit longer than was completely necessary.

"Mrs. Hix, Brian wants you to avoid the north trail by the reservoir and says for you to stick to First Hill today," Rick told her.

Jennifer gathered up her reins clumsily, betraying the fact that she was not a very experienced rider. "I know, I know. Is he still fishing with the Texas guys up there?"

"Yes, ma'am. Says he will be gone all day, and not to ride below them in case they decide they want to plink prairie dogs."

"I told him that Marley and I would be out riding today," she said peevishly.

"Stay away from the reservoir." Rick's tone was sharp. He took ahold of her horse's bridle and gave her a stern look. "You hearing me, ma'am?"

Jennifer tried to jerk the reins away, but Rick held the bridle firmly.

After a stare down that lasted a full minute, Jennifer sighed and nodded. "God forbid we disturb the men plinking prairie dogs."

We headed towards the sloping tree line west of the stable, and when I glanced back over my shoulder Logan was watching us with his arms folded tight across his chest. His expression was difficult to read. Logan squinted at us, enduring the bright sunlight, and he looked pensive.

Rick put a hand on Logan's shoulder, leaned in and said something that I didn't catch. Logan nodded and spun away, heading down the slope towards the cinder block building below the stables. The long row of fans thrummed loudly from the roof of the building, just as they had the last time, and they must have been burning a fortune in electricity.

Rick bounded up the steps leading inside the house, and I guessed he was going to take advantage of the fact that Jennifer was out, and he and Holly would have a few hours to themselves.

I turned forward again and watched as Jennifer fumbled with her reins.

"Dang nammit," she said.

"Here, like this." I held up my right hand so she could see how to properly hold a set of reins.

"I'm sorry. How the hell do you do this again?" she asked.

"Hold the top rein between your thumb and your first finger. Hold the second one between your second and third finger," I said, steering Peanut beside her so I could help her position her hands.

"There, that's good. How long have you been riding?" I asked.

"This is my third time," she said.

I looked down at the buckskin she straddled. The mare looked like she was about twenty years old, and in no hurry to go anywhere. I doubted the blast of a cannon would be enough to startle her. If Rick was in charge of choosing the mounts for folks to ride on the Bybee ranch, he'd certainly done his homework when it came to picking a horse for Mrs. Hix. I wondered if the buckskin would make it a mile before she had to stop and rest.

I wanted to be cordial, even though I was feeling anything but. Somehow the riding invitation from her felt forced, almost like Jennifer had asked me to come see her simply because she didn't have anything else better to do. Or because she wanted someone to amuse her for a few hours.

I forced myself to smile and nudged Peanut's flanks. The little mustang perked up and we trotted down the slope away from the big house and headed for a stand of cottonwood trees marking the edge of the football-field-size yard.

We rode side by side for over an hour, Jennifer chatting away like a happy hummingbird and Peanut swiveling his ears back and forth with curiosity. He had never seen this place before and he was taking it all in. Our pace was slow. Jennifer was still having a difficult time managing her reins.

My thoughts kept drifting back to what Loy and I had talked about the last time I'd seen him, about the loose morals of the crew on the Bybee ranch. Maybe Holly and Zane had made eyes at each other at some point and Rick had slashed him to bits in a jealous rage? Maybe—

"Marley, I said what did you wear when you got married?" Jennifer asked impatiently.

I jerked myself back to the present. "Oh? Ah, it was a very pretty crocheted top. Funny, but it was white. I mean, who am I kidding, right?"

"Girl, you are a thousand miles away," Jennifer told me. "You haven't said two words since we left."

I debated telling her about my speculations concerning Zane and Holly. I didn't know Jennifer all that well, but she was so personable and seemed so agreeable, she would probably volunteer any gossip she had.

I was about to explain what was going on inside my head when shots rang out. I reined Peanut to a standstill and swiveled my head, trying to get a line on where the shots were coming from.

Not surprisingly, they came from the north. Presumably from the direction of the reservoir.

I stood up in my stirrups and tried to see as far as I could.

The rolling hills sloped down until they reached the river and I could see glints of sunlight play across the surface of the rolling water below on the valley floor.

The hills rose up sharply on the other side of the river, culminating in a high plateau far above us. It was too high to see clearly. Stands of aspen trees crowded the ridgeline of the plateau, creating a perfectly private retreat for Texas businessmen looking for an authentic Western experience.

"Plinking prairie dogs?" I asked.

Jennifer shrugged. "I imagine. I thought they would be fishing all day. But sometimes they get bored."

The shots echoed across the river, bouncing around the foothills like the calls of lost ravens. And then, they simply stopped. There couldn't have been more than four shots fired. Who only fired four shots when they were shooting at prairie dogs?

I scanned the edge of the plateau. Something caught my eye and I squinted against the hot afternoon sun, trying to get a good look at it. A dark brown line snaked along the outer edge of the plateau and it was clear that it was a man-made structure.

"Jennifer, what is that?" I asked.

"You mean along the ridgeline? That's our buffalo fence," she said.

She kicked her buckskin, urging the mare forward. Peanut pulled at the reins with impatience. Finally I tore my eyes away from the long brown fence and let him follow the mare. He trotted to catch up.

"Didn't you tell me you and Brian are raising buffalo?" I was finally holding up my end of the conversation.

"Well, we only have about a dozen. Not enough to make that much money off of, but enough to supply the local butcher. I wouldn't really call it a herd yet. It's more like an experiment."

"That must be some fence," I said. "The plateau is a long way off, and I can still see it all the way from down here."

"Those buffalo are mean as snakes," she said. "I hate them. That fence cost a fortune, but Brian says there is real profit in raising buffalo meat. At least, over time there might be. I wish we had never got them. They tear up the corrals and they are really hard on all the equipment. Not to mention how hard they are to move from one place to another."

"Are buffalo more difficult to raise than beef cattle?" I asked.

My experience with buffalo was limited. I'd seen them occasionally at special events at the fairgrounds But other than that, I really didn't know that much about them.

"Are you kidding?" Jennifer asked. "They will kill you if they get the chance. Brian thinks that they are primeval, sort of like the way the Old West used to be. He likes them because Zane turned him on to the idea of having the ranch look more like it did two hundred years ago, before all the white people showed up."

"What else did Zane try to turn Brian on to liking?" I asked cautiously.

This was the first time Jennifer had opened up about Zane Ackerson, and I wanted to keep her talking.

It was a crazy idea, but it had crossed my mind that Zane might have tried to pull a wild stunt and bring a wolf onto the ranch.

It was unlikely, but it was the best explanation I could come up with at the moment.

"You name it," she said, steering her mare over a jagged patch of rocks.

She chatted on. "Zane wanted Brian to leave the coyotes alone and not shoot them. He wanted Brian to cordon off the whole Third Hill last summer because he found a den of foxes living up there. They had a huge argument one time about a beaver dam Brian found blocking up a section of the Snowy. Brian shot the beavers and Zane went ballistic."

"It must be hard to balance the needs of the wildlife and the needs of the domestic stock on a ranch this size," I said.

It came to mind that Brian Hix probably didn't have a fur trapper's license for shooting the beavers. It was one more thing not to like about the man.

"It's a nightmare," she admitted. "I never knew it was so much work to hold on to a place like this. But even someone as rich as Brian needs to balance the budget. He's more worried about money than whether or not we have a nice habitat for field mice."

"How big is the Bybee ranch?" I asked.

"Twenty-five thousand acres." She grabbed her saddle horn as her mare stumbled down a steep spot on the trail.

I let out a low whistle. "And I thought my father's little thousand-acre spread was a lot of work."

Jennifer pulled back her reins. "My ass is killing me. Let's go back and have a cocktail."

I looked at the sloping hillside we were riding on and tried to determine where we were in relation to the ranch. "Is this the Third Hill?" I asked.

Jennifer cracked a smile. "We haven't even gotten off of First Hill yet. There are three main hills, and since we don't really have anything else to call them, we just say First, Second or Third Hill and everyone knows what area you are talking about. First Hill is closest to the house, and Third Hill is the farthest away. On the other side of the Snowy River is the plateau. When we talk about it we say we are going up by the reservoir. You can't see it, but there is a big body of water up there. It's fed by a spring, I guess. It's always full, even when it doesn't rain for weeks and weeks."

"Who's your closest neighbor?" I maneuvered Peanut around and followed Jennifer's mare.

"Well, Tatiana is, but I don't really know which way her property is from here. I still get lost up here all the time."

We rode back towards the house at a much quicker pace, and Jennifer was uncharacteristically silent. After a few minutes of blessed quiet she stared off into the distance. She looked like she was thinking about something.

"Marley," she said at last. "You are friends with Loy, right?"

The little hairs on the back of my neck started to prickle up. "I went to high school with him."

She leaned down and fiddled with her left stirrup, even though there didn't seem to be anything wrong with it. "What's he like? I mean, is he a nice guy?"

"I think he's a great guy. He's a good sheriff, if that's what you mean."

She sat back up and rubbed the end of her nose. "It's just that, well, he has been really leaning on Brian about this thing with Zane. Coming out at odd times, calling. It's annoying. I mean, we've already told him everything we know."

"It's just procedure," I said evasively. What did Loy know about the Bybee ranch that he wasn't telling me?

"And you know how I feel about Logan," Jennifer added. "But, I don't think it's really fair for the sheriff to single him out and pick on him so much. Logan isn't my favorite person, but I still don't think Loy should assume things about him just because he has a sketchy past. It doesn't make him a criminal."

"Has he assumed something about Logan?" I asked.

"All I know is that Logan is really frustrated. He told me the sheriff has it in for him, keeps asking him about his alibi the night Zane got killed."

My ears pricked up at that statement instantly. "Why in the world would Logan need an alibi? It was just an accident, right? Tatiana Phelps says it looked to her like Zane was mauled by a wolf."

"That's what we all thought. So, why is the sheriff holding Logan under a microscope? Maybe you could ask the sheriff to lay off of him. You know, friend to friend?" she said.

I deliberately avoided her gaze. "I'm sure it will all be cleared up in no time."

Her expression relaxed and she kicked her mare into a canter. "Let's get out of this heat!"

We rode back to the ranch in quick time, and when we stopped in front of the stables both horses were lathered with foam and sweat. Rick sauntered over to lead the horses inside and cool them down. I followed Jennifer up the wide steps leading to the house.

As we pushed through the front doors I glanced back and gave the vast yard and stable area a thorough exam. As expected, Logan Hiser was nowhere to be seen.

I had a strong feeling that the Texas hunters were not really plinking prairie dogs up on the plateau. And I had an equally strong feeling that the ranch's gamekeeper was with them, cleaning up whatever mess they had made by missing what they had been shooting at.

I'd promised Loy I had no intention of getting involved with what had happened to Zane Ackerson, but there was something not quite right about the Bybee ranch. By chance I had made friends with the wife of the owner, which just happened to put me in a perfect place to observe the crew. If I managed to see or hear something important while I was socializing, that wasn't really my fault now, was it?

CHAPTER 12

"You must be the gold-digging hussy who conned my dad into marrying you."

I froze, my hand halfway to the light switch in the kitchen. Not only had I about peed myself, I'd almost grabbed the closest heavy object and started swinging.

My hand found the switch and I flipped it on.

A young man was sitting at the kitchen counter, swirling a glass of red wine with one hand. He took a swig of wine and set the glass on the counter before turning to offer me a withering stare.

I took a deep breath. "You must be Scott."

His blond hair and narrow face bore a striking resemblance to those of Virginia Gable, Leif's ex-wife.

He'd been sitting in the dark drinking. Alone.

Never a good sign.

His clothes were ready for a Ralph Lauren photo shoot. His tie was narrow, creamy white, and tucked inside his black wool blazer. His slacks were rumpled from the flight, but still looked more like something you would wear while addressing a congressional subcommittee than what would hold up at a street dance during rodeo weekend.

I did what I could to paste a smile on my sunburned face. "This is a nice surprise."

"He's upstairs taking a shower," Scott told me, obviously talking about Leif.

He ignored the wine glass and focused on me like a cobra.

I had ridden with Jennifer for several hours in the blazing sun, had endured the taunts and teasing from the gang of Texas hunters after they had gotten back from their fishing/plinking expedition, witnessed a classic argument between Rick and Holly about whether or not her blouse was too transparent, and topped it off by getting a nip on the shoulder from Peanut when he realized I was leaving him at the Bybee ranch.

I wasn't in the mood.

"Gold-digging hussy?" I said, looking at him with equal animosity.

He had the decency to look a little ashamed, and glanced away just as Leif came into the kitchen behind me.

"I see you two are getting to know each other." Leif gave me a squeeze on the shoulder. It was the shoulder Peanut had bitten, and I winced but didn't say anything.

"We sure are," I said cheerfully, my grin so wide you could hang a lasso off my dimples.

Scott was Leif's stepson, and due to an unfortunate set of circumstances involving Virginia getting pregnant when she was only nineteen, I was barely six years older than Scott and now I was officially his stepmother.

Goody.

Scott smiled back, giving his stepfather every impression that he was pleased as pie that I was his new stepmother. "Marley was just telling me how

171

nice it is I will be staying with you for the whole week," he said, his tone dripping honey and ice cream. He gave us both a peachy grin.

Leif's expression brightened and he gave me a quick smooch on the cheek. "That's good. I was hoping to introduce you two, but I've probably talked enough about you both that you must already feel like you know each other."

"Oh, I think you could say that, Dad," Scott said, one corner of his mouth curled up.

"Did you two have supper yet?" I asked.

"We had a bite to eat in Billings," Leif said. "But don't let us stop you from fixing something up. I'm sorry, Marley. I forgot to tell you I was picking Scott up at the airport today. We always have him come to Killdeer for rodeo weekend and it never occurred to me to let you know about it in advance."

On a scale of bad things that had happened to me the past few days, this didn't even come close to being the worst. I shook it off with a shrug. "It's no trouble at all. This is Scott's house too."

The kid actually looked up at me with surprise. I went to the refrigerator to grab a snack, and I could feel Scott's eyes boring between my shoulder blades. When I turned back around he was staring at me like he was trying to figure out my angle.

"I would love to sit and visit with you two for a while," Leif told us. "But it's Friday night and I am sure there is something going on downtown this evening. Why don't the two of you head to Main Street and check out the sights?"

Scott looked at me, I looked at him, and we both looked over at Leif's hopeful, sincere expression, and simultaneously nodded with false enthusiasm.

"Sure, that would be fun," I said.

"Great idea, Dad," Scott said. "Aren't you coming with us?"

Leif gave us both a pleased smile, but shook his head. "Not tonight. I am bushed from the drive. But you two go have some fun and get to know one another. We can have breakfast together in the morning and catch up."

Bless his heart, but Leif was oblivious to most awkward social situations. He was brilliant when it came to business deals, but his stepson was certainly a blind spot for him. Leif had the notion that since he and Scott were so close, and since he and I had such a good relationship, it was a given that Scott and I would get along splendidly.

In all the time that Leif and I had been a couple, I'd never even spoken to Scott on the telephone. This wasn't exactly an ideal situation, but the two of us had to get acquainted at some point.

I took a bottle of water out of the fridge and drank half of it before motioning towards the kid and nodding at the door. "We should leave now. It will be tough to find a decent parking place if we wait much longer."

"I'm ready," Scott said, sliding off the bar stool and giving his dad a hug. "It's great to be back. See you in the morning, Dad."

I didn't bother to change before we left. I was a mess, and I knew it. But where we were headed, getting into nice clothes wasn't a very smart move to make.

Scott and I slid into my SUV and I backed out of the driveway.

"How are you liking my mother's car?" he asked.

I glanced down at his shoes. Polished black leather. Probably Italian. I knew from experience

173

that they would be totally trashed by the end of the evening.

"How is Virginia these days?" I asked, deflecting his question.

Scott ignored me and looked out the window.

We drove in silence until we reached the edge of town, and I managed to find us a parking spot only a few blocks from the action.

When we stepped out of the car the air was suddenly sharp with the smell of beer, heavy with dust, and loud music blared from somewhere down Main Street.

I could hear the distinct twang of fiddles and guitars, accompanied by the slurred drawl of some intoxicated local singer doing his best Merle Haggard impression.

The entire length of downtown Killdeer was blocked off. A stock fence had been set up to contain the revelers and prevent any cars from traveling on the road, and underage kids hovered around the single entrance hopefully, looking for any opportunity to dart past the police and sneak inside the barricade.

Police dressed in blue manned the entrance, checking each ID scrupulously. A stage was set up in the middle of the street, circled all around with speakers and garbage cans, and an impromptu dance floor had blossomed over the parking places. Couples two-stepped and jitterbugged to the music, not able to hear each other yell over the noise, and loving every minute of it.

Down Cemetery Road, a side street just off of Main, the Broken Spoke Saloon was alive with a different kind of music, and a long row of Harley-Davidson motorcycles guarded the bar's perimeter. Usually cowboys and bikers avoided each other, but once a year the bikers let their hair down, as it were, and mingled with the cowboys in relative peace.

I was exhausted but not about to let it show. This outing with Scott obviously meant a great deal to my new husband, and the last thing I wanted was to ruin the night by cutting it short.

"I've never been to the street dance before," Scott said, hands thrust inside his pants pockets. He had forgotten about his animosity towards me for the moment and was scanning the crowd with a game expression.

Maybe this wouldn't be so bad after all.

"Didn't you ever come down here with your mom and Leif before tonight?" I asked.

"We always went to the pancake breakfast and the bed races, and usually somebody ended up bothering my dad for a donation to some Rotary Club thing or another. But we never came downtown at night."

Scott's eyes sparkled as he watched the dancers in front of the stage.

I tugged his shirtsleeve. "Let's go in."

He hesitated, but after watching the revelers, his courage spiked and we pulled out our driver's licenses so that we could get inside the barricade.

They carded everyone.

I even saw them card Lewis Pritchett, and I knew for a fact that he was fifty-two years old.

As we half-walked, half-shoved our way inside the barricade, I realized I knew almost every person inside.

Killdeer had a population of 901, when everybody was home, and at least 801 of them were at this street dance whooping it up.

"Do you have a girlfriend?" I asked Scott.

"Why, are you cruising for a piece?" he asked, eyeballing me. But his tone was light, and he smiled to show he was teasing.

"Just curious." My eyes slid sideways until they fell on a cute brunette who had spotted Scott. She stood beside a plump blonde girl with short hair, and the two of them were watching him with intense curiosity. It was a safe assumption that they had never seen anything like him before.

He saw the two girls staring at him and his cheeks colored. "Well, I did have, but we broke up."

It occurred to me that I knew absolutely nothing about Scott, other than the fact that he was Leif's stepson. I didn't even know what he did for a living.

"I should warn you about Killdeer," I said.

"Warn me about what?" he asked.

At that moment the brunette marched forward and grabbed Scott by the arm. "Wanna dance?"

He looked absolutely stunned.

I leaned over his shoulder, shoving him towards her. "He'd love to!"

The brunette giggled and tugged him towards the mob of two-steppers.

I felt a little guilty about his obvious discomfort, but not guilty enough to do anything about it. After a few awkward moves, he started to loosen up and looked like he was in danger of actually having a good time.

In Killdeer during rodeo weekend, the women asked the men to dance. It was an old tradition going way back.

Well, he'd figure it out.

I hadn't drunk nearly enough water today to compensate for the heat, and started to head for the fresh-squeezed lemonade stand when I felt a strong pair of hands circle around my waist and swoop me onto the dance floor.

"Hello, Cookie."

A pair of sharp blue eyes appeared before me, and I felt a wide palm pressed to the small of my back intimately.

"Logan, I'm a married woman." I grabbed both his hands and forced him into a more proper dance position.

He put his mouth beside my ear. "What did you do to my brother?"

My shoulders slumped. "Why do people keep asking me that?"

Logan leaned back and studied me. "He quit his job. He loves his job. What did you do to him?"

I took his wandering right hand and placed it in a more appropriate position on my waist. "Haven't you asked him?"

"He won't talk to me."

Logan swung us around, and for a man with obvious bloodstains on the toes of his boots, he was a surprisingly good dancer.

"Where's your big hunting knife?" I asked.

He looked disappointed. "They wouldn't let me bring it inside. Can you believe it?"

"I'm astonished," I said.

"Now, about my brother," he began.

"I don't know what to tell you, Logan. He's a grown-up man and he can tie his own shoelaces and everything."

"He's also a bit of a prat," Logan said.

"I won't argue with you there."

We drifted further from the stage, and it was getting more and more difficult for me to keep an eye on Scott. I did what I could to steer us back towards the center of the dancers. Leif would kill me if something happened to his son.

"You a pretty good shot, Logan?" I asked.

He slowed his movements and deliberately didn't look at me. "I'm fair."

The song ended, the music stopped and the dancers around us clapped and shouted out requests. The band members said they would take a five-minute break, but to keep our dancing shoes on.

I tried to step away from Logan but he kept his hands on me. "Why?"

I raised one eyebrow. "That prairie dog blood on your shoes?"

His grip tightened on my right hand and his steel blue eyes focused sharply. "I'm going to give you a piece of advice, Cookie. The next time Jen calls you to come out to Bybee ranch and go riding tell her you can't."

I tilted my head back and returned his gaze. "And why would I want to do a thing like that for? It's not very neighborly."

"For your health." His voice came out a hiss.

"There's nothing wrong with my health, Logan," I said, not backing down an inch.

He released my hand and stepped away, his eyes mere slits. He looked me up and down speculatively. "Now I see what Finn was talking about."

Without another word he turned and disappeared into the throng of dancers, leaving me standing there like he had been a figment of my imagination.

What in the world had all of that been about?

Scott appeared at my elbow, a lopsided grin on his face. "I got a phone number."

My hands were shaky, but I masked it as best I could. "Let's go get a drink. I'm parched."

He seemed less antagonistic toward me and trailed at my heels. I stopped at a lemonade vendor trailer and Scott scanned the drink list. After a moment his face fell. "Lemonade or iced tea? Don't they have a nice pilsner or something?"

"I think you should stick to the light stuff tonight," I suggested.

We paid more for our two cups of lemonade than I normally paid for groceries for the entire week, and went off in search of a quiet place. I found an alley that was only occupied by a young couple making out and three members of the band taking a smoke break.

I leaned my tired back against the wall and Scott propped himself beside me.

"I don't know where my mom is," he confessed suddenly, his mouth a few inches away from his cup. He took a hasty sip of his drink.

I hadn't seen this conversation coming at all. "How long has it been since you spoke to her?" I asked.

"Six months. I can't get her to return my phone calls. Dad says he hasn't heard from her either. Does she . . . I don't know . . . does anyone ever call the house and hang up if you answer the phone instead of Dad? Or have you gotten any mail addressed to her?"

I thought hard about the last year and a half and tried to recall anything that might be helpful. "No. Nothing. She really hasn't contacted you in all that time?"

He stared into his cup. "She's done this before. Dad thinks she may have a new boyfriend. I don't know. Listen, I'm sorry I was so snotty towards you back at the house. This hasn't been easy for me to deal with. I'm used to taking care of my mother and it worries me when I don't know where she is."

I felt a pang of sympathy for Scott. Virginia couldn't have been the warmest person to be raised by, and truthfully, Leif was probably the only stable force the kid had ever had in his life. I reminded myself not to think of him as a kid. He was almost twenty-nine, after all. But in spite of the fact that he was technically a man, he still looked like a kid to me.

"You know she was a dental hygienist? That's how they met. After Leif got back from Iraq, he hadn't been to a dentist for a year. He met my mom when she was cleaning his teeth."

I tried to picture Virginia Gable sticking her fingers in my mouth and had to suppress a shudder. "How old were you then?"

"Eight. Leif married my mother not long after they met. But right after we moved in with Leif he acted like we had been there all along. He took me to Little League. He went to all the parent-teacher conferences. Hell, he even put me through college. He has been my dad ever since."

Scott took another long drink of his lemonade, his eyes focused on a memory. "He was gone a lot, too. Running off to Boston, London, or wherever. But whenever I really needed him he was always there for me."

I did some quick math in my head. So, Leif had met Scott when the kid was only eight years old. That was over twenty years ago. No wonder Scott looked up to Leif like a true father. He had been involved in Scott's life long enough to qualify.

"She hated it here," he said, choking out a sad laugh and casting his eyes around the town. "She tried to fit in. But it's so small."

I couldn't argue with him there. "Sometimes it's easier to live in a city where nobody knows who you are."

He cast a rueful glance my way. "Like D.C., right? I can go for weeks and never see another person I know."

I laughed out loud at that. "I can't go ten minutes without seeing someone I know."

"Why did you marry my dad?" he asked abruptly.

There was only one right answer here, and I wanted to make sure he knew I meant it. "Because I love him."

He rolled that around in his head for a moment, his face a mixture of skepticism and bemusement.

"I think my mom married Leif because she thought it would be a good move," he said, dropping his gaze back to his cup.

"But, she loved him too, right?" I asked.

He nodded unenthusiastically. "As much as my mom can love anyone, sure. If she didn't have me to look out for her, I don't know what would happen to her. Sometimes she just doesn't know when she should use her head. I wish I knew where she was!"

"If she has done something like this before, disappeared I mean, I wouldn't worry too much, Scott. Virginia is tough. She will turn up."

He nodded and took another drink. "This is terrible."

"Don't worry. I am sure she's just fine."

"No. I mean the lemonade. Really, can't we go find a beer or something that doesn't taste like warm water with a yellow crayon dipped in it?"

I laughed.

"Well, this is probably a really bad idea, but do you want to go to the biker bar?"

He cocked a smile. "There is a biker bar in Killdeer?"

"Nonbikers are allowed in during rodeo weekend, grudgingly."

He tossed his cup in a nearby garbage can. I had counted seventeen gigantic garbage cans since we had stepped inside the barricade and wondered where they got them all.

"Let's go," he said. "I want to tell everyone when I get back to work next week where I went."

We squeezed our way outside the barricade and headed for the Broken Spoke. An old wagon wheel, missing one spoke, hung over the door on the end of an ox yoke that had been installed like a sign handle.

"Very quaint," Scott remarked.

"I'll bet you don't have anything as fancy as this in D.C.," I said proudly.

He actually laughed.

I managed to fight my way to the bar, receiving at least one blatant grope for my trouble, and shouted my order to the bartender.

Scott accepted the bottle of beer I hustled outside for him and the two of us sat down on a concrete parking barrier to enjoy the ambiance of the dust-filled parking lot.

He looked down at the label.

"Pigs Ass Porter? Is this for real?"

"Comes out of Belt, Montana."

"I'm not sure I can drink this," he said, taking a tentative sip.

"I don't blame you."

In spite of the name, he managed to enjoy the beer, and after we'd sat together in silence for several minutes, Scott gave me a sideways smile.

"I think we may have stayed out long enough to make Dad feel better," Scott said. "He wanted us to get to know each other, but I had a terrible flight down from D.C. and we should call it a night."

We ambled back towards the car and I didn't detect a whiff of his previous animosity. It was obvious that Scott practically worshiped his dad, and I couldn't blame him. As far as I was concerned, Leif was worthy of a little hero worship. It seemed clear to me now that Scott's initial hostility towards me was due to overprotectiveness.

Maybe it was the way I was dressed, with my tattered and stained clothes and dusty boots. Maybe it was my sense of humor. But for whatever reason, Scott seemed to have come to the conclusion that I wasn't as pretentious as he'd expected. He behaved as if the best course of action for dealing with me was to call a truce. As long as I didn't do something stupid like start insulting his mother, something I would never do, there seemed to be a ray of hope that the two of us might actually be able to get along.

As we rounded the corner of the bank building and headed for the car, I could see through the dim glow of the streetlight that someone was sitting on the bumper of my SUV. I touched Scott on the arm and took a few steps ahead of him. He slowed his pace, letting me take the lead.

Some intoxicated idiot had decided to plop themselves down on my bumper like it was a public picnic bench. That's what I got for parking close to the action.

"Can I help you?" I asked.

When I was close enough to distinguish features, I saw right away it was a woman. She looked up, with a soiled and stained bar napkin pressed to her face and both eyes leaking tears. That she had been crying wasn't the only thing making her face wet. Red oozed from her nose and one hand shook when she tried to dab it dry.

It was Holly Koltiska. And someone had just beat the bloody hell out of her.

CHAPTER 13

I sat on the open tailgate of Loy's sheriff's truck. He stood beside me, one hip propped on the fender. We sat in the parking lot of the Stockyard grocery store. The store was closed, but the parking lot was bathed in a soft glow of streetlights and it was enough to see by.

"Her nose is busted," Loy said. "Luckily for her, it's rodeo weekend."

"You are a silver lining sort of guy, aren't you Loy?" I asked.

He shrugged. "There are paramedics every twenty feet in Killdeer until Sunday morning, which is the lucky part, and unlucky because it's probably all the booze and action that led to her getting pounded in the first place."

Holly was taking some sort of painkiller, washing it down with a paper cup of water, and wincing. A harried paramedic stood next to her, looking like he'd had about four hours of sleep in the past two days. She had a blanket wrapped over her shoulders and she was clutching Scott's hand like he was a rescue swimmer and she was drowning.

Scott sat right beside Holly, hovering like a parent, even though he had only known her for twenty minutes.

"She seems to feel pretty comfortable around that kid," Loy said.

"When he saw her sitting on my car, he walked right up to her and sort of took charge," I told him. "I sure didn't expect him to do that. But Holly hasn't let go of his hand since."

"Criminetly, what a night," Loy said, rubbing his forehead.

"This isn't the worst thing you've had to deal with?" I asked.

Loy turned slowly and looked at me, his lips twitching. "Marley, I hear it right that you and Jennifer Hix are Killdeer's newest power couple?"

I looked at my hands. "Maybe."

He blew out a long breath. "I wish you'd stay away from the Bybee ranch. They are not exactly strangers to those of us in law enforcement."

"Jennifer Hix stole Peanut from Tatiana," I said.

"Who's Peanut?" he asked. "You been drinkin' tonight, Mrs. Gable?"

"Dearcorn. And no. Peanut is Tatiana's mustang she keeps at the ranch for her niece. I took a shine to him, and the next thing I know, Jennifer has hauled him out to the Bybee ranch and we are going riding together."

Loy gave me a long, deep stare. "Tatiana's mustang, huh? That's funny."

It was my turn to give him a long stare. "What's so funny?" I wasn't laughing and neither was he.

"Tatiana called me tonight and said she found some of her sheep, tore to hell, about three miles away from where we found Zane's body."

I sat up. "What? How many?"

"Three." He spat on the ground. The air was so thick with dust you could draw pictures in it.

"I'm doing what I can to keep it quiet. The last thing we need right now is a repeat of the great coyote bait run of 2012."

"What happened to the sheep?" I asked.

"It looked like they had been mauled. Not eaten. Just mauled."

"Like Holly," I said, half joking. "I don't suppose you happen to know where her boyfriend is at the moment."

"Hun, I can't prove it was Rick who hit her," Loy said, looking towards the ambulance.

"We both know it was," I said.

A pickup truck full of teenagers breezed by, music blaring and tires chirping on the asphalt as they goosed the engine.

I heard the distinct sound of beer cans rattle in the bed of the truck.

"I'm pretty sure that was Richie Williams. Sounds like they have been drinking. He's seventeen," I said.

"I don't have the energy to chase him right now," Loy told me. "I'll call his mother in the morning and let her crucify him."

I wiped a layer of dust off of my face with the tail of my grungy shirt. "Three sheep, mauled. Jennifer Hix making herself my new best friend forever, and now Holly gets a busted nose. Not to mention what happened to Zane. Loy, what in the hell is going on around here?"

"Speaking of what the hell is going on, what did you do to Finn?"

I rolled my eyes. "Not you too?"

"Irene told me he's put in his notice at the weather station," Loy said.

"I don't want to talk about it," I said, meaning every single word.

"I only ask because my deputy has been hounding me for days, trying to get in touch with Finn."

"Why is Nick needing to talk to Finn?" I asked.

"He won't tell me. I thought you might know."

"Has everyone in Killdeer just gone pure crazy?" I asked.

"You mean, more than normal?" he said.

"It was a rhetorical question."

"I don't want to say it," Loy said, propping one hand on the butt of his pistol.

"Say what?"

"Wolves," he said, looking at me pointedly.

"Dammit, Loy. We talked about this. If you really do think it's wolves killing Tatiana's sheep, call the Fish and Wildlife office and have them send over a biologist."

"I'm not particularly interested in doing that. I want to know what it is you think is going on," he said, his voice deceptively smooth.

I made a feeble attempt to tuck in my shirt. "I don't know yet. But, I've got some thoughts on that."

"Maybe you could see your way towards sharing those thoughts with the local sheriff?" he asked.

Holly and Scott were talking quietly inside the ambulance. Scott carefully helped her out and slowly started leading her towards us. I knew Loy was pumping me for information so he could figure out just how deeply I was involved with the Bybee ranch, which I couldn't blame him for doing, and I didn't have a lot of time to tell him everything.

"Listen," I said, talking fast. "What did Holly tell you happened tonight?"

He grimaced, but after taking a long breath he relented and answered. "She said it wasn't Rick. She said it was someone she didn't know, at the street dance. Her and Rick had a spat, and he took off. The next thing she knows, some stranger is hitting on her, won't take no for an answer and she tries to ditch him, and is rewarded with getting punched in the face."

"Your take on that?" I asked.

"She's lying. But, I can't prove it. I can't find Rick Lee anywhere. And I mean, anywhere. He's disappeared."

"Do you think it was Rick?" I asked.

"Hun, I know it was. He goes into a frenzy whenever he thinks Holly is getting too much attention from another man. I seriously cannot believe he hasn't killed her, or someone else for that matter, before this."

Holly and Scott were nearly close enough to hear our conversation. But I only had one more question anyway. I lowered my voice. "Loy, I know this might sound like a really stupid thing to ask. I need to know where Todd Ramsey is right now."

The sheriff looked at me like he was contemplating administering a sobriety test to me. "The brand inspector? What do you want to talk to him for?"

"I'll let you know later," I said. There was a very specific reason I wanted to get in touch with the local brand inspector but I didn't have time to go into it with the sheriff at the moment.

Holly and Scott came to my side and when Loy got a close-up look at her face again, I could see veins pop out on his neck. "Holly, Marley said she will take you over to the women's shelter in Parkman. That alright with you? Just for tonight.

We can talk about other arrangements tomorrow when things look better."

Holly glanced over at Scott. He was still holding her hand and I was astonished that the kid had stepped up to the situation so calmly. "It's just for tonight," he said, giving her a reassuring smile.

Holly didn't say anything, but she nodded and let herself be led to my SUV. Scott helped her inside.

"Todd?" I asked Loy, backing away towards my vehicle and pulling out the keys.

Loy kicked a discarded soda can at his feet and tried not to meet my eyes. After a moment's hesitation, he sighed and shut the tailgate of his truck. "He's in Killdeer. As far as I know he is still planning on being out to the L Bar T day after tomorrow. But why do you want to know where the brand inspector is?"

I called over my shoulder. "I'll tell you if it turns out to be important."

I climbed inside my vehicle and noticed that Scott was sitting in the backseat with Holly. She had stopped crying, and was silent as a stone as we drove the half hour into Parkman. Any thoughts I'd had of asking her questions evaporated when I saw how defeated she was. We dropped her at the women's shelter and to my relief she let go of Scott's hand when it was time for us to leave.

I told myself the next time I had extra money, the women's shelter was getting a big fat donation.

On the drive back to Killdeer Scott was quiet.

"You were a real lifeline for Holly tonight," I said.

Scott tilted his head a little to the side. "Well, you can't grow up being Virginia Gable's son and not know a thing or two about how to deal with a drunk, battered woman."

I jerked my head towards him.

He looked over, sheepish. "No, not Leif. He'd never hurt a fly. But the string of losers she went through before she found him was no picnic."

By the time we pulled into the garage both of us were physically and emotionally wrung out. I was a little surprised to find Leif sitting on the patio, a ring of candles beside him on a small table illuminating his face. He smiled when he saw us.

"How was the street dance?"

Scott and I looked at each other, not sure how to respond.

"It was fun," Scott said brightly, jumping in with both feet. "I got a phone number from a cute girl."

"Good for you," Leif said.

I saw a tall glass of red wine sitting beside him on the table. Underneath it was a fat manila folder. An ink pen rested at his elbow.

"Well, son, why don't you turn in and get a good night's sleep. You must be tired from your flight."

I was surprised once again when Scott turned and gave me a quick hug. "Night, Marley. It was really nice to meet you at last."

He went inside the patio doors and I sat down beside Leif in one of the wrought iron chairs.

He reached for my hand and gave it a kiss. "I couldn't sleep. Did you two have a good time?"

"We had a very interesting time," I said, with all sincerity.

He set his wine glass aside and pulled a stack of papers out of the folder. "Sweetie, I need you to sign these."

"What are they?" I asked, scooting forward and taking the pen he offered me.

"Just bank stuff. One of them puts you on my safe-deposit box. One of them is for some life insurance. Just busywork I need to get taken care of now that we are married."

I didn't bother to read any of the papers. I trusted Leif implicitly and whatever he was putting in front of me I knew it was necessary and important.

I signed a half a dozen documents with a blue ink pen and handed them back to him. There wasn't enough light to read any of the papers, and barely enough to find the dotted lines to sign. But I forgot about the documents the moment I handed them off to Leif.

"Did you know Virginia is missing?" I asked.

He frowned. "I did. If she doesn't turn up soon I will take steps to locate her. Scott worries."

We sat beside each other, holding hands and taking in the night sounds from the forest around the house. Somewhere off in the distance a fox called out, talking to its companion.

"So tell me what's bothering you, my dear wife," Leif said, patting my hand.

I debated about how much I would say. It wasn't as if I could actually do anything about what had happened to Zane. And as far as I knew, Jennifer Hix really was interested in spending time with me out of sheer loneliness. Holly's tortured life didn't seem like a good topic, so I settled on saying only what I knew for certain.

"There is a rumor in Killdeer that we have a wolf issue," I said.

"Hmm. What do you think?"

"It's possible. But not very likely. I am trying to stay out of it."

He chuckled. "Sweetie, you need to take care of you, and expect that other people will be able to take care of themselves. Sometimes I think you try too hard."

I couldn't argue with him there. "What about you? How is work going?"

He sighed and leaned back in his chair. "I have almost got it to the point where I can wrap it up. I'm selling off several of my holdings, and the lawyers are not making the process easy on me."

"I don't suppose there is anything I can do to help?" I asked.

"I wish there were. But no, it's only a matter of slogging through the mounds of paperwork and convincing my partners that I know what is best. By the time I am done with this matter we will have fewer worries."

He looked tired.

More tired than I had ever seen him. Well, it had been a very busy few days.

"Marley, I know that you and Scott have only just started to get to know each other. But I was hoping that you would be able to open yourself up to having a good relationship with him."

After the evening's events, the possibility of Scott and I having a friendship didn't seem too remote.

I smiled at him and squeezed his hand. "I think we have gotten over the worst of it. He's a good kid."

"He is a good kid. But, he's fragile. I would like it very much if you would take it upon yourself to view him as my son. He isn't my biological child, but that makes no difference to me. I know how important family is to you, and he is my family. Does that make sense?"

He was trying to ask me something, in his own way. "Would you like me to think of him as my family too?"

"I know it's a great deal to ask of you after such a short time. But I would like to see you take on a protective role in his life. He has not always lived in the most stable of home situations. It would mean more to me than you know that he can turn to you if need be."

"Of course he can lean on me. He is your son. I think you underestimate him, though. Scott's no hothouse lily. I think he has more resilience in him than most people give him credit for."

Leif blinked with surprise. "You do?"

"He's a lot tougher than he looks. But I'll let him know that if he needs me for anything he can count on me."

Leif relaxed and gave the back of my hand a kiss. "That's all I could ask for."

We sat together in silence, basking in the cool night air and hearing the soft whisper as the breeze moved through the pine needles. An owl hooted with surprise from somewhere deep in the trees and we both laughed. The last week had been rife with troubles, but sitting with my new husband taking in the peace and quiet of home somehow managed to make them all go away.

CHAPTER 14

The phone rang and I scooped it up, chewing my pancakes as quickly as possible so I didn't answer the phone with my mouth full.

"Hello?"

"Hello, Marley."

The woman on the phone was familiar, but I couldn't place her. For one horrible moment I thought it might be Leif's ex-wife, Virginia, and I nearly choked.

"How can I help you?" I asked, hoping my ignorance wasn't too obvious.

The woman laughed and her voice sounded like bells. "You don't have any idea who this is, do you?"

"Tammy?" I stammered.

It was all coming back to me now.

"I got your number from Allen. He said he got it from Irene. She must have gotten it from your dad. Apparently your new husband doesn't like to be found."

"How the heck are you?"

I was delighted to talk to Tammy. She was a biologist with the Fish and Wildlife branch office where I had worked, and I had gotten to know her well during my tenure.

Apparently, someone from my old life was still speaking to me.

"I'm doing the same," she said.

"That bad, huh?"

She laughed again and I could hear the creak of her office chair as she swiveled back and forth.

Leif and Scott were trying to beat each other to the pile of dirty dishes. Stacks of syrup-laden plates were scattered across the black granite countertop, and half-empty mugs of coffee sat in random places. We had just finished breakfast.

"So, how's married life?" Tammy asked.

"So far, so good," I told her, rescuing my coffee before Leif could snatch the cup and start washing it.

"You've only been married, what? Three days?"

"And he still seems to like me," I said, mock wonder in my voice.

"Go figure."

"What are you doing in the office on a Saturday?" I asked, taking the phone out of the kitchen and tucking myself on the living room sofa.

"Looking for another job in Hawaii. Surfing for porn on the Internet, the usual."

I chuckled. "Right. What are you really doing at the office on a Saturday?"

She was quiet for a moment and I could almost see her expression shift from teasing to serious. Finally she cleared her throat and took a breath. "Marley, where exactly did you find that tick that you gave to Allen?"

Her tone was suddenly all business. Apparently Allen had gotten over our spat in the parking lot in Three Forks, had put a crowbar in his heart and pried it open wide enough to do me a favor. He'd driven over to Helena and given Tammy my tick after all.

I switched gears to match her. "I found it on the Deep Creek Ranch. It was crawling on the sheriff's deputy after he had just finished processing a crime scene."

I could hear the rustle of papers. "Where, exactly, is the Deep Creek?"

She must have been pulling out maps. No wonder she was at the office.

I closed my eyes and tried to draw a mental picture of the location. "Northwest of Killdeer. Deep Creek butts up against that piece of Forest Service land where the public access trail leads up to the old tie flume historical site."

More rustling.

"Oh, yeah. I see it. Jesus, that's a long way from where you are in the valley," she said.

"It's a big ranch," I said.

She was quiet again.

"Tammy. You gonna tell me what kind of tick it is?"

She coughed. "It's called a Lone Star."

"A what? Come on."

"No, really. Amblyomma americanum. The Lone Star tick. It's called that because of the white dot on its back. The females have it, and what you found was a big fat female."

"Is this the part where you tell me that global warming is increasing the mean temperature of the planet and allowing species that are not native to Montana to get a foothold and colonize new territories?" I asked, quirking a smile.

"Not exactly," she said. "This is the part where I tell you that it is physically impossible for that tick to be here."

I lost my quirky smile. "What do you mean, physically impossible?"

"It's indigenous to the state of Texas. It can be found in some parts of the Midwest, but this species lives primarily in Texas. It is not found in Montana. It isn't even found in Wyoming. The environment up here is too alien for this tick to survive. It can't even get a toehold in Colorado."

A shiver of warning crept up between my shoulder blades. "So, how did it get here?"

"I have no idea."

"Do you have any theories?" My brow wrinkled up.

"I was just going to ask you the same question."

"Could it have been dropped by some Mexican drug dealers when they off-loaded a bale of hash?" I asked.

"Marley, this is serious," she said.

"I was being serious," I said.

She snorted. "Like that will ever happen. Listen. I don't want to rattle your cage, or anything. But your ex-husband has been poking around here for the last few days."

"Allen? What's he poking into?" I asked, confused.

"Bruce."

"I don't follow," I said, suddenly getting a very bad feeling.

"Allen has been sitting in Bruce's office, with the door closed, a lot."

I had to swallow a tight feeling in my throat. "What have they been talking about?" I asked.

She snorted. "They haven't been talking. Bruce isn't even in the office. Allen has commandeered it while Bruce is away on that training seminar."

"I know you Tammy, you probably have the room bugged," I said.

She laughed outright at that. "It's possible that perhaps, just maybe, I may have accidentally been outside the window on the patio having a smoke while Allen was in there talking on the telephone with the window open."

"You don't smoke," I said.

"I thought I'd give it a try to see what I've been missing for all these years," she told me.

"Well? What was Allen saying?" I asked. "Is he investigating something?"

"You," she said, her voice amused.

That sounded worse than bad. "What about me?"

"If I knew, I'd tell you. But all I could catch was your name from time to time, and then Allen requested a copy of your letter of resignation."

"I got fired," I told her.

"That's not what Bruce said," she replied.

A sharp retort was on the tip of my tongue, but in the background I heard someone say something to Tammy.

She must have covered the phone with her hand, because the reply was muffled. When she spoke to me again, I could tell she wasn't alone any longer.

"I have to go. Unlike you, I have a life. It was good to talk to you after all these years."

"It's been two."

"Whatever. Don't be a stranger, alright? I know that people don't get much stranger than you, as a general rule. But you know what I mean."

I felt a small warm glow fill my chest. It seemed that my old contacts from my previous life didn't hate me the way I'd always imagined. "Count on it. Next time I am in Helena I'll buy you a greasy hamburger."

"I'm a vegetarian now," she said.

"You are kidding me."

"Congrats, girl. Give your new hubby a squeeze on the tush for me. Hugs!"

She hung up the phone before I could reply. Very Tammy.

I punched the button on the handheld and set the phone beside me on the couch.

Texas? What was a tick from the southern region of the US doing all the way up here in Montana? More importantly, what was Allen doing snooping around my old office? His jurisdiction did not include Helena, and he was obviously into something that he shouldn't be.

"Sweetie, we are going to go into town and watch the bed races. Maybe even place bets," Leif said, poking his head out of the kitchen door. "Want to come?"

The rodeo events had officially begun. Saturday morning, teams made up of staff from local businesses donned their best pajamas, rolled modified four-post beds on wheels onto Main Street, and tore down the center of the street as fast as their legs could go. For whatever reason, Speedy Printers staff always seemed to win, no matter how juiced up the local bank managed to make its bed. It was a famous rivalry from way back.

I smiled and scooted to my feet. "I think I'll go see Irene and catch her up on all of the happenings as of late. Is it alright if I let you and Scott have a father/son day today?"

Leif beamed at me, a grateful smile spreading across his face. "Thanks, my dear. Scott and I would like that. Dinner tonight? I'll grill something."

I gave him a quick kiss, and a squeeze on the tush.

"What was that for?" he asked, laughing.

"Tammy says hi," I said.

"You'll have to introduce us sometime," he told me.

I shook my head. "Not a chance. See you tonight."

They were gone by the time I had dragged myself out of the shower. I was sore, head to toe, from riding with Jennifer. The prospect of facing the day was daunting. Everything hurt and I chastised myself for letting my riding form get so degraded.

Maybe I would start going out to Tatiana's more regularly and riding Peanut after Jennifer took him back over to the Deep Creek.

It certainly was good exercise.

By the time I got to Lil's it was already close to eleven-thirty and the place was packed.

When Irene saw me push through the café doors she hastily cleared off a place at the counter, and held up her hand to a hung-over Rodeo Queen contestant before the girl could sit down. "It's reserved," Irene said, pointing to another stool further down the counter.

The girl wandered away from the stool, her big hair slightly lopsided, and I sat down fast before someone else tried to take the spot. Lil's was crawling with rodeo fans.

"You'll be able to retire after the profits you earn this weekend," I said.

Irene smirked. "I could probably retire twenty minutes from now if I really wanted to. You are having the French dip."

"I just ate breakfast," I said, protesting.

"And now you are eating lunch."

Her short blonde hair was flat from steam and I could see that her hands were wrinkled. "Did your dishwasher quit again?"

She practically ground her teeth. "Quit last night during rush. This happens every rodeo weekend. I swear, I will have to start importing them from Canada or something."

Irene leaned back towards the cook's window and shouted out my order.

She pulled her small stool out from beneath the counter and propped herself up by one hip. "So. Spill it, Marley."

I poured myself a glass of iced tea from the communal pitcher. "Spill what?"

She glared at me. "Don't give me that. What did you do to Finn?"

I held out my hands innocently. "Why do people keep asking me that?"

"He's leaving Killdeer. What did you do?" she demanded.

"You mean, besides making important life choices that will contribute to my personal happiness by getting married to a wonderful and stable man who loves me?"

She blinked. "Don't be cute. What happened that all of a sudden, Finn is putting in his notice and fleeing from Killdeer like his tail is on fire?"

"What do you mean, fleeing?" I asked, stirring sugar into my tea.

Irene shoved the stool back under the counter and leaned on both elbows next to me.

She lowered her voice, which was a considerable feat.

"The way I heard it, Finn put in his two weeks' notice at the weather station," she began.

"Yes, yes. It's all my fault. He has fourteen days to clean out his locker. What does this have to do with me?"

Irene heard the bell behind her and reached back without even looking to snatch my French dip. She set it in front of me, resuming her position.

"But that's not what's really going on," she said. She leaned so close to me I could count the veins in her bloodshot eyes.

I took a bite of the sandwich. Irene's nose was inches away from my hands. "Do you mind?"

"Not at all. And, the two weeks' notice thing? That's not what he's really doing," she said, not moving back a centimeter.

"He's not putting in his notice?" I asked, feeling foolish. Why was this important to me?

"No, he's quitting. But he's not going to be here for much longer."

"So, he's leaving in ten days instead of two weeks. So what?" I said, taking another bite.

"More like ten hours."

I stopped chewing. "What are you talking about? Ten hours?"

Irene dipped her head and let her voice fall to practically a whisper. "You know Martin Shelly. He owns the hotel?"

"I know Martin Shelly," I said.

"Well, Martin's granddaughter, Penny, works up at the airport," Irene said, leaning into her story.

"Okay," I said, not sure where this was headed.

"She told her dad, Marshall, who told Martin that a charter jet is coming into the Killdeer airport to pick up a single passenger."

I shrugged. "So?"

"That single person chartered a private jet in order to take an extensive gun collection on board. Why do you think he can't fly commercial? It's Finn. Got to be. He's bugging out."

"The Bybee ranch has hunters fly up from Texas all the time in private jets, and they bring big gun collections," I said, pointing out the obvious. "Everybody knows that. It could be the latest group of hunters leaving after their Montana safari."

"Chartered to go to Newark, New Jersey, international airport?" she asked. "How many hunters fly into Killdeer from Newark?"

She had a point. I very purposefully took another bite of French dip. "Again. What does this have to do with me?"

"Are you seriously going to sit there and tell me that you have no earthly idea why Finn is leaving like this?" she asked. "Everyone in town has sort of gotten used to him. He's like our pet foreigner."

The parking lot erupted with the sounds of honking horns, and I turned around in time to see a man in a beat-up Chevy Cavalier, dressed like a rodeo clown, parked nose to nose with a three-quarter-ton Dodge Ram sporting a massive chrome grille guard on the bumper. He was fighting with the Ram's driver over a single parking place.

The rancher behind the wheel of the Dodge shouted loud enough we could hear it inside the café. "This parking lot isn't big enough for the both of us!"

The clown shouted back. "Yeah? I got kicked by a Brahma last night! You think I'm scared of you?"

"Maybe you should sell the parking spaces in your lot this time next year," I suggested.

She glared at me again. "Marley. Aren't you just the least bit curious about it?"

I slid my empty plate across the counter. "No."

"Liar. I am telling you. If you had five minutes alone to talk to him, he would spill it all. Is he wanted by the IRS? Was he hiding out in the witness protection program? It's killing me that I don't know what's going on."

"Maybe you should take up watercolors, or something," I said.

She slapped the counter between us. "Go talk to him. You deserve an explanation. You are the only person in Killdeer who ever talked to him and got more than three words in response."

I leaned back and thought about the envelope that Leif had given to Finn the night we had gotten married. A team of stampeding horses couldn't drag that piece of information out of me, but putting it together with Finn's quick departure, it did seem like something very strange was going on with him.

"Irene. I would if I could. But I have no idea how to get ahold of Finn even if I wanted to. He doesn't have a telephone number where I can call him. I never know where he will be. What do you propose I do about it? Go apply for a job up at the weather station?"

"I already sort of took care of it for you," she said.

My eyes narrowed. "What did you do?"

Her head bobbed back and forth a few times. "I called in a favor. It's not that big a deal."

"Irene . . ."

"All I did was ask Dean Tisdale if he saw Finn up at the airport to give you a call. He's up there all the time since he got that job doing animal control on the runway. He's sweet on Penny and hovers over her like a shadow. Not that the girl doesn't need it. She's too pretty to be left alone up there all evening by herself."

"Irene," I said, my voice dangerous.

"Well? What was I supposed to do? Wait for you to take the initiative?" she asked.

"It's really none of my business what Finn does. And if you think he would tell me what he is doing, even if I had the bad taste to ask, I think you are overestimating his patience."

"Promise me you will tell me what he says," she told me.

I leaned back and rubbed my temples. I could feel a headache coming on. "How was your buffalo burger special? Do you think you will put buffalo meat on the menu full-time now?"

"Who cares about buffalo burgers?" she asked.

"I do."

She grabbed the empty iced tea pitcher and started brewing another batch. "It was a mess. I ran out. We had to change the menus. This is the last time I try some novelty item for rodeo weekend."

"You ran out?" I asked, leaning forward.

"I don't know what happened. I was getting it from Legerski Processing, and then all of a sudden I wasn't."

"He say when he will get some more?" I asked.

"Honey, are you going to vacate this stool for a paying customer?" she asked, giving me a hard look.

I gulped. "If you want me to."

"Don't come back in here until you find out why Finn is ditching out on all of us."

She said it like he belonged to the entire town of Killdeer.

"I won't make any promises." I got to my feet.

"Ten hours," she said, pointing at me. "Don't blow it. We are all counting on you."

When I finally reached my car the rodeo clown and the grille guard lover were still arguing about who had gotten there first. With the heat the way it was, no wonder everyone's nerves were so on edge.

The bed races had been over for a couple hours, but Main Street was still crawling with people while everyone queued up in anticipation of the parade. Somewhere in the crush, Leif and Scott were probably up to their necks in corn on the cob on a stick and cotton candy. The sun beat down relentlessly and not for the first time I wished that the town council would consider moving rodeo weekend to a cooler time of year. But I knew that would never happen.

I climbed inside my SUV and turned the air conditioner up as high as it would go. Off in the distance, a dark wall of rolling thunderheads was creeping across the horizon to the west. I watched the clouds boiling above the valley, poised to swoop down on Killdeer and dump a heavy load of rain. There was a very good chance we would be getting a thunderstorm in a few hours.

That's what this town needed. Some cold water thrown in its face.

CHAPTER 15

Two thoughts rattled around inside my skull, nagging me to take a closer look at them. The first thing that bothered me was the tick. There had to be a logical reason why a tick from the state of Texas had been deposited this far north. It hadn't occurred to me until I'd spoken to Irene about the hunters that Brian Hix imported from Texas on a regular basis. It was possible that one of them had unwittingly transported a tick in his gear when he had come to Montana. It was possible, but the explanation felt wrong to me somehow.

The second thing that bothered me was the buffalo meat. If Brian and Jennifer were so determined to make a go of it with raising exotic meat for the local market why hadn't they been more careful about having enough supply during the busiest time of year?

On impulse I drove over to Legerski Processing. It was a little hole-in-the-wall local meat processor located a mile outside of town in an abandoned coal miner's house, and they did amazing sausages. During hunting season they could hardly keep up with the parade of hunters demanding elk burgers.

Legerski's didn't have a sign on the door. If you were a local you simply knew when they were open. I parked in the dirt parking lot and peered through the window. Old man Roger Legerski was leaning on the counter smoking a cigar.

Yep. They were open.

I went inside and pretended to check the long freezer that squatted beside the door.

Roger chewed his cigar. When he didn't have the cigar, the shop was closed. It was a horribly inefficient form of business management, but we all abided by it.

"Help you?" he asked.

"You got any buffalo burgers?" I asked.

"Nope. Plumb out till next Tuesday."

He shifted the cigar from one side of his mouth to the other.

"Thought you got those from Bybee's?" I went back to staring at the freezer case. Polish sausage was on special.

"Nope."

I glanced up. "Where do you get your buffalo from, then?"

He lifted a scarred hand and plucked the cigar from his mouth. "North Dakota."

I frowned. "So Bybee's ranch just keeps buffalo for pets?"

He smiled then. His mouth was so jagged from tooth loss he looked like a hockey player. "Don't know what they do with them. Maybe they feed it to their wolves?"

Oh brother. Everyone in the valley was picking at that scab. I didn't bother to argue with him.

I bought a pound of frozen Polish sausage and thanked him.

Since it was just past noon, getting anywhere in downtown Killdeer at the moment would be a hassle. The parade was about to start and for the next hour Main Street would be crawling with horses, floats, kids scrambling for candy and runaway balloons. Instead of heading home, on impulse, I drove out of town and stopped when I got to the junction.

I sat on the side of the road, staring at the sign marking the turn towards Deep Creek Ranch. Loy's admission to me the previous night that three of Tatiana's sheep had been mauled concerned me. What about just having a quick look at them to see what I could see?

I threw my SUV in gear and headed west towards Tatiana's.

It took longer than usual to get there, fighting the traffic of gooseneck trailers coming and going from Killdeer. But when I pulled into the dusty courtyard in front of Tatiana's house I felt a stab of disappointment. Nobody was in sight.

No doubt everyone from the ranch was in Killdeer enjoying the festivities. The place was completely deserted.

I parked and went inside the stables, feeling a small pang of regret that Peanut was still trapped out at the Bybee ranch. After rodeo weekend was over, I'd help Tatiana go out and bring him home.

Tatiana's big roan mare, Shiloh, lifted her head and nickered at me in greeting as I walked through the stable. She tossed her head, eager and game to get a scratch or a treat.

"Hey, girl. Everyone's gone off and left you all alone, huh?"

I rubbed her neck and she leaned into the scratch like a thousand-pound kitty cat.

"Want to go for a quick ride?" I asked.

Her ears pricked forward and it was almost as if she could understand me.

Tatiana would kill me if she caught me borrowing Shiloh. The mare was her baby. Her prized possession. But it was only a short ride, and I figured we could be back in an hour. It was possible Tatiana was out on horseback someplace close by, and if I rode out maybe I could find her and ask her about those three sheep she'd lost.

Shiloh tossed her head happily when I opened the stall and slipped on her bridle. The saddle was a problem. Shiloh's height forced me to use a groom stool just to get the saddle over her withers.

I made sure to give her a good long drink before starting out. It was hot, again. I didn't want the mare to get dehydrated.

Once in the saddle, I barely touched Shiloh with my heels and she tore from the stables like she'd been shot. The saddle was all that kept me on her back and I had to lean forward to regain my balance.

"Damn, you are quick!" I said, gripping her mane with my left hand.

This wasn't the brightest idea I'd ever had, but driving my husband's expensive BMW out into the cactus-infested prairie seemed even worse, and Shiloh was more than game for a good sprint. Holding on, I gave her plenty of rein and before long, tears were rolling down my cheeks from the wind.

It couldn't have been more than ten minutes before we reached the prairie dog town. I'd always known Shiloh was fast, but I had not expected her to be Secretariat.

I reined her in when we approached the area where Tatiana and I had found Zane's body. She blew out a satisfied puff and bent her head at once to snatch a tuft of grass. The grass was so dry it sounded like she was munching potato chips, but she didn't seem to mind.

I hopped to the ground, my thighs protesting at being back in the saddle again so soon, and tied Shiloh to a tough sprig of sagebrush.

She didn't even look like she had worked up a sweat.

I felt like I'd been beat on a rock.

Limping slightly, I headed for the place we had found Zane's body and started scanning the ground.

"What are you even looking for?" I asked myself out loud.

This was the place where Deputy Wilcox had managed to pick up that Lone Star tick. How it had managed to get here was a complete mystery to me.

The thick stand of junipers was exactly how I remembered it. I turned around and stood with my back to the clump of thick vegetation, looking out across the sloping hills.

Now that I was more familiar with the area, thanks to riding with Jennifer Hix for a few hours, it was a surprise just how close we actually were to the Bybee ranch.

I squinted beneath the bright light as I tried to determine where the Deep Creek Ranch ended and the Bybee ranch began. It suddenly didn't seem like that far after all. From where I stood, I could see it would have been a relatively easy ride on horseback to this prairie dog town. Maybe it was Zane himself who had transported the tick to this spot when he had come out to search for ferrets?

I looked over at Shiloh, her jaw working a tough clump of grass, and I kicked the dry ground at my feet. Eight miles was nothing for a horse like her.

Why not ride to the edge of the Bybee ranch, just the edge, and see what I could see?

As I walked back to the big mare the ground radiated heat. This would have to be a quick trip or the two of us would cook under the August sun.

When I mounted up I checked the ground for any signs of human activity. The odd-shaped depression that I had pointed out to Loy was long gone. It still bothered me. What in the world could have been kicked out of a truck and set on the ground that would make such an indentation? I recalled the long, round depression in the soil and tried to imagine what sort of object would make such a mark. I came up with nothing. Not that it would have been helpful had I managed to figure out what the object was. It most likely wouldn't have pointed me in the direction of what had really happened to Zane that night. It was one more puzzle piece that I couldn't place, and it bothered me. Everything about this situation bothered me. More than anything, I wanted answers.

Shiloh tugged the reins and I pointed her east.

She chewed the bit, anxious to run. It was then that I remembered Tatiana used Shiloh to reenact the Pony Express run down in Wyoming every year. Each leg of the run couldn't have been more than ten miles. For Shiloh, an eight-mile gallop was probably her usual workout.

I wrapped both hands in her thick mane and leaned forward.

Bracing, I touched her flanks with my heels.

Shiloh bolted across the prairie like an antelope. She ate up the ground with each stride and tore across the landscape, chewing it up and spitting it out like it was her own personal speedway.

The sun had barely moved by the time we reached the edge of the Bybee ranch. I recognized the long slope of what Jennifer had called Third Hill, and I walked Shiloh to cool her down as we approached the fence line. As incredible as it was, Shiloh had covered the distance in a little more than a half-hour. She looked slightly pleased with herself.

I led her along the fence line, pausing as she bent her massive head to chomp tufts of grass. The fence was a standard barbwire job. Nothing special about it.

We walked a few paces along the strands of wire, and suddenly I noticed a section of fence had been cut. The wires had curled up, leaving an area of open ground between posts. It was enough to drive a vehicle through, but I didn't see any tire tracks. Still, with the wind and lack of rain, the soil was so dry any tracks probably would have blown away days ago. When had this happened? Did Tatiana know that the fence was down between her place and the Hixes'?

I shaded my eyes, wishing that I had had the sense to bring a hat with me, and looked down the valley towards the river.

The Snowy River meandered through the lush valley, making the entire landscape look like a picture-perfect postcard. No wonder Jennifer could afford the best clothes money could buy. The cost of spending a week hunting and fishing on this ranch must have run in the multiple thousands of dollars.

As I let my eyes take in the view below, the plateau caught my attention. Although the eastern edge of the formation was steep and daunting, the western edge sloped gently to the top. It wouldn't be that difficult to summit from this side.

Shiloh looked thirsty, and the river was only a half-mile below us in the valley.

The entire area looked completely deserted. Most likely, everyone from the Bybee ranch was in town watching the parade and eating free hot dogs. I knew that Rick wasn't stupid enough to stick around the ranch when Loy was looking for him, and the last place Jennifer would be on a hot day was up riding under the sweltering sun. Nobody sane was likely to be riding up in these hills on this day. Present company excluded.

It was probably a stupid thing to do, but I tossed the reins over the mare's head and mounted up. I nudged her through the hole in the fence and we trotted down the slope towards the river. There wouldn't be anyone around to care that I was trespassing. Besides, all I wanted to do was take a closer look at the buffalo fence. It wasn't as if I was there to steal their cattle.

After a long cool drink and a splash through the water, Shiloh blew through her nose happily and the sound scared up a small herd of whitetail deer from the brush. The three does, three spry yearling fawns in tow, watched us indignantly, then darted away, their long white tails waving like flags as they retreated.

The air smelled like aspens and old wood. It had been years since a fire had cleaned out the debris from all of the old trees in this valley. Someday a grass fire would sweep down through this place and gut the pristine forest. I made a mental note to tell Jennifer that she and Brian should think about having some mitigation done at some point. Better safe than sorry.

I led Shiloh across the river. The last thing I wanted to do was risk her twisting an ankle on a river rock and taking us both down. The water felt blessedly cool on my tired feet. My legs were soaked above the knee by the time we crossed to the other side, but since I was wearing an old pair of boots, I didn't care about the wet.

Had this been early June the river would have been raging and if we'd attempted to cross it we probably would have drowned. But August this year had been so dry we forded the river with little trouble.

Up the bank on the other side, I mounted and urged Shiloh up the gentle slope leading towards the plateau. She seemed to be just as fresh as when we had left the stables.

It was an easy climb for her powerful legs. We crested the tree line quickly and I found a deer trail winding up to the top of the plateau that was almost wide enough for two horses side by side. Shiloh leaned into the task and it wasn't long before I caught sight of the long buffalo fence at the top of the ridge.

Shiloh stopped when she saw the fence. Her ears swiveled back and forth, uncertain. It was not like any fence she had seen before, I was certain of that. It was much taller than usual, and it was covered with something that made it impossible to see through it.

"It's alright," I told Shiloh reassuringly. "I know you have never seen one like that before, but it can't hurt you."

I patted her neck. She seemed to take little comfort from my gesture, and she danced beneath me, nervous.

"Whoa, Shiloh. Easy, girl."

I dismounted and held her bridle firmly.

She swished her tail with her head down and her ears cocked back, horse-speak for I'm terribly unhappy just now.

She wasn't thrilled about it, but she allowed me to lead her up the last leg of the climb until we reached the buffalo fence at last.

"Would you look at that," I said.

The buffalo fence was made of double-duty chain link and stood at least ten feet high. A quick examination told me that the chain link was buried in the ground and each post was set in a wide circle of concrete. The fence itself was covered with heavy brown fabric, top to bottom, making the surface look like a solid wall. I tried to peer through the gaps where the fabric met the posts, and found to my irritation that I couldn't see very much. The fabric was completely opaque and pulled tight to each post, but if I squinted I could see through it a little, but not well enough to see what was on the other side.

Why did they need a wall of fabric like this? Were buffalo less likely to tear down a fence if they simply thought it was a solid object?

"Shiloh, come here," I said, leading her close to the side of the fence.

She blew through her nose with irritation. Obviously, the mare did not want to be anywhere close to the fence.

I managed to get her to stand still next to the posts, climbed into the saddle and coaxed her to stay where she was.

I still couldn't see over the top of the fence. The upper edge was several inches above my head.

Taking care not to move too quickly and startle Shiloh, I tucked both feet underneath my butt and stood up in the saddle slowly until I could grasp the top of the fence.

The jagged metal was razor sharp. "Yikes!" I pulled my hands back quickly, one finger bleeding from a cut.

When I tentatively held the top edge of the fence again, more carefully this time, I could see that a long steel arm was attached on the top of each and every post. The steel arms hung inside the fence at a forty-five-degree angle, and looped strands of barbwire were strung between them. It reminded me of the pictures I'd seen of the border fence in East Germany, with the loops of barbed wire attached to the top of each fence. It was designed to prevent anything from climbing up and getting outside.

"Good God," I said, taking in the sight.

Shiloh's flank twitched and she swished her tail menacingly. A huge horsefly was harassing her and she batted at it with her hind legs.

The other side of the fenced-in plateau looked exactly like the outside. A few trees dotted the area. Some shrubs. Off in the distance I caught a glimpse of the reservoir Jennifer had told me about.

I inched up to the balls of my feet to see if there were any ducks floating in the water and at that moment Shiloh squealed and bolted.

I let out a cry as she tore away from the fence and it was all I could do to snag the top and hang on.

The barbwire tore into my palms and I scrabbled my feet across the chain link trying to get a toehold. The toe of my left boot caught and I managed to push up with my leg just enough to lift my hands off of the wire.

My hands came free and I plummeted to the ground, landing hard on both legs and crumpling like a straw doll.

I lay on my back, groaning, and listened to the sounds of clomping hooves.

Shiloh stopped beside me, her muzzle inches from my face. She blew horse snot on my forehead and mouthed her bridle sheepishly.

"Thanks a lot," I said.

Her ears swiveled back. Apologizing.

"Damn horseflies," I said, sitting up gingerly. The bite Shiloh had gotten must have been a doozy.

I rubbed my bloody hands on my jeans and inspected the damage. Not as bad as it could have been. When I got back to town I thought it might not be a bad idea to get a tetanus booster.

Just as I was about to toss the reins over Shiloh's neck and get back in the saddle, I heard something that should not have been there.

The sound of an engine. Not just one, but at least two.

A brief flash of panic shot through me. Where were they?

I turned my head back and forth, trying to pinpoint which direction they came from. The familiar sound of two ATV's echoed across the plateau.

When I realized they were coming from inside the fence I froze, not at all certain what to do next.

It was only at the posts that daylight could pass thorugh the fence. If we stayed between the posts and didn't move a muscle, there was a good chance that whoever was coming wouldn't even know we were here.

I led Shiloh to a spot on the fence where the brown fabric looked solid and in good shape. I squatted down underneath her head and held her reins tight so if she moved her bit wouldn't rattle and give us away.

"Don't move girl, whatever you do. Sit still."

I stroked her cheek slowly, hoping to calm her down.

She swished her tail once, furiously. Then she stood still and let her head droop down so that she could rest.

I practically held my breath.

The two ATV's trundled straight for us and I closed my eyes with dismay when they stopped, practically on top of us.

Both engines died.

Perfect.

Two voices drifted towards me, carried on the breeze. I heard footsteps. They stopped only yards away from us.

"What did I tell you? Look here. This is exactly where I said it was."

It had to be Logan. I recognized his voice.

"What does this prove?"

That was Brian Hix.

They walked closer, their footsteps rustling through the dry grass.

Shiloh let out a tired sigh and I cringed.

The mare's eyes closed partway and she cocked her back foot, resting.

There was no reaction from the other side of the fence. I could hear the two men start walking, and luckily they were heading away from me.

"See? What did I tell you? This is not a mistake."

Logan's voice again.

Brian let out an exasperated sigh. "Do I pay you for this? Just fix it, right?"

Logan didn't reply immediately. It was quiet for a moment. But then Logan asked a question, and Brian answered with another testy response. They started arguing.

Another volley of heated words was exchanged, but the wind had shifted and I couldn't understand what was being said. Whatever it was, clearly they were not happy about it.

What had they found?

The voices stopped altogether and I flinched when the engines on the ATV's started up again. One of them pulled away from the fence, turned sharply and sped off, while one stayed still for a moment.

I chanced a quick peek through the tiny gap between the fabric and the post, and I could barely see Logan sitting on his ATV, one hand on the throttle and the other resting on his thigh, staring straight at me.

I pulled my head back and swallowed. My heart was hammering in my chest and I told myself that there was no way he could see me. I hadn't moved a muscle. He wasn't looking at me; he was simply looking in my direction. There was no possible way for him to know I was here. Was there?

After another tense moment, the ATV clicked into gear and I heard him drive away.

The moment I was certain they were driving fast in the opposite direction, I waited for a count of one hundred before moving again. It was time to get the hell out of there before they came back, but before retreating, I led Shiloh toward the spot on the fence where I'd heard the men stop and argue.

I crouched down in the dry dirt and saw a hole cut in the fabric. The fabric was sliced clean, and when I peered through it, I saw the chain link had been severed with bolt cutters. A hole had been cut through the fence and some dirt was disturbed underneath it, but it was barely large enough for a sheepdog to slither through. It certainly wasn't big enough for large livestock to escape, so what had they been arguing about?

More importantly, what if they came back to fix it? Realizing I had bigger problems at the moment, I tossed the reins over Shiloh's neck and leapt in the saddle. The mare's head jerked up with surprise as I grabbed the saddle horn and she rolled her eyes back at me.

"Let's go, girl."

She jumped away from the fence and we slid down the hillside, scattering stones and shaking clods of dirt loose that rolled down ahead of us.

I urged her on, trotting when we could and walking fast when we had to slow our pace. By the time we reach the river Shiloh was thirsty and I let her have one minute to bend her head and drink.

I stopped her from overdoing it, and urged her to wade across the river, leading her behind me as fast as I could.

He shouldn't have been able to see me, but Logan Hiser was Finn's younger brother, after all. The two of them were probably gifted with some sort of supernatural abilities brought on from years of working in dangerous places, and I wasn't about to take any chances. Not that I thought Logan and Finn had superpowers, but they certainly did seem to be a lot more observant than the average man.

I wasn't sure what drove me to retreat from the Bybee ranch so quickly. I was technically Jennifer's friend, and if someone saw me it wouldn't have been the end of the world.

But some inner voice whispered to me that it would be far better to beat feet than hang around and tempt detection.

I led Shiloh up the bank and as soon as her hooves were on dry land I hopped up and pulled myself into the saddle. She was already running by the time I managed to gather up the reins and it was clear she sensed my urgency.

I pushed her as hard as I dared, and probably looked back over my shoulder a dozen times before we made it to the fence line marking the boundary to Deep Creek Ranch. Nobody followed us that I was able to see. When we crossed the downed fence that marked the boundary between the ranches I heaved a sigh of relief.

Shiloh was lathered and laboring by the time we clopped into the stables at Tatiana's place. I was red from too much sun and dying of thirst.

By the time I pulled off her saddle and bridle, walked her to cool her off and washed her down, it was well past five and I hadn't eaten anything since lunch. For once, I was grateful that Irene had force-fed me back at Lil's. It was all that was keeping me going.

The thunderheads that had been far away a few hours ago were now hanging overhead menacingly. The air was heavy with humidity and before long the rain would fall.

I checked Shiloh head to toe to make sure her shoes hadn't lost any nails, her legs looked alright and she looked happy. I let her have a few oats and drink enough to satiate her thirst, and then I dragged myself into my vehicle and started the drive for home.

I was surprised there hadn't been a soul on Deep Creek the entire time I'd been there. Maybe there were some good points about rodeo weekend after all. Eventually I would explain to Tatiana that I had borrowed her prize pony, but not today.

As I pulled into the garage, having navigated the snarl of traffic in downtown Killdeer, I thought about what I had seen and my gut feelings were practically yelling at me to pay attention to them.

The buffalo fence at the Bybee ranch was impressive. In fact, it was probably the best damn buffalo fence in a tri-state area.

There was only one small problem.

There weren't any buffalo inside.

CHAPTER 16

The phone was ringing when I bounded up the back steps and pushed through the door into the utility room. The house's alarm went off and I tried to punch in the code to deactivate it while reaching for the receiver.

"Hello?" I said, cradling the phone and stabbing at the blaring keypad box with one hand while holding the melted package of Polish sausage in the other.

Finally I found the proper sequence of numbers and the thing shut down, quiet at last.

"Miss Marley?"

I gulped air. "Dean? How are you?" I tossed the sausage in the trash can beside the back door. It had been ruined sitting in the car at Tatiana's and there was no salvaging it now.

Dean cleared his throat loudly. "I'm okay. I'm calling you because Irene told me that if I was to see Finn at the airport that you would want to know."

"Finn is at the airport now?" I asked.

"Yes."

"Alright, thanks, Dean."

He hung up the phone. I stared at the receiver, listening to the dial tone for a moment.

Dean Tisdale was a man of few words.

I set the receiver in the cradle and leaned against the door.

Why did I care that Finn was leaving? So what if I would never see him again? It wasn't like it would be that big a loss. We had shared a brief fling, and that was all.

I listened intently to the rest of the house. No one stirred. Leif and Scott were probably enjoying the silliness of rodeo and hadn't come home yet. No wonder the alarm had been set.

It was impossible to say what time they would be getting back.

My head ached, my stomach ached and I didn't want to admit to myself that a part of me was truly angry with Finn for bugging out with no explanation.

"Dammit."

I turned around and went back out to the garage, punched the button to open the door and climbed back inside my vehicle.

If I was going to make a complete ass out of myself, I had to hurry because the window was closing.

The Killdeer airport was little more than a steel building, a row of private hangars and a good place to watch the bears get into the garbage dumpsters in the springtime.

An ancient battered fire truck sat next to the putty-colored steel building. There was a fifty-fifty chance that it actually still ran.

I pushed through the glass door leading inside the office area, and black rain clouds overhead broke open. Fat raindrops started pattering on the bone-dry ground.

One angry streak of lightning cut the sky above, but the bulk of the clouds were still rolling in from the west. In a few minutes the valley would be engulfed.

I saw a low desk opposite the door and a young woman with big blue eyes and perfectly straight black hair smiled when I came in.

"Hello, Marley. Whatcha doing up here in this weather?"

"Hey, Penny. Where do your charter jet passengers wait for their planes?" I asked.

I'd been to the airport a dozen times, dropping Leif off or picking him up, but I'd never actually flown out myself. No commercial flights came into Killdeer, so private pilots had a free run of the place. I glanced through the second set of doors that led outside and could see the tail of a white jet parked on the tarmac.

Penny Shelly, the daughter of Marshall Shelly, the granddaughter of Martin Shelly, pointed towards the jet.

"He's out there. The plane had to take on fuel. Shouldn't be but a minute more and they can take off if they hurry. It's stupid, because of the storm. But the charter pilot says that a plane on the ground is a plane not making any money and he's chomping at the bit."

"Thanks."

The door leading to the tarmac was so heavy it took both hands. I was bent over, shoving it open with a heave, when I came face-to-face with Finn.

His eyes blazed fire when he saw me. He didn't move, but his face was a mask of sudden fury.

"Hey," I said, letting the heavy door close slowly behind me. The rain began in earnest then, wetting my face and trickling down my hair and under my sweat-soaked shirt.

227

He didn't say anything. His face was rigid.

I had no idea what to say. I'd never seen him look so hostile.

He refused to speak and would hardly look at me.

Finally I couldn't take his silence any longer. "What kind of jerk leaves without even saying goodbye?" I wiped my soaked hair out of my eyes.

He looked like he had just run a marathon he was breathing so hard.

"Marley. You can't be here," he said, his voice ragged.

"And you can't find the time to drop by and let me know you are going?" I said.

His eyes darted everywhere but on me.

"Finn. It's alright," I said, holding up one hand in a gesture of peace. "I don't know why you feel like you have to go. But if that is really what you want to do, I'm not going to berate you for it. I just wanted to say goodbye."

"I cannot be talking to you," he said helplessly.

"What do you mean, you can't? Never mind. I never understood half of the things that came out of your mouth anyway. Do you want me to go?"

"Of course I want you to go!"

I took a step back with surprise. He'd shouted the words.

"Did I do something wrong?" I asked stupidly.

Finn turned his head to the side as the small jet started its engines. The fuel truck was backing away and heading for the garage area.

Finn stared at the ground, shaking his head from side to side. "No."

"So, I didn't do something?" I asked. "Why can't you tell me what's going on?"

"I cannot explain it." He took two steps backward. "I have to go. Do not follow me. Do not talk to me. Do you understand?"

He turned his back on me and started walking through the rain towards the jet.

"What was in the envelope, Finn? Was it money? Did Leif pay you to leave and never talk to me again?"

He froze in mid-step, turned back slowly and came at me, both fists clenched so tight I backed away from him until my heels hit the building. He stopped, his face inches away from mine.

His voice was so soft I had to strain to hear him above the rain.

"Do you really think Leif Gable would pay another man to stay away from his wife? Do you? Because, if you do, I think you don't know him as well as you should."

"No, I don't think that Leif would do that," I said, embarrassed at my outburst.

"Do you really think that I'm the sort of bloke who would accept money as a bribe? You know me better than that."

I couldn't tell if he was sad or torn. He looked away from me, his gaze drifting across the tarmac, looking for something that wasn't there.

I blinked water from my eyes. "The crew at Lil's is going to miss you. Killdeer has taken a shine to you, Finn."

"And what about you?"

His question stopped me short. "What about me?"

"Friend. Am I anything other than that to you?" He searched my face, scrutinizing me intently.

"You will always be more than simply a friend," I said cautiously.

"And you can't bring yourself to say anything other than that? Can't you say the words?"

I held out both hands. "What do you expect me to say? I don't know how else to put it. I gave you every chance when we were together, and you walked away from me. What was I supposed to do? Sit around and wait for you to get over your messed-up past and sweep me off my feet?"

His eyes shifted back and forth. "I never expected you to understand why I had to keep you at a distance."

"And that's the difference between you and Leif Gable," I told him flatly. "He always tells me the truth. About everything. No matter how hard or ugly it is. He knows that I can take it. But you? All you did was bend over backwards to protect me from the big bad world, protect me from your horrible past, all that time not realizing that what you were actually doing was pushing me away."

I lowered my head, surprised at my own anger.

"He doesn't tell you the truth about everything," Finn said, his teeth clenched together.

My eyes met his. "What are you talking about?"

His mouth clamped shut and he looked distressed.

"Nothing. Maybe you are right. Maybe he does have more faith that you can deal with pain than I ever did."

"I've been handling rough situations since the day I was born. You never gave me any credit for being able to cope, but it's not in my nature to fall apart. Why couldn't you ever see that?" I asked.

"And it never occurred to you that I wanted to keep you safe for my sake?" He looked down instantly, almost ashamed.

"For you? I don't understand."

"Where I came from," he said, the words coming out like he was being tortured. "What I did before I came here. It . . . it was not a good place."

"That was a long time ago," I said.

"Not long enough that they forgot about me," he said.

He looked down at the palms of his hands, staring at them like he would find the answers there. Finally he closed his hands and met my eyes with such a wounded expression it looked like he was in physical pain.

In an instant all of my anger washed away.

Standing right in front of me was a man who represented the road not taken.

In a flash I realized that I would never know what could have been for us and it hit like an avalanche.

My throat tightened with remorse.

I thought of Leif and his unselfish commitment to me.

My new wedding ring gleamed underneath the hangar lights and the diamonds shimmered in the rain. I had made a promise to him that I would always keep.

For me, there was no going back.

Leif was my future, and Finn was my past.

Finn had made his choice about me a long time ago. And I had made my choice, too.

I knew it was time to let go of the hope that it could have been different.

I'd never really grieved for our lost connection. Well, I was grieving now.

"Did I ever tell you how beautiful you are?" he said suddenly, reaching up and cupping my cheek with his hand.

If it hadn't been raining he would have seen the tears rolling down my face.

"Take care of yourself, Marley Dearcorn."

He bent forward and kissed my forehead.

When he stepped back his eyes were mournful, not angry.

"Mr. Hiser? We need to take off now."

I glanced over his shoulder. A soggy pilot was standing behind Finn, beckoning.

"I'll be right there," Finn said.

I must have looked confused because he paused and gave me a half smile. "Angus Finn Hiser. I should have told you my name the first day I met you."

"Where are you going?" I asked.

He shuffled his feet back and forth. Debating? Deciding?

"I'm going back to the beginning," he said.

Then his face seemed to change. Some thought had come to his mind because he started to pat the pockets of his shirt, searching for something. On impulse he took a quick step towards me, his hand retrieving something from inside his front pocket.

"What is it you Yanks have plastered all over the fire extinguisher boxes in this country?" he asked.

"I don't know. Service unit every six months?" I asked stupidly.

He cracked a smile and took my hand in his. He carefully set a small pouch in my palm and closed my fingers around it. "I-C-E."

I looked down at the small gray pouch in my hand. "What does that mean?"

I looked back up and he was gone, striding towards the plane through the pouring rain. He disappeared inside the jet and I backed away as the engines roared with urgency.

I stood there like a fool, feeling the chilled rain soak through my bones, and watched until the white jet had taxied away from the building and lifted off into the black sky. It banked sharply to the east and flew like a falcon out of the valley and straight through the heavy clouds until it vanished. The pilot was a madman, counting on being able to break out of the clouds and get above the weather quickly, but it looked like that was exactly what he was doing.

When I couldn't see the tiny white dot any longer, the only thing left to do was drag my soaked body back to my car and climb inside.

A Dairy Queen napkin was tucked in the car door and I used it to wipe off the worst of the rain from my face and eyes. When things weren't so blurry, I looked at the pouch in my hands, flipping it over, but there was nothing special about it.

I pulled the drawstring open and tilted it up. A cell phone fell into my hand.

It was ordinary, very plain and not sophisticated. It looked like any generic throwaway phone that could be purchased at the counter of a filling station.

When I flipped it open, there was one number programmed into the contact list, and only one. There was no name associated with it. The number didn't even look like a telephone number to me: 011-27-11. That sequence of digits was followed by seven more numbers that didn't make any sense at all. Was it a date? An e-mail address? And what did he mean by I-C-E anyway?

I stared at the silver cell phone in my hand. "You never could give me a straight answer about anything, could you?"

I held my thumb over the off switch until the cell phone powered down and then I flipped it closed, shoved it back inside the pouch and tossed it in the glove box. Maybe if I got a flat tire on the side of the road I could call a tow truck. It obviously wasn't going to be good for anything else. As usual, Finn had managed to say something without actually telling me anything at all.

"At this point, I would expect nothing less," I said, shaking my head.

The rain came down in torrents and I drove home through the muck and the mud until I managed to make it back inside the garage and drag myself up the back steps.

Leif and Scott still hadn't made it home, and I took the opportunity to shower and drink about a half a gallon of water.

When I finally padded down the stairs it was nearly seven and I heard the sounds of bustling coming from the back door.

Leif and Scott swooped through the back door, laughing and drenched. Both of them were soaked through and filthy.

I crossed my arms and scoffed at them standing in the middle of the utility room, dripping on the tile like a couple of teenage boys. "What happened to you?"

"We went to the butt-darts championships," Scott announced. "I won a duck!"

My eyebrows shot up. "A duck?"

Scott produced a purple stuffed animal shaped like a duck. He practically vibrated with excitement. "My prize for being runner-up in the competition."

"You entered the butt-dart finals?" I asked, incredulous.

Leif clapped his son on the back. "It was the proudest I've ever been. Well, except for that whole Harvard thing."

"This was a lot more fun than college," Scott confessed.

"Really?" Leif asked.

"No, no," I told them. "I can see how winning a purple stuffed animal could be as rewarding as graduating from Harvard."

Leif was smiling, Scott was giddy, and the two of them looked like the rain had only added to the occasion.

They began stripping down right in the middle of the floor, and I left them to pile up their dirty clothes and clean up.

There was nothing to grill. The butt-dart competition had gotten out of hand and Leif had forgotten to pick up something for dinner. We ended up raiding what was left in the refrigerator. The only thing inside were eggs and bacon, and so we stirred up a batch of pancakes and had breakfast for supper.

The rain eased back after we'd eaten, and soon the only sounds from outside on the patio were the patter of small raindrops pinging against the wrought iron chairs.

Leif and I said goodnight to Scott, who was still on D.C. time and exhausted by nine-thirty. The kid disappeared upstairs and we sat down on the sofa in the living room, one wide window open to the fresh smell of evening rain.

We didn't need to talk. Taking in the night was enough.

It had been a long time since I had seen Leif so content. His issues at work had taken such a toll. I could see the difference in him now that he was close to having his business dealings wrapped up at last.

Maybe it was selfish. Maybe it was wrong. But I decided not to tell him about going to see Finn one last time before he left Killdeer. There was no point to it. The truth was, I would never see Finn again, so why drag my husband through my own personal drama?

It did cross my mind, the comment Finn had made about Leif not always being honest with me, but only fleetingly. What could he possibly have meant by that? Truthfully, I doubted I'd ever know what he had really meant and I was beyond caring now. I could have asked Leif what he thought Finn had meant by the statement, but why? What difference would it make?

Besides, Leif looked so happy and at peace, bringing up such a sad scene would only spoil the moment.

No, this was a burden I would have to bear alone. For the sake of my marriage, for the sake of my own sanity, the best possible thing that I could do now would be to forget about Angus Finn, forget about our past, look to the future and vow never to contact him again.

It was the right thing to do.

CHAPTER 17

The rain stopped at midnight. Killdeer should have felt washed clean, but instead the heavy thunderstorm had left the valley humid and hazy.

It was barely noon and already pushing 100 degrees. With the muggy air bearing down, my arms and legs felt like they weighed a thousand pounds.

"Hand me the hoof pick," Tatiana said.

I dutifully jumped up from my hay bale and grabbed the pick, passing it to her where she was bent underneath the weight of Shiloh's back leg. Inside Tatiana's stable it was sweltering. At least it was out of the direct sun.

"Great God almighty, nag. You weigh a ton," she said, shouldering the horse.

Shiloh had gradually eased her weight off of her left hind leg and was putting most of it on Tatiana. The ranchwoman cleaned a stone from Shiloh's hoof and then dropped her back leg without preamble. The mare grunted her disapproval.

"Don't look at me like that," Tatiana said. "It's not my fault you are getting so fat."

Shiloh swished her tail and proceeded to ignore us both like an indignant cat.

"She's probably tired from the run I gave her yesterday," I said, coughing up my secret.

Tatiana didn't bat an eye. "Probably. Great lazy beast. I think it did her some good. She needed a workout and I've been too damn busy with this business of the wolves and the effect it is having on my crew to pay much attention to her."

I sat back down hard on my hay bale. "You knew I rode Shiloh yesterday?"

"I came back to the house for dinner before going out to the fairgrounds to watch the barrel races. Saw your car. Saw Shiloh gone. Don't have to be a detective to figure that one out, Marley."

My cheeks flushed with color. "Is it alright that I borrowed her? I wanted to have another look at the dogtown and see if there was anything I missed."

"And?" Tatiana appraised me, her left hand busy digging dirt out from underneath her fingernails with a long buck knife. "Was there anything you missed?"

I swung my legs like a twelve-year-old. "Wish I could say. There was one thing that has been bothering me about this whole deal."

"You mean, aside from a guy getting his head chewed off?" she asked.

"Aside from that."

"What's been bothering you?"

She folded the buck knife and shoved it back in her pocket.

"Loy and I saw something on the ground next to a set of tire tracks. It was like someone had set an inner tube on the ground and sat on it with the back tire of a truck."

She squinted at me, wiping away a bead of sweat from her lip. "An indentation? Sort of shaped like watermelon?"

"Yeah. How did you know?" I asked.

"It's a tire jack, silly girl."

I frowned and my legs stopped swinging. "How can a tire jack be shaped like a watermelon?"

"Because it inflates underneath the truck. You slide it under a flat tire while it's deflated, and then you inflate it. Like a blow-up doll."

"Can we use another analogy, please?" I asked.

"Fine. Like a beach ball. You carry them around in the back of yer outfit like any other jack. If you get a flat tire someplace that is real sandy, you try to jack up the truck and a regular jack just sinks, right?"

"So, this inflatable jack sits on top of the soil and doesn't sink," I said, the picture coming into focus.

"You stick the tube attached to the beach ball on the end of your tailpipe, start the motor." She spit on the ground like a minor league baseball coach. "The truck lifts off the ground. You change the tire and that's that."

"Anyone on Deep Creek have a set of wheels with a tire jack like that in the back?" I asked.

She laughed. "We have horses, remember? They get a flat and you have to shoot them."

I rolled my eyes at her. "Like you would ever shoot one of your horses."

She looked across the stall from Shiloh and I could see her thinking. "That reminds me. Why don't you go back out to the Bybee place and get Peanut for me? I know you won't believe this, but I miss the little bugger."

"You miss him? I thought you wanted to sell Peanut if you could find anyone stupid enough to buy him."

Her face grew wistful.

"You do miss him," I said, surprised.

JESSICA McCLELLAND

"I guess you don't know what ya got until it's gone. Anyway, I'd send one of my own crew but I'm a man down."

"Did somebody quit on you?" I asked.

It happened to all employers during rodeo.

Tatiana shook her head. "Nope, I had to fire Justin. He shot Harvey Wilson's German shepherd day before yesterday and we almost had another range war on our hands."

My eyes bulged. "He didn't."

"Right behind the left shoulder. Killed him almost instantly. Justin thought it was a wolf and that was all she wrote. Damn shame, too. That shepherd was about a hundred and fifty years old, if you count the miles on him. How he managed to make it this far is a mystery. And then Justin goes and shoots him because he can't tell the difference between gray and brown."

"I'll bet Harvey was a bit upset."

"Homicidal," Tatiana said. "But I fired Justin, with Harvey standing there. Wrote Harvey a check to compensate him, and to show him I'm a good neighbor, I threw in a couple loads of hay."

"I would imagine the wolf hunt is now officially over," I said.

"Harvey let it be known that if anyone else went out shooting people's dogs, he'd get the sheriff to take away their guns."

"Wow."

Tatiana laughed. "Lucky for me, we don't have dogs here on account of Peanut hating them so much. I swear, those jackals are so dumb if I'd had a poodle they woulda shot it too."

"So, Peanut earned his keep after all," I said.

"And how. So, if you could go pick him up, I'd be grateful," she said.

"I'll borrow Dad's truck and trailer and go pick him up soon. I haven't seen or heard from Jennifer Hix since we went riding that one afternoon, but I would imagine it's alright if I go out there without calling first. I swear, I think the only reason she wanted to pal around with me is so she would have an excuse to ask me to beg Loy to lay off of her crew. Can you believe she actually said that?"

"Asked you to talk to Loy for her? Sure I can believe that. Jennifer has always struck me as a woman who believed in the power of being nice to get you what you want. Must be a Texas thing."

I frowned and looked at the dirt covering the toes of my boots. My biologist friend, Tammy, had said the tick I'd found had come all the way from Texas. I'd kicked around the likelihood that someone had brought the tick with them on an airplane when they came here for a hunting trip, and had since discarded that notion. It didn't seem likely to me. Since I was fairly sure that a tick hadn't hitched a ride with an airplane load of Texas businessmen, maybe Brian Hix was getting some of his livestock from Texas and the bug had ended up in Montana via the back of a buffalo.

Except for the fact that I hadn't seen any actual buffalo on the Bybee ranch.

"What time did you say Todd Ramsey would be here?" I asked, thinking about all the loose ends I still hadn't managed to tie up.

She chewed her bottom lip. "Should be anytime. How did you know he was coming today, anyway?"

I kicked a layer of horse manure from the bottom of my boots. "I called the L Bar T and they told me he was finished up out there. They let me know he was coming here next. But I thought you had already done your brand inspections for the year."

"Todd wants to get appointed to the Livestock Loss Board and he is out stumping. He wanted to look at my three ewes and see if he could tell if they were killed by wolves."

"Well, Todd would know. In his line of work I imagine he has seen it all."

We sat in silence for a moment, and I could feel Tatiana's eyes on me.

"Something eating you?" she asked at length.

The last thing I wanted to do was bring up all the crazy thoughts I was trying to sort through. At this point, nothing I'd come up with explained what had happened to Zane.

I still had a lot of information left to uncover if the truth was going to come out.

I shrugged and leaned against the rough boards of the horse stall. "I suppose there's a few things eating me. But it would take too long to explain them all."

Luckily for me, we both heard the sound of a truck engine and the conversation ended before it started.

Todd Ramsey pulled his big dual-exhaust diesel pickup to a stop in the courtyard and climbed out of the cab.

His classic cowboy boots hit the ground and I swore I felt an impact tremor.

"Ladies," he said, his voice a deep rumble.

As he was dressed in an ordinary gray T-shirt that exposed his arms, I noticed that one of his biceps was as big as my entire thigh.

"Todd," Tatiana said, moving to shake his hand.

He rotated his huge head around and looked down at me. "Miss Dearcorn. How's your father?"

"He's the same. Ornery as ever," I said, straining my neck to look up at him.

If Todd ever decided the brand inspector life was no longer his cup of tea, he had a great career in his future as a construction crane.

I recalled that Tatiana had told me the story of the day Todd had pulled my friend Dean off of one of her ranch hands who had insulted her niece in an unkind fashion. If there was a human being on the planet who could handle Dean Tisdale in a fair fight, it was this man.

"Show me your lambs," Todd said, slamming the door of his truck.

"They're ewes. Adults," she told him, leading us both around to the back of the stables.

As soon as we turned the corner the strong smell of death hit us.

It was a smell I was used to, having grown up on a ranch, but it was never pleasant.

The three of us walked to the end of the stable and Todd knelt down on one knee beside the fluffy white bodies. The ewes were stretched out alongside the building in a row, looking like discarded winter coats. Black flies crawled indiscriminately over the corpses. It had been hot, so the ewes were shriveled, but not to the extent that their wounds were not discernible.

"How long ago did you say this happened?" he asked, straightening up again.

"Friday," Tatiana said, studying Todd's expression. "I would have gotten rid of them by now if'n you hadn't asked me to hang on to them. Stink to high heaven. You see something odd here?"

He rubbed his stout jaw with a calloused hand. "Nothing on the legs. Just marks on the back of the neck. I suppose I'm used to seeing them hamstrung. But these three were bitten, and then left. Not fed on at all."

I felt the blood drain out of my face and had to take a few steps away from the pungent carcasses. Not fed on, and bitten on the back of the neck. I had a flashback to the moment we had found Zane's body underneath the sprawling juniper.

Todd had just described the wounds suffered by Zane and the memory of his mangled neck flashed into my head. After a few deep breaths of fresh air, I managed to get myself back under control.

"Is that unusual, Todd?" I asked.

The big brand inspector tilted his head back and forth. "A bit. I expected to see stomach lacerations. Leg trauma. But, it's not impossible that a local predator would hunt using this strategy."

I had a sour feeling in my stomach. "Do you think it's likely these animals were killed by a wolf?" I asked.

Todd gave me a slightly patronizing look. "More sheep are killed each year from noxious weeds, disease, lightning strikes, feral dogs, bears and mountain lions than by wolves. By far. This almost looks like a cat to me."

What had Finn told me about his brother? He'd said that Logan was better than he was at identifying the species of a predator by looking at a kill.

I felt the flicker of a thought tickle me for attention. Something brewing in my head was bubbling to the surface at last.

I felt like I was suddenly very close to getting an answer to one of my questions.

Why would Logan have knowledge about multiple different species of predator kill techniques? Because he was a game master and that was his job.

So, why would Brian Hix specifically hire a game master who had been born and raised in South Africa?

Well, there was only one answer that fit.

Brian Hix had hired a game master from South Africa because they were not hunting game animals from Montana behind that buffalo fence on the Bybee ranch, and they were hunting something else instead.

I started backing away from the stable. "Tatiana, I've got to go. I'll go get Peanut this afternoon or tomorrow. That alright with you?"

She glanced over, surprised at my sudden desire to leave. "Didn't you have something you wanted to ask Todd, here?"

I stopped, feeling certain I already knew the answer to my question, but it wouldn't hurt to be absolutely sure. "Todd, did you do the brand inspections for the buffalo out at the Bybee ranch? I wondered if you need special permission to raise them, or if they are considered normal livestock?"

Todd shook his head once, looking confused. "The Bybee ranch never applied for a bison permit, that I know of. And I think I would know."

I was already jogging towards my SUV. "That's what I thought. Thanks. See you later Tatiana!"

I drove back towards Killdeer, and I had to force myself to keep my speed under control. The roads were nearly dry from last night's rain, but patches of mud cropped up here and there, and hitting one too fast would send the SUV into a skid.

It was all starting to come together in my head at last.

It was no wonder with all the prickly pear cactus on the Deep Creek Ranch that someone had gotten a flat tire driving out by the dogtown. But on the night Zane had been killed, someone had gotten a flat tire not a hundred yards from where his body had been dumped. That was too much of a coincidence to ignore.

And right beside Zane's body were sets of tracks from an animal that I didn't recognize. An animal that nobody in Killdeer would ever recognize.

The barbed-wire fence that separated Tatiana's ranch from the Bybee place hadn't been cut because someone was driving out there to look for ferrets. It had been cut because something a lot bigger than a ferret on the Bybee ranch had escaped, and the crew had gone after it.

Zane had gone after it.

And that had cost him his life.

An inflatable jack was an anomaly in Killdeer. I'd never even heard of them before today. Somebody on the Bybee ranch had one, though. The night that Zane had been killed, they had been forced to use it. All I had to do was find out who it was, and I would know who had been responsible for trying to dispose of a body.

Brian Hix and Logan Hiser hadn't wanted anyone going up to the reservoir. It was obvious, now that I really thought it through. They were hunting something inside the buffalo fence that was probably illegal. Something that rich men from Texas were willing to pay a lot of money to travel all the way to Montana to shoot.

I had a perfect excuse to go to the Bybee ranch and poke around until I got more answers. I could go see my good buddy, Jennifer. And maybe I could take a peek inside the back of the ranch trucks while I was there.

CHAPTER 18

When I pulled into the compound behind the stables at the Bybee ranch, relief washed over me. No vehicles sat in front of the house, and nobody seemed to be around. Brian's enormous red truck was nowhere in sight, but Logan's black Humvee and Jennifer's gleaming Audi were parked side by side behind the stables.

The last thing I wanted to do was be conspicuous, so I pulled my SUV beside Jennifer's Audi and tried to park the nose as close to the back of the stables as possible. Unless someone was really looking for it, they wouldn't see my vehicle.

I closed the door on my SUV as quietly as I could. Jennifer's Audi was always unlocked, so I slipped up to the back and opened the hatch.

Two huge department store shopping bags, empty, lay in the back and I shoved them aside quickly to see what sort of spare tire was underneath the hatch cover. I pulled up the carpeted flap and saw a standard metal tire jack tucked inside. Not a speck of dirt anywhere. It was a cinch that this vehicle had never been four-wheeling it around the ranch.

Disappointed, I dropped the flap back into place and pulled the shopping bags back to the same position.

Not that I'd expected Jennifer to have an inflatable tire jack in her Audi, but it had been worth a shot.

The hatch closed with a soft click, and I went to the back of Logan's black Humvee and fumbled with the handle, trying to open the back.

It was locked

A huge off-road spare tire hung on the back door of the Humvee, and a cargo rack was bolted over it. There wasn't much room between the tire and cargo rack to see inside the back, and on top of that, the windows were heavily tinted.

I tried the driver's side door and found it locked too.

How the hell was I going to get a look inside?

A fine film of sweat was starting to coat my upper lip. There had to be a way to get a look inside the Humvee without drawing attention.

Aside from smashing the back window, I didn't have that many options left.

Grumbling, I decided to check the stables to see if anyone had thought to hang a key rack inside. And in any case, it would be good to see Peanut again and give him a scratch. It would perk the little mustang up to see a friendly face.

Inside the stables I was disappointed once again. There was nothing by the front doors that looked like a key rack. Most likely, Logan had one set of keys for his Humvee. In his pocket.

I would have to think of something else.

Peanut nickered a greeting when he saw me. Even though he was stone deaf, I talked to him when I reached across the stall door to give him a good scratching.

"Hey, boy. Miss me?"

He nuzzled my palm, searching for treats. When he didn't find any he blew slobber all over my hand and tossed his head impatiently.

"What are you doing in here?"

I spun around. Brian Hix was standing in the double doors of the big stable, looking at me with a murderous expression. His wide frame blocked out a distressing amount of sunlight and his thick neck throbbed with anger.

My heart nearly dropped out of my chest. "Brian! Hey. You startled me."

"I asked you a question."

"I wanted to take Peanut back to Deep Creek this afternoon." I smiled, forcing my voice to stay perky.

Brian stomped forward, his curly blond hair streaked with sweat and rivers of dirt stained his temples. He'd been working outside and radiated heat. His forearms and face were scorched with a deep sunburn.

I tossed my hair like I had seen Jennifer do, cocked my head to the side and showed off my dimples. "Tatiana doesn't want to impose on you anymore if she can help it. Peanut here was cross-bred with a hog and eats like one."

I giggled as girlishly as possible and blinked my eyes like a cupie doll.

Brian looked at the mustang, looked back to me and grumbled an uninteligible response.

"Sorry?" I said.

"I said it's fine. Does Jen know you are here?"

"I was just about to go say hello," I told him.

He glared at Peanut because glaring at me any longer would have been bad manners. Somehow I got the impression Brian Hix didn't care about manners as much as he did about how things looked. He was a toad, but at least he knew better than to be abusive towards his wife's new friend.

"She's upstairs," he said, dismissing me.

He turned to go but stopped and looked over his shoulder at me, the eyes still dangerously narrow. "You seen Holly around lately?"

The question was deceptively casual.

I shrugged, stupid grin still firmly in place. "Can't say I have. She disappear on you?"

He watched me, speculative. "Haven't seen her since Friday."

"She's just sleeping it off somewhere. The last time I saw her was when I was out here visiting Jen."

Which was a big fat lie. The last time I'd seen Holly Koltiska, she's been bleeding all over the bumper of my SUV.

Brian worked his jaw like he was thinking, then spun away without another word and stomped out of the stables.

I felt my legs go rubbery and somehow managed to start walking towards the house like I belonged there. Climbing the steps leading up to the front door was not easy but I managed to do it without stumbling and looking like I was half-smashed.

Truthfully, just being on the Bybee ranch was giving me the heebie-jeebies. Something about the place felt unnatural and threatening.

The last person I'd expected to see was Brian. His truck was nowhere in sight and having him walk in on me while I'd been contemplating breaking into Logan's Humvee had jangled my nerves.

Almost the same moment I raised my hand to knock on the door, it flew open and I saw Jennifer standing in the doorway, a wide grin spreading across her face.

"Well, Marley, what are you doing here? It's so good to see you!"

She took my hand and pulled me inside the house. "Come in out of that heat. Want a Jack and Coke or something to drink?" She led me through the entryway into the vast living room.

She was already drinking, and I could smell that she had been at it for a few hours.

"No thanks. How about just a Coke?" I said, smiling back at her.

"You sit your little ol' self down and catch me up on all the goings-on around here," she said, wobbling slightly as she headed towards the bar.

I sat down on a pristine leather sofa and looked down at my outfit. My jeans didn't have holes in them, at least. The same could not be said about my sleeveless T-shirt, and I folded my arms self-consciously over a tear on the waist.

An oil painting hung over the sofa. It was photo-realistic in its detail, and nearly as long as the sofa itself. The nose and eyes of an African lion peered at me from the canvas, looking like the lion was actually crouched there, waiting to pounce. The image sent a chill down my body despite the heat.

Jennifer was, as usual, dressed like a mannequin in a department store window. Her chestnut hair was loose and flowed down her back in a cascade of perfectly teased curls. Her spotless white slacks draped at just the right angle to make her long legs look even longer. She wore a jet-black cropped top with geometric sleeves, and a silver coin necklace that hung down to her waist.

Her white sandals clacked on the wood floor as she went to the bar and grabbed a soda out of the small refrigerator. She popped it open and managed not to spill it all over herself, poured the can into a tall crystal glass and tossed in a couple of ice cubes.

Jennifer could have been a bartender, her motions were so deft.

Even as drunk as she was, she handled the drinks in her hands smoothly.

She came back to the sofa and plopped down beside me.

"Jennifer, it's good to see you," I said.

She took a swig from her glass and eyed me with a loopy smile. "Me too. I mean, you too. It's good to see you, Marley."

She didn't ask why I had come out.

I took a long drink from my Coke and tried desperately to think of something to say.

"So how are you?" I asked, wincing inside at the pathetic question. Why did I always feel like a second-class citizen around Jennifer?

Luckily she was too intoxicated to notice that my conversational skills were completely nonexistent.

"I'm . . . good."

She wasn't looking at me. She was looking at a spot on the sofa between us.

Her mind was a thousand miles away.

"How's Holly?" I asked on impulse. Maybe if I asked after Holly, Jennifer would pass along to her angry husband that I was as clueless as the rest of them as to the cook's whereabouts.

"Holly?" she asked, looking straight at me. "She got fired. Didn't I tell you? Brian fired them both, Rick and Holly. He got so tired of them fighting all the time."

"Wow. I guess they both had it coming, though. When was the last time you saw them?" I asked carefully.

"Saturday. Rick cleaned out his room over at the bunkhouse."

"Did Holly clean out her room too?" I asked, my nose in my drink.

"You know," Jennifer tilted her head to the side, "I never saw her. Isn't that just awful? She never even came to say goodbye. Brian wouldn't let me talk to Rick so I never got a chance to ask him where she was."

Rick was probably hitting the Mexican border right about now, was my guess. The chances that he would stick around Killdeer after pounding Holly black and blue were remote.

"Too bad you didn't get a chance to talk to her before she left," I said.

She took a lazy swig from her glass. "I guess Brian knows what he's doing."

"First Zane, now Holly and Rick? That's just bad luck, Jennifer."

She locked her eyes on me, piercingly. "It is bad luck, isn't it?" Suddenly, Jennifer looked very sober.

My muscles quivered with adrenaline. It wasn't easy, but I kept my legs from bobbing up and down with nervous energy. I'd just had an idea for how to sneak a look inside Logan's Humvee and I forced myself ahead with it before I lost my nerve.

"Hey, do you remember that night at the fairgrounds? Wasn't that just crazy?" I asked, changing the subject.

She laughed. "That was such a train wreck. But, come on. You have got to admit it was a blast."

"It was memorable," I said. "But I think I lost a bracelet in the backseat of Logan's car. Is he around today? Do you think he would open his Humvee so I could look for it?"

"Honey, you don't need Logan. There's a spare key in the kitchen. It's not Logan's, anyway. It belongs to the ranch. He just drives it."

I had a sneaking suspicion that Logan drove the Humvee exclusively.

"Could we go look for it? Leif gave me that bracelet and it would break my heart to lose it."

Jennifer swirled her drink languidly. "Break your heart?" She downed the rest of her drink and set the glass on the table. "Then we should go have a look."

A wet ring started to stain the pristine wood of the coffee table almost immediately. She didn't seem to notice.

"Thanks," I said, getting to my feet. "It means a lot to me."

She held out her hand and insisted that I pull her to her feet. She wobbled slightly, but righted herself and smoothed down the front of her perfectly pressed slacks.

"The kitchen is this way."

She led me through a swinging door to the right of the main living room and we walked into a kitchen worthy of a Las Vegas celebrity restaurant. Two state-of-the-art stainless steel gas ranges sat side by side in the center of the counter. The kitchen had four sinks. One sink was standard, another was deep and wide and obviously made to accommodate huge pots and pans. Two dishwashers sat side by side, and the countertops were all made of red granite of a striking shade. The ranch was equipped to serve dinner for a small army.

I momentarily forgot what we were looking for. "This place is incredible."

She took in the décor of the kitchen and shrugged it off. "It's not like Brian designed this place. Personally, I never went in for all this macho decorating with horns and dead animals on the walls, nonsense. But it was his father's pride and joy, and even though this damn ranch costs him a fortune Brian wants to keep it going. I think it reminds him of his dad, or something."

"Brian's dad passed away?" I asked.

"Dropped dead of a heart attack out of the clear blue. You know, now that I think about it, the whole thing is sort of sad," Jennifer said. "Brian's dad had this place built while he was still living in Texas on their ranch outside of Austin. When this house was finally finished, the old man up and died without ever having gotten the chance to live in it."

"That is sad," I said.

She seemed resolute and put on a brave smile. "Brian inherited everything. He sold the ranch in Texas and we moved up here full-time, since it was way too expensive to run both places."

"I think it's beautiful," I said, not sure if I was awed by the opulence or by the obvious care that had gone into making the house.

No matter what room we went into, it always seemed to top the last in terms of lavishness.

"Here we go," she said, tottering over to a drawer and rummaging inside.

She pulled out a silver key and held it up. "Spare. Want some help looking?"

I took the key from her and tried to give an enthusiastic smile. "I'd love some help."

The two of us stumbled together down the long front steps and it was all I could do to keep Jennifer upright when her high-heeled sandals hit the gravel of the compound.

She flailed wildly but I caught her arm and steadied her as we ambled across the compound. "Damn wedge heels," she said under her breath.

She didn't seem to notice, but I probably looked over my shoulder a dozen times as we made our way to the Humvee. As far as I could see, we were alone.

"Oh, why on earth did you park back here behind the stables?" she asked, coming up short when she saw my vehicle.

"I wanted to put it in the shade," I said.

I felt a sudden stab of guilt for using Jennifer like this. She had no reason to doubt that my intentions were honest, and I was tangling her up in my scheme. I swallowed my guilt and helped her to lean against the side of the Humvee while I unlocked the door. This little adventure would give me some very important answers and it would all be over in a minute.

"I'll just climb in back and see what I can see," I said.

She looked like the heat was getting to her, and she pinched the top of her nose with two fingers while she waved me inside. "Go, go. I'll wait."

Her eyes were both closed and she was breathing hard. Apparently, for Jennifer, alcohol and hot weather did not mix.

"So, where is Logan today, anyway?" I asked, flopping into the backseat and pretending to search the carpet.

"I don't know. He's . . . away," she said vaguely. "Something about a broken axle on one of the trailers."

I looked up over the top of the seat, but Jennifer was leaning against the side of the Humvee with her eyes closed.

"A broken axle?" I said, snaking a hand over the back of the seat into the cargo area and pulling aside a blue tarp. "What a disaster."

"Speaking of disasters," Jennifer said caustically. She leaned her head back against the door, and it looked like her eyes were still closed. "I thought you were going to talk to your sheriff friend and tell him to stop bothering us? If anything, he's been coming around even more lately. Said something about getting a warrant. What did you tell him, anyway?"

"Loy? I didn't tell him anything," I said with surprise.

I rummaged faster behind the seat, hoping to catch a glimpse of the tire jack.

I was surprised at how little room was in the cargo area. The blue tarp seemed to go on forever, and it was tangled up around a heavy toolbox tucked underneath a battery charger, and I was making so much noise looking for the damn tire jack it was a miracle Jennifer hadn't turned around once to ask me what the heck I was doing.

Then I saw it.

I pushed the tarp aside and got a good look at the jack to make sure I was really seeing what I had been looking for.

A yellow tube was coiled around a deflated orange plastic ball. The end of the yellow tube was designed to fit over the tailpipe of the vehicle, and after I uncovered the orange ball I could see letters printed in black on the surface. The letters said 4x4 Jacklift.

There was no doubt that this had been the vehicle out at the scene where Zane had been killed.

I hastily covered up the cargo area and scooted out of the Humvee.

Logan Hiser may not have been the one who was responsible for Zane's death, but he sure as hell had been the one responsible for trying to cover it up. I guessed it had been Logan who'd stumbled across Zane after he was mauled, and in a panic, he had most likely tried to hide the body in the junipers while he and Brian Hix got together and got their stories straight.

Maybe it was a good thing that Finn had left Killdeer in such a hurry. Finding out his brother was an accomplice to a crime would make his opinion of Logan sink even lower.

"I couldn't find it," I said.

Jennifer looked disappointed and leaned on me. "Oh, I'm sorry."

"It's okay. Let's get you out of this heat."

I led Jennifer back inside the big ranch house and set her on the sofa in the living room once again.

"You look like you could use a nap," I said.

She flopped on her side and tucked her feet, shoes and all, up underneath her on the sofa. "That's a great idea."

I knelt down beside her and patted her shoulder. "Everything alright with you, Jennifer?"

She rummaged for a cushion and tucked it underneath her head. "I wish I knew why everyone is acting so damn strange around here. First Holly and Rick disappear, and now Logan is stalking around the ranch like he's ready to kill someone."

"You mean, more than usual?" I asked, half-joking.

"Marley," she grabbed my hand, "Logan is really starting to creep me out. I get the feeling that he's not a nice man at all."

"Why do you say that?" I was actually thinking she was right about him not being a nice man.

"He is the only one who can handle the tranquilizer darts," she told me. "He keeps them

259

locked up. The darts are all really old, and way beyond their expiration dates, so they aren't that effective anymore. But, still, Brian likes to keep track of them."

"I remember," I said. "Logan keeps the tranquilizer pistol in his backseat."

"Yeah, but some of the darts are missing," she said with a shudder. "And Logan has been really stonewalling Brian about telling him where they are. I think he used them for something but he won't tell us what it is."

She looked genuinely afraid.

"Jennifer, it might not be a bad idea to take some time off and leave this place for a few days."

"I should go home to Texas and never come back," she said.

"Well, I'll come out later and pick up Peanut. Is that alright? How about tonight? Then we can sit and chat after you've had a chance to rest and maybe figure out where you should go next."

She blinked her eyes and clutched my arm. "Oh, Marley. That would be super. Please do come back. This place feels so damn empty."

I reassured her I would be out that very evening and left her tucked on the sofa.

Things had to be pretty bad at the Bybee ranch if Jennifer was drinking at three o'clock in the afternoon.

I did feel a twinge of guilt for tricking her into helping me look inside Logan's Humvee, but the information I got was something I was sure Loy Shucraft would be very interested to know.

When I went back down to the compound and rounded the corner of the stable all I could think about was that I had finally unraveled the truth about what had happened the night Zane Ackerson had died.

Then I looked up and my mouth went completely dry.

Logan Hiser was leaning against the side of my SUV, looking supremely unhappy.

In fact, he looked more than unhappy. He looked furious.

"Hey, Logan. How are you?" I said in a chirpy voice as I stopped.

He looked almost exactly like his brother Finn when he was angry.

For the first time, I could truly see the resemblance in their features.

"Don't tune me cack, Cookie. What the bloody hell do you mean by coming around here and snaking me like that?"

"Like what, Logan?"

"Did you and the boss lady find whatever it was you were looking for in my backseat?"

My cheeks colored. "I thought I lost a bracelet. Jennifer was helping me look for it."

"You bloody well didn't lose a bracelet."

"Logan," I told him evenly, "I think you need to calm down a bit."

"I told you not to come back out here. Didn't I?"

I probably should have been worried, or at the very least cautious, but after the emotional roller coaster I'd been on lately my patience had evaporated.

My mouth engaged before my brain even had a chance to stop me. "What's the matter? Afraid I would see something in your backseat that you don't want anyone to know you've got?"

"See what in my backseat?" he demanded.

"Something that proves you were there the night that Zane Ackerson died."

261

Logan's face twisted with confusion. "What are you talking about?"

"You know what I'm talking about," I said hotly.

He glared like a viper. "I'm telling you this again. Don't come back here. Sometimes bad things happen to little girls who stick their noses into places they don't belong."

He spared me one last withering glance before disappearing around the edge of the stables.

I climbed inside my vehicle, slammed the door and tore out of the compound with all four tires slinging gravel.

I was mad enough to chew nails and spit bullets.

Who the hell was he to tell me what to do? I wasn't the one who was going to be arrested soon. Zane's death had probably been an accident, but stuffing his body in a juniper stand to conceal it was tampering. Now I knew that it had been Logan who had hidden the body. Even though he was most likely just following Brian's orders, it was still a crime.

"Stupid, bullheaded swindler," I said, stomping on the gas pedal.

Logan had really put his foot in it up to his knee. I doubted he had expected things to get this bad. But his true colors were showing.

He had come to Montana to see his brother, no doubt. But he'd taken a job working for a man who had a huge secret.

That's why they had built the buffalo fence. And that's why they were able to maintain a ranch house worth multiple millions of dollars.

Brian Hix had obviously been flying in rich businessmen from Texas so that they could have a once-in-a-lifetime experience of hunting some sort of exotic animal he'd had shipped up from his old home state. The Bybee ranch was remote. It was isolated enough to hide just about anything. But unfortunately for him, one of the exotic animals he'd imported had managed to escape. Zane had suffered the consequences of that accident, and nobody would have thought his death was anything other than a freak incident if Tatiana and I hadn't been checking the dogtown for the plague.

I would have thought Zane had died from a wolf mauling too, if it hadn't been for that tick.

Who did Logan think he was, telling me what I could and could not do? I wasn't the criminal here. And it wasn't as if Zane had been deliberately murdered. Why go to so much trouble to cover up an accident? Well, they would have had to, in order to protect their illegal hunting scheme.

I wondered what sort of animals they were importing for the canned hunts. For all I knew, it really could have been a wolf after all. But it hadn't been a wild wolf. Whatever had killed Zane was most likely captive bred.

And Jennifer had been unwittingly caught up in it, not having any idea what was actually going on around her.

I felt sorry for her all over again. And I felt furious at Logan for helping to cover up Zane's death.

Finn had been right. Logan was nothing but a pirate.

It still wouldn't stop me from going back out to the Bybee ranch that evening to retrieve Peanut.

After all, what was Logan going to do? His secret was out now. Unless he fled the United States and went back to Africa, he'd be charged with some sort of crime, probably in a matter of days. There was nothing more Logan could do at this point. All the damage had already been done. The least I could do was get Peanut out of there before everything went down.

CHAPTER 19

"Dad, are you ever going to clean out this truck?"

I rummaged behind the seat for a pair of gloves.

My father made a hurt face. "Think of all the history."

"There's a candy wrapper in here from 1979," I said, sifting through the garbage.

"When was the last time you could buy Necco wafers at the grocery store?" he asked.

"When was the last time anybody wanted to buy Necco wafers?"

I pulled up a small can of something marked with angry red letters. "What the heck is this?"

"Careful!" he said, lunging forward. "It's bear spray. Don't point that at your face."

He took the can from my hands and gently set it back behind the seat.

"Why do you have bear spray in your old truck? And, more importantly, why can't I just take the new truck to pick up Peanut? It's got power steering."

"Because the new truck doesn't have a gooseneck trailer hitch," he said, shoving the seat back to hide the mound of trash that had accumulated over the years. "If you don't like the way it looks back there, don't look back there."

I struggled with the ignition. "Are you sure these are the right keys?"

He reached across the seat and twisted the key back and forth, jiggled it twice, and twisted hard until it fit. "See? You just have to finesse it."

"I wish you could finesse your way into putting a gooseneck hitch on the new truck."

He ignored me and concentrated on the task at hand. "Okay, this thing doesn't like to be in first gear. But it won't pull the trailer uphill unless it's in first gear. It will buck like a bronc unless you really give it the gas. Don't be worried if black smoke shoots out the back. That's normal."

I slumped against the seat. "Peachy."

"If someone pulls up behind you and starts honking and carrying on, just wave them around. Four generations of Dearcorns have been slowing up traffic on these roads, the locals can darn well keep their shirts on. People drive too fast these days anyway."

"Right. Wave them around. What if they think I am actually on fire?"

"Just keep on driving. They will figure it out."

I tried to put on a brave face. "I'll bring the truck back tomorrow. Thanks for letting me use it."

"You sure you can back this thing up?" he asked, squinting at the long gooseneck trailer.

"I won't need to back it up. The Bybee ranch has a huge lot in front of the stables. I can park and load up Peanut and pull out without ever putting it in reverse."

"Wear your seat belt, Kiddo. Don't ride the clutch, and try not to drop the transmission out the bottom."

"Thanks," I said, starting the engine.

A cloud of bluish smoke shot out the back.

My father watched it. "Huh. Looks like we might have a bad piston ring."

"Will it get me all the way out to Tatiana's hauling Peanut?" My brow crinkled with worry.

"Take the saddle. If it dies you can ride him home. See you tomorrow!"

He waved over his shoulder as he headed back inside the ranch house to finish doing his dishes. I'd caught him right after supper and getting the trailer hitched up had taken longer than I'd expected.

The old transmission groaned when I slammed it into first, and the truck bucked forward, lurching down the driveway like a wounded sow.

"Come on, baby, hold together," I said to the truck.

My seat belt strap was twisted, and as I fumbled with it, I had to shift into second gear to keep the engine from exploding. The thing drove like a pig trying to climb a barbwire fence.

I bounced down the dirt road as fast as I dared, keeping to the side as much as possible so that angry drivers could pass me on the left. Surprisingly, not very many vehicles darted around me on the drive out to the Bybee ranch.

By the time I pulled the big gooseneck around the tight corner at the junction that led east, the smoke shooting out the tailpipe had died down considerably.

Whether that was a good sign or not, I didn't know. At least the truck was still moving.

I'd wanted to get back out to pick up Peanut well before dark, but hitching the trailer had taken longer than I'd bargained for and as I crossed the cattle guard marking the edge of the Bybee ranch, the sun was nearly gone below the horizon.

Both windows were wide open, the truck having been built before air-conditioning had been invented.

A fat bumblebee flew in through the passenger-side- window, bounced a couple of times on the windshield, buzzed with annoyance and zinged by my nose on its way out the driver's side. Evidently, the bumblebee had taken one look at the truck and determined that it was a piece of junk, and wanted nothing more to do with it.

"Don't blame you," I muttered.

The truck groaned and bounced its way long the dirt road, heat jetting inside the cab like a blast furnace.

I would probably weigh about ten pounds less by the time I got there. So much sweat was pooling in the small of my back it felt like I was sitting inside a sauna.

A hot breeze blew through the windows, doing nothing to cool down the cab. As the sun retreated further below the foothills, the landscape turned orange and the dry prairie grass almost looked as if it was burning with a smokeless fire.

I saw the Bybee ranch house come into view and shifted out of second gear. The last thing I wanted to do was attempt to back up with a gooseneck trailer, so parking close to the stable doors was out of the question. Instead, I settled on pulling up alongside the stable and leaving myself plenty of room between the building and the house. After I loaded Peanut into the trailer, it would be relatively easy to flip a wide U-turn and pull out of the compound without the worry of backing up.

I shut off the engine and it began to ping and whistle like a calliope as the hot metal started to cool. Hopefully the thing would start again when it was time to leave.

Jennifer's little white SUV had been moved. It was parked directly in front of the house, the bumper inches away from the front steps.

That was odd.

Maybe Jennifer was still tipsy from drinking all afternoon and she had tried to park her car close to the house, and nearly managed to park it on the porch. One light glowed inside. Someone was upstairs in the huge mansion. Probably Jennifer sleeping it off. Aside from that single light, the rest of the house was completely dark.

I slammed the door on the truck, since that was the only way to get the thing to close, and headed for the stable door. The big double doors of the stable faced the front of the house and when I got closer something seemed out of place. One of the doors was open, swaying slightly in the hot breeze. I frowned and came to a stop. The heavy door had been left ajar and the latch was undone. Was someone inside?

I listened hard to the land around me. It was quiet, like the whole prairie was holding its breath, waiting for something.

Not even a meadowlark sang.

The only sound I could hear was the low hum of motors coming from the refrigeration on the cinder block building down the slope from the stables. The big fans on the roof thrummed loudly, keeping a monotonous vigil.

The hot wind shifted and the stable door creaked as it swung closed. Turning, I gazed back at the house, the feeling that something wasn't quite right even stronger now.

Why was it so quiet?

Dusk draped the compound in near darkness, but enough light remained that I could make out a shape lying in the courtyard just off to the side of Jennifer's car. I hadn't seen it before, but now that I was really paying attention to my surroundings I noticed. It looked like a pile of dirty clothes had been dumped on the ground next to the car.

"What the . . . ?"

A loud whinny echoed from inside the stable and I jumped. A crash erupted from the stalls and I practically leapt a foot off the ground. I listened for a moment, a cold feeling snaking up my skin. I could hear the horses kicking the walls of the stable and spinning circles inside their stalls. They sounded frantic.

I turned back to the rumpled shape lying in the compound beside Jennifer's car and swallowed hard. Something told me it wasn't just a pile of laundry.

As I walked towards the dark shape, it suddenly came into focus and I found myself running.

I dropped to my knees on the ground. "Logan! What happened?"

Logan Hiser was sprawled facedown in the dirt. For one terrible moment I thought he had been mauled like Zane. I checked him for wounds but didn't find anything. Rolling him to his side, I saw that he was still breathing.

He moaned and tried to focus on me.

"Where are you hurt?" I asked, my hands running over his arm and legs, checking his chest for blood.

"Marley." His arms flailed helplessly. He tried to move his legs, but they seemed too heavy for him to lift. It was like he was having a stroke, or some sort of seizure.

"You need a doctor," I said. "Hold on."

I jumped to my feet and reached for the passenger door of Jennifer's vehicle but it was locked. I lunged for the driver's side and jerked up on the handle with both hands. It was locked too, and all the windows were rolled up tight. There was no way inside.

I ran back to Logan and dropped to the ground next to him. Something sharp gouged my knee and I jerked back, feeling in the dirt for the object. A thin dart with a feathered tail was half buried in the dirt beside Logan, and it had jabbed my knee as I'd skidded to a stop beside him.

It was a dart from his tranquilizer gun.

Someone had shot him.

I yanked the dart out from underneath his leg and threw it as far as I could. There was no way to tell how long ago he'd been drugged. He could have been lying here for hours for all I knew.

"Logan, listen to me. Who shot you?"

I shook his shoulders. His eyes fluttered and he tried to focus on me, but he only managed a mumble. "Run, Cookie."

I shook him again. "Was it Brian? Where is he? Logan!"

Then I heard a sound that made my heart grow cold.

Inside the stable the horses were screaming.

I stood up slowly. Something was very, very wrong.

I looked towards the mouth of the stable and saw something moving through the open door.

Through the blue twilight I saw a shape lope across the compound and come to a halt only fifty feet away. Whatever it was, it ran with an unworldly gait on long front legs and a barrel chest.

My eyes refused to believe what they saw. This was no wolf.

All I could focus on was the massive mouth, glimmering teeth and the black eyes of a creature that should not have been there.

An African hyena stood in the compound, its black muzzle leering at me with a greedy smile. It lowered its massive head, sniffed the air once, and growled like a dog.

Then it charged straight for me.

I turned and bolted up the steps for the front door as hard as I could. The moment I turned the knob I knew it would be locked.

I didn't waste a second. I took two running steps towards the left, grabbed the top rung on the banister, and jumped.

Claws scrabbled on the porch behind me and I sailed over the banister and hit the ground running. Panting sounds chased me across the packed dirt and I didn't dare turn around to look back. I sprinted for the stable door with my arms pumping madly. The hyena was so fast it was almost on my heels.

I crossed the threshold of the stable and leapt for the first stall like my life depended on it. The wood cut into my palms. I heaved myself up and over the top of the empty stall and fell head first inside, landing hard.

As soon as I had my wind back I cautiously stood up and peered over the top of the stall gate.

The horses were going wild around me.

The hyena paced the gate outside my stall, snuffling and pawing at the wood, digging at the hinges impatiently.

"Holy Mary Mother of God," I said.

At the sound of my voice the hyena glanced up and let out a growl. It was enormous. Far larger than any dog I'd ever seen. The black eyes watched me expectantly, anticipating.

Right away I noticed the smell. Musky. Like a wolverine.

It stared at me hungrily, its wide mouth working the air as it tried to paw the stall gate loose. It stood up on its hind legs, front paws scrabbling at the wood. It was tall enough to peer over the top of the gate and it looked at me without a shred of fear in its eyes.

The wood rattled against the onslaught, but the gate held firm. In spite of the fact that the hinges seemed to be holding I still backed up to the corner of the stall, trying to put as much distance between me and the animal as possible.

The hyena dropped back down to all fours and I could hear it moving up and down the stalls, snuffling and digging randomly as it tested each gate it came to. There were a dozen horses housed in the stable. They pawed and paced, some of them frozen completely still with fear, their eyes wide and rolling.

Off to the right, I saw Peanut with his head sticking over the top of his gate. His eyes were as big as silver dollars and his lips were rolled back from his teeth. His short ears were plastered against his head and he rammed the stall gate with his chest. Peanut was in a frenzy.

The hyena focused on a stall straight across from me and hefted its bulk up on short hind legs. Its massive paws clawed for purchase on the top of the gate as it eyed the terrified horse inside.

But all it could do was lean against the wood. It didn't seem able to jump. As long as the hinges held, the horse would be safe.

For the moment I was safe, too. Apparently, hyenas couldn't climb. As long as I kept the door closed I would be alright.

Then I remembered Logan.

"Oh no."

He was still in the courtyard. And he was practically helpless. The moment I thought it, the hyena seemed to lose interest in the horses and started working its way back toward the stable door.

When I'd sprinted away from Logan he was half-conscious and barely able to move. He would be easy prey.

The same thought seemed to occur to the hyena, too. It loped past me, rolling its great head almost playfully. It trotted through the stable door towards Logan, a growl escaping its huge maw.

I searched the stall frantically for something I could grab and use as a weapon. There wasn't even a pitchfork propped against the wall. Not a shovel. Nothing.

I scanned the stalls across from me. I couldn't even see a stock whip.

"Hey! You ugly beast, over here!" I shouted.

I waited to see if my calls would bring the hyena back but it didn't reappear.

Logan didn't stand a chance. I had to do something.

I figured he had about sixty seconds to live.

Frantically, I dropped to my knees and felt along the bottom of the stable.

I turned up two small rocks and stood up quickly, clutching them in my hand. Even if I could hit the thing, a couple pebbles wouldn't slow it down. I needed something with more stopping power than a couple rocks.

Maybe I could make it to the truck? The can of bear spray was inside behind the seat. If I could get to the bear spray it might buy Logan enough time to get inside the stable.

It was a horrible plan, but it was the best I could come up with. I dropped the small rocks and put both hands on the stall gate.

How was I going to make it to the truck without getting killed?

Even at a dead run I couldn't hope to beat something with four legs. It would catch me before I was even halfway there.

At that moment Peanut draped his head over his stall gate and pawed at the wood frantically. He snorted, tossed his head, and rammed the gate with his chest.

My eyes locked on the little mustang. I didn't need to outrun the hyena. I just needed to be on the back of someone who could.

"Bridle, bridle," I said, checking the hook outside my stall.

There was no bridle hanging on the hook, but two gates down I could see one draped over an empty stall.

Logan yelled suddenly from the courtyard. Had he cried out in pain?

If I was going to do this, I had to do it fast.

Every fiber of my being told me not to open the gate, but if I didn't, a man would almost certainly die. I took two deep breaths and slid the bolt.

My feet carried me to the bridle and my hands seemed to lift it from the hook without any help from me. My body was so charged with adrenaline it seemed to move without any direction from me at all, and I was inside Peanut's stall with the gate locked so quickly, it was like I'd levitated across the ground.

I heard a yip of excitement come from the hyena outside in the courtyard, and Logan let out a yell of pain.

I couldn't stop to see what was happening. I had to move.

Peanut lifted his nose as I held up the bridle. He snorted with rage and tossed his head madly.

"Hold still," I said, trying to shove the bit in his mouth.

He wouldn't cooperate, and I had to throw an arm over his neck to get him to take the bit. Finally he held still long enough for me to slide the bridle over his ears. The instant I tossed the reins over his neck he pawed the ground.

Before angling the little mustang so that I could unlock the gate, I paused.

There was a very good chance that the hyena would attack Peanut the moment we left the stable. He might be able to get me to the truck. But after?

But if I didn't do something, Logan would die.

"Sorry, boy. I'm so, so sorry," I said, taking a split second to stroke Peanut's neck.

He danced sideways. I threw my leg over his back and sat up.

I angled Peanut so that I could open the gate. My fingers found the bolt and slid it back. I kicked the wood and the gate flew open.

If my hands hadn't been wrapped in his mane I would have rolled right off his back.

Peanut charged from the stall like a bull.

We galloped the length of the stable and by the time we reached the front door tears rolled down my cheeks from the wind. Peanut clipped the door with his shoulder, sending it careening open with a crash.

All I could do was suggest which direction he should go. Peanut was possessed. I reined the mustang hard to the right, trying to point him towards the truck.

But Peanut was having none of it.

"Whoa! No not that way!"

Ignoring my furious commands, the little mustang opened his mouth and screamed a warning. He turned away from the truck and looked straight at the hyena.

It turned to focus on us, jaws open, eager. But when it saw twelve hundred pounds of angry mustang heading straight for it, the hyena stopped with uncertainty. It swayed back and forth, dropped its head, and then tucked its tail and ran for it.

I pulled on the reins like a maniac. "Peanut! Stop!"

But he caught the bit between his teeth and yanked it forward.

All I could do was hang on for dear life.

Peanut caught the hyena in six strides, rolled it with a strike from his front hooves and sent it spinning.

The hyena somersaulted to its back and yelped, trying desperately to right itself, but Peanut lowered his head and advanced like a tank. He kicked out with both front legs and flipped the hyena onto its chest.

My legs were trembling with fatigue, and they gave out when he reared. I slid off and hit the ground inches away from Peanut's back legs. I managed to crawl away from the carnage on my hands and knees.

Behind me, the mustang unleashed his fury. Frantic yelps of pain, squeals of terror and the sounds of breaking bones made me crawl faster.

When I was several yards away I slowed my retreat and chanced a glance back.

Peanut stomped on the hyena with both front hooves, and kept stomping until there was no more movement.

He lowered his muzzle and sniffed the carcass of what was left. The hyena was nothing more than a bloody heap.

Satisfied, Peanut blew out through his nose, swished his tail and turned back towards the stables, looking for all the world like he'd just done a good day's work.

The little mustang ambled back towards the stables and walked casually through the door, trailing his reins beside him.

I stood up and headed for Logan.

I didn't bother to look behind me to see if the hyena was dead. Even if the animal was still breathing, it would never get up again.

I knelt in the dirt beside Logan and took his hand. "Who did this to you? It was Brian, wasn't it?"

He blinked up at me, his right hand dripping blood. For the first time I noticed his big hunting knife was missing from its sheath. Whoever had unleashed the hyena had also taken the time to remove Logan's knife after he'd been knocked out.

"Logan, where is he? Where's Brian?" I asked.

He shook his head once, trying to form the words. "It was Jen."

It was like getting kicked in the chest. "Jennifer? I don't understand."

His words came out like his tongue was swollen. "She lied. About Zane. Told me it was an accident."

I felt the blood rush to my face with anger. My hands clenched into fists.

278

Zane had been murdered? She had set the hyena on him deliberately?

"Are you sure?" I asked.

He nodded weakly. "Zane wanted the hunting trips to stop. Said he would tell we had these exotic animals. Jen shut him up. It was a lot of money."

"She killed him?" I asked with disbelief.

"She must have cut the fence. The hyena got out. We went looking for it, split up into teams. She was with Zane. She must have locked him outside the Humvee with the hyena at the prairie dog town."

Logan had nearly died. And I had almost been killed trying to stop it. And why? All because Jennifer didn't want to give up her lifestyle?

She wasn't just a greedy liar. She was a cold-blooded killer.

My eyes must have glazed over with rage, because Logan reached for my arm and took hold of me. He was beginning to recover his strength and I had to force him to let me go. I stood up and walked straight for the house.

I heard him trying to claw his way to his feet. "You don't want to be here, Marley. Its all coming apart."

The door was locked. I wasn't about to let that stop me.

Tall picture windows ran the length of the porch, and my foot smashed the glass easily. I reached inside and unlocked the window, slid it open and climbed inside the house.

The last thing I heard was Logan stumbling up the front steps, imploring me not to go inside.

CHAPTER 20

I hadn't come inside to talk to Jennifer. I didn't care what she had to say for herself. All I could think about was getting my hands on her.

No one should be able to get away with murder. The unfairness of it all was simply too much. If it hadn't been for sheer stupid luck, and Peanut, Logan would be dead now.

Something had obviously gone terribly wrong with her plan. She knew I was coming back out to the ranch, and she had meant for me to discover Logan's body in the courtyard. She had meant for me to assume it was Logan who had been responsible for Zane's death, and that while he was trying to move the hyena tonight, it had killed him too. But for whatever reason, the hyena hadn't managed to dispatch Logan before I'd arrived.

That must have been a nasty surprise for Jennifer.

I wasn't about to let her talk her way out of this. I was going to pin her down and keep her under my knee until I could call the sheriff. Something told me her first move would be to make a run for it.

Not a sound could be heard anywhere inside the huge mansion. Not a creak of a board or the scrape of a chair on wood. Light from the upstairs bedroom ghosted through the house. It created long shadows, but it was enough to see by.

She knew that I was still alive. And she knew that I was inside now.

I slipped around the corner of the living room and stood stock-still.

Jennifer was smart. She was smart enough to fool everyone around her into thinking that she was an innocent, sweet girl who was a victim of circumstance.

I knew almost at once that she wouldn't be waiting upstairs for me. The light was on in the upper bedroom because she wanted me to go there.

Like all things with her, it was a diversion.

I closed my eyes for a moment and pictured the living room area of the house. The stairs leading up to the second floor were beside the library. All she had to do was wait inside until I walked past the library and started going up the steps. Then she could shoot me in the back. I was almost certain she still had the tranquilizer pistol, and the library was a perfect place for an ambush.

I knew where she was. All I had to do was get to her before she saw me.

She expected me to walk quietly by the library and head up the stairs. If she stayed pressed against the wall around the corner from the stairway, unless I made it a point to look inside I would never see her.

Now I knew exactly where she was standing.

The hallway leading to the library was long, dark and totally silent.

Everything looked gray as I moved as silently as possible across the floor.

The walls over my head were lined with busts of trophy animals. A bear. An elk.

A set of perfect mule deer antlers was mounted on a heavy base of solid oak and it hung like a painting over my head.

I knew the instant I stepped around the wall into the library she would shoot me with the tranquilizer pistol. Unless I could get her to shoot something else instead.

I backtracked a few paces and lifted the head mount of a black bear carefully from its hook and eased it into my arms. It was heavy, maybe twenty pounds. But I could hold it at arm's length for a few seconds, which was all it would take.

My boots made very little sound as I eased to the corner of the library doorway.

I shifted my stance, and the floor let out a small creak. A sudden, sharp intake of breath told me that she was standing directly where I'd thought she would be, around the corner, waiting for me to make my move. Her quick inhalation told me she had just figured out that I was there.

It was now or never.

I crouched down and shoved the bear snout around the corner with both hands.

A deafening crack rang out and the bear head was shot from my grasp. It spun away and clattered to the floor. Another shot boomed in my ears and the bear head skidded to the left from impact. She sure as hell wasn't using a tranquilizer pistol.

Before I had time to think she wheeled into view holding a revolver with both hands. She'd expected me to be standing up and she hesitated. The split second it took her to realize I was crouched down was just enough time for me to lunge.

I hit her in the stomach with my shoulder and the two of us careened across the floor in a wild skid.

The revolver flew out of her hands and clattered to a stop underneath the sofa.

I managed to snag her by the ankles and pull her toward me. Jennifer screamed and backed away, scooting across the floor frantically, but I jumped for her and grabbed both her wrists.

She fought with everything she had.

She twisted in my grasp, shoved at my face and tried to throw me off with her legs. "Marley stop! I thought you were the hyena!"

I pressed my knee to her chest and pinned her to the floor. "No you didn't."

Her eyes bulged with fear when she realized I wasn't backing down. She had counted on my forgiveness.

"Please," she begged. "It was an accident. I swear it."

Her hands flailed against my arms as she tried to escape.

"I suppose killing Logan was supposed to look like an accident," I said, my voice a snarl.

She caught my arms with both hands and strained against me with all of her strength.

Half a lifetime of bucking hay bales and stringing barbwire had given me arms stronger than the average woman's, and Jennifer was no match for me. Her arms slowly buckled as I got her under control.

"Alright!" she yelled. "Alright. I'll tell you the truth."

"Like I will believe a word that you say."

She struggled futilely. "The hyena got loose. We all went to look for it. Zane and I found it first. I got scared when we found the hyena and I panicked. I locked the doors and it killed Zane, but it was an accident."

"How did it get loose, Jen?" I asked with a hiss. "I know you cut the fence. You don't expect me to believe that was an accident?"

"Please, wait," she said, struggling. "It must have been Logan."

"You make me sick," I said.

I pushed down harder, straining until the blood rushed to my ears.

She gasped for air and kicked her legs underneath me. "Please! Stop, please. I'm so sorry. It was a mistake. A mistake!"

"It's way too late for sorry."

I had her well and truly pinned. If Logan could make it inside, he could call the sheriff while I held her. She wasn't going anywhere now.

"Marley, please," she gasped. "You're crushing me. I can't breathe!"

Totally by reflex, I loosened my grasp a tiny fraction, and she heaved with every muscle she had. I felt my legs rotate to the side and my hands slipped off her wrists as she rolled out from underneath me. When she pivoted to her knees, I turned to find myself face-to-face with Logan's hunting knife. The blade was inches from my nose.

"Alright," she said, not taking her eyes off me. "You are going to sit here and let me walk out."

"Because after all that, I'm what? Too tired to stop you?" I asked.

She eased to her feet and started to back away. "Don't follow me, Marley. I'm not going to ask you twice."

"You know what the difference is between you and me, Jen?" I asked. "I'm not afraid to get hurt, and you are."

I reached out with my right hand and grabbed the knife.

Her eyes bulged with shock when she saw me holding the blade. I knew she would jerk it back and the instant she pulled I swung my left fist as hard as I could. My knuckles hit her temple and she yelped with pain.

I'd been cut. I could feel the blood on my palm, but the pain hadn't registered yet.

Jennifer reached for her face with her left hand and her grip on the knife loosened. I jerked it from her grasp. She staggered backwards and I rotated the knife so I was holding it by the hilt.

Before she could scurry through the doorway I snagged her arm and kicked both her feet out from underneath her, sending her crashing to the floor in a heap. I landed on top of her and had her pinned once more.

The knife was slippery and I brought it to Jennifer's chest so I could adjust the hilt and get a better grip on it.

At that moment Logan tackled me from behind.

I flew off Jennifer sideways and slid across the wood floor. I crashed against the wall, the knife falling from my grasp and spinning across the room.

I scrambled to regain my feet but Logan landed on top of me and pinned me down. He was drugged, and moving slow, but he was still twice as strong as me.

Jennifer stood up, her face white and frozen in shock. She looked at the two of us, looked at the knife, and then turned and ran out the back door as fast as she could move.

"She's getting away," I said through clenched teeth. "Get off of me!"

"Marley you need to get ahold of yourself," he said calmly, holding me down.

I struggled but Logan kept me from chasing after her.

The sounds of an engine starting, tires on gravel and a splash of headlights from the courtyard told me that it was too late.

Jennifer was gone. It would be impossible to catch her now.

Logan stared at my face, his arms gripping me until he could see my breathing start to return to normal.

Cautiously, he let me go and had the good sense to pick up his knife again before letting me sit up.

He half-sat, half-collapsed on the floor beside me, breathing like a bellows.

My mouth was dry and I could barely swallow. Blood pooled in my palm and dripped on the floor. I flexed my hand, relieved that I still had all my fingers attached.

My hands shook violently when I held them out.

"It's the adrenaline," he said, resting his forehead in one hand. "It'll pass."

I managed to scoot back and prop myself against the wall. "I wasn't going to kill her."

He was still panting with effort. "That's not how it looked from where I was standing."

He was finally getting his breathing back under control and he wiped a slick of sweat from his face.

"Why did you do that?" I asked. "Why did you stop me?"

"I didn't do it for you," he said, pushing himself to his feet with effort. "I did it for Finn. It would wreck him if you went to prison. Which is why you are getting out of here. Right now."

He pulled me to me feet and pushed me towards the door. My legs would barely hold me up and my hand was beginning to throb with pain.

"Go load up your mule," he told me, staggering after me with immense effort. "Drive home, and don't ever, ever come back here."

"I should call Loy," I said. "He needs to know what happened."

"My fingers are fine," he said, shoving me towards the door again. "I can dial a telephone. Go!"

Maybe it was the shock. Maybe it was the adrenaline wearing off, but I felt sick and my eyes drifted in and out of focus.

Logan marched me into the courtyard and left me next to my father's truck, and wordlessly dropped the gate on the gooseneck trailer. He went inside the stable and came back out, leading Peanut by the reins. He led the mustang inside the trailer, tied the reins in a knot and looped them over Peanut's neck.

He staggered and had to rest against the side of the trailer when he came out, but he refused to give up. Wordlessly, he untucked his shirttail and tore off a long strip to wrap around my palm. He cinched it tight. "That will get you home, at least."

"What happened to Brian?" I asked, wincing with pain as he knotted the cloth.

"Locked in the refrigerated holding pens down where we keep the animals," Logan said, grimacing as he closed the trailer and locked the gate.

"Why would she do that?" I asked.

"She had to get him out of the way while she took care of me." He waved a hand over the courtyard. "Would mess up the whole deal if she accidentally got him killed too."

"That means she acted alone, and Brian had no idea what she had been doing."

"That'd be my take on it, too," he said.

"I can't leave you here like this, Logan. What if she comes back?"

He scoffed. "She won't. Marley, listen to me. Get in your truck and drive out of here now. Do not call the sheriff. I will take care of that. Do you understand?"

He grabbed my arm and steered me to the cab.

Then he pulled open the door and physically shoved me inside, slamming the door closed and turning to walk towards the stable.

"I can't just leave," I told him.

"You broke into this house and tried to kill Jennifer Hix with a knife."

"That's not what happened," I said. "She confessed it all to me. She said she killed Zane."

"You think she will tell the police the truth?" he asked. "It'll be your word against hers. And believe me, Jennifer is very good at getting other people to take the blame. She might have told you she killed Zane, but there's not a thimble full of proof to back it up."

"You can tell them what really happened," I said.

He gave me a pitying look. "No, Cookie. I can't. Once your sheriff does a background check on me, I'm the last person anyone will believe."

Logan turned his back and moved towards the stables.

"This isn't right," I said. "I'm not the kind of person who can walk away."

He whirled and took two giant steps toward me. "You are not walking away. You are trusting that I will take care of it."

"You know what Finn would say about trusting you?" I asked.

Logan let his head fall forward. "I know exactly what he would say. But right here, right now, you've got to take my word for it. Go home and tell Loy you picked up your horse this evening, and when you left, everything was fine. And that's all you need to say."

"I don't understand," I said.

"Are you still here? I'm not gonna say it again. Go!"

I started the engine of my truck and breathed a sigh of relief as it fired to life without choking out.

As I pulled away from the courtyard and drove towards the road leading back to Killdeer, the last thing I saw in the glow of my taillights was the ranch horses running out the front of the stable. Logan was setting them free.

I turned back towards the road and kept my eyes focused straight ahead. The only reason I could think of that he would turn out the horses was because he was getting ready to run himself, and there would be no one on the ranch to feed them. He didn't want them to die inside the stalls after he was gone.

I drove away, knowing it would take my hands days and days to finally stop shaking.

CHAPTER 21

The sun was hot and high overhead, baking the ditch grass dry as paper.

I was parked on the side of the road leading to my father's ranch, sitting inside my sweltering SUV, with the door hanging open so that I wouldn't bake to death inside. Heat waves drifted up from the road, and I rested my chin in my palm, wondering what I was doing there when I had a perfectly good air-conditioned house to go to.

It was three weeks to the day since I had last seen Logan Hiser.

Knowing that he was planning to bolt the night I'd left the Bybee ranch, I'd given him twenty minutes to bug out before driving into Killdeer, and I'd only waited that long simply due to the fact that he was Finn's little brother. I had called Loy from Lil's café and met him at his office more than an hour after I'd watched the horses running from the Bybee stables.

I'd told Loy everything, not leaving out a single detail. He agreed with Logan's assessment, much to my frustration, that it would be practically impossible to prove anything. But he had promised to do the best he could.

Luckily my hand hadn't required stitches. It didn't mean the healing would hurt any less.

The story hit the press three days after Loy had wrapped up his investigation.

To the dismay of the locals, it had come out that Zane Ackerson had not been killed by a wolf, as originally thought, and had in fact been killed by an exotic game animal the Hixes had been keeping on their ranch illegally. The local members of the anti-wolf militia were, needless to say, a little disappointed.

Loy had driven straight to the Bybee ranch after I'd told him my story. Brian Hix had been found locked inside his own holding pens. He was happy to be arrested after not having any food or water for over twelve hours.

Behind the pens the local game warden from Parkman had uncovered two dead adult male African lions and three dead hyenas. Brian had been trying to bury the animals to hide the carcasses. He had shot them shortly after his last group of hunters had gone back to Texas, hoping in vain to keep his canned hunting operation a secret.

Jennifer Hix had vanished. But Loy had confided in me that she would soon be arrested in Austin, and was being charged with homicide. She wasn't being shipped back to Killdeer to face a trial for the murder of Zane, she was standing trial in Austin. As it turned out, a lengthy investigation had been going on in Texas for months, looking into the sudden death of her father-in-law, Brian's father, and had resulted in a murder charge against her. It seemed she hadn't wanted to wait for her husband to inherit the wealth of his father any longer, and had sped up the fragile heart condition suffered by the old man with a generous dose of barbiturates. The case was strong and she would most likely be convicted.

Loy had also confided in me that proving her guilt in Zane Ackerson's death would be something he would only try to do if she was acquitted. As far as he was concerned, the case of Zane's death was unsolved, still open, but considered cold.

Logan Hiser was listed as a person wanted for questioning for the transport of illegally purchased exotic animals across state lines, but the likelihood of locating him was remote. By one account, he had managed to make it out of the country, and since he wasn't a murder suspect the chances that he would ever be extradited from wherever he ended up were slim.

No one ever saw or heard from Rick Lee again.

I knew for a fact that Holly Koltiska had moved back in with her mother in Billings and was working at a swank downtown restaurant as a sous chef. Her broken nose had healed, but we would have to wait and see about her heart.

I flexed my right hand and saw with satisfaction the cut I'd received was healing nicely. It would scar, but Logan's knife had been so sharp the cut was clean and small. Over time, I probably wouldn't even notice it.

A lone cricket trilled from the brush beside the road, calling me back to the here and now.

I'd come to the place where I had met Angus Finn for the first time. Sitting on the side of the road, I didn't expect to see him, but for some odd reason, perhaps nostalgia, I felt compelled to rest in the spot for a few minutes while I thought about everything that had happened since he'd left town.

Scott had gone back to D.C. at the end of rodeo weekend, and Leif had counseled me not to reveal to his stepson the part I'd played in the downfall of the Bybee ranch. Leif and I had decided the best course of action from that day forward would be to only bring it up if the sheriff suggested it. Tatiana as well had no idea the extent of my involvement.

But I found it hard to believe the sly ranchwoman was not, at the very least, just a little bit suspicious.

I was about to pull my door closed and start for home when I heard the familiar sound of heavy tires on road gravel.

I squinted against the sun, not sure that the vehicle coming down the road towards me was really the vehicle I imagined it was.

But as the familiar black Jeep came into view, my heart sped up a beat or two. It looked exactly like Finn's Jeep, and for a moment I was stunned to see it arrive.

As usual, the black Jeep drove by, flipped a U-turn, and parked behind my SUV.

When the driver's-side door opened, I stood up and gaped with astonishment. It wasn't Finn behind the wheel.

Deputy Nick Wilcox stepped out of the Jeep, hoisted his gun belt and sauntered over to my car with a swagger worthy of Chris LeDoux.

He came to a halt a few feet away, appraising me through his mirrored sunglasses.

"Shut the front door," I said.

"You are in a restricted area," he said, cocking his hip. His uniform was black, but it definitely had a more Western bend to it than Finn's ever had. He wore a perfectly shaped black Stetson.

"Is this Halloween in August?" I asked, my mouth still wide.

"I'm the new security chief up at the weather station. And you are in a restricted area."

I didn't even know what to say. It took all of my strength not to laugh.

"Is this why you wanted to get in touch with Finn so badly a few weeks ago?" I asked.

He rocked back on his heels, cocky. "The real money is in the private sector. Loy was never going to make me his undersheriff. He even told me that to my face. So if I want to get into forensics in any serious way, I need a résumé with something listed on it besides deputy in a pissant little town. This was as good a place as any to start."

He scrutinized the roadway, doing his best imitation of a Secret Service agent.

I did laugh then. "How in the world did you ever get this job?"

He acted like it was nothing special. "Finn recommended me. He gave me a letter and everything."

I shuffled my toe in the dirt. "I don't suppose you know where he is these days?"

Nick gave me a slick grin. "Classified."

"In other words, you have no idea," I said.

He shrugged. "Nope. But if I did, it would be classified. Anyway, you can't park here. You have to move your vehicle. This really is a restricted area."

"That's just ridiculous."

"Hey, hey. Just doing my job, Marley. Just doing my job."

He tipped his hat to me and went back to the Jeep. It was the first time Nick had ever called me Marley. Usually he addressed me only by my last name, derisively.

As he drove away I watched the rooster tail of dust float up behind the Jeep and shook my head.

Nick had actually seemed happy. He was still a toad, as far as I was concerned. But he was a content toad.

"I guess some things really do change for the better."

I took one last look at the ditch, feeling silly at my melancholy nostalgia for such a barren and useless stretch of road.

I drove back home, trying to decide what Leif and I should have for supper, and thinking that it would be nice to be normal for a change.

STANDING ON THE SHOULDERS OF
THOSE WHO CAME BEFORE.
THANKS MOM.

A fourth generation Wyoming native,
Jessica McClelland is a librarian, avid archer and
spent a decade hunting dinosaurs in the
Jurassic formation in the foothills of the
Bighorn Mountains, a stone's throw away from
where the Johnson County Cattle Wars occurred.
She is the author of the Marley Dearcorn novels,
a series of murder mysteries set in
South Central Montana.